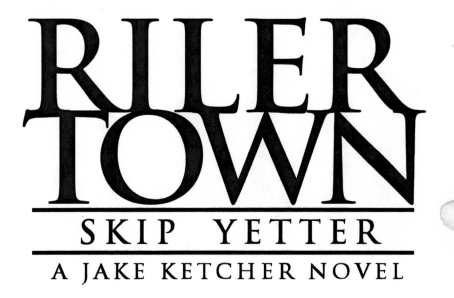

RILER TOWN

SKIP YETTER

A JAKE KETCHER NOVEL

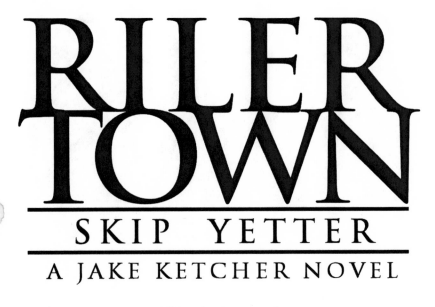

RILER TOWN

SKIP YETTER

A JAKE KETCHER NOVEL

Cover and book design by Dave Bricker.

ISBN: 978-0-9962370-1-7

To Gabi: the woman who brings pop, sizzle,
meaning and rhyme to every word of my life

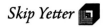

Contents

"The average newspaper, especially of the better sort, has the intelligence of a hillbilly evangelist, the courage of a rat, the fairness of a prohibitionist boob-jumper, the information of a high school janitor, the taste of a designer of celluloid valentines, and the honor of a police-station lawyer."

— HL Mencken

"All the news that's fit to print."

— *New York Times* slogan since 1851

"All the news that fits, we print."

— Anonymous, *Rilertown Post-Recorder*, Rilertown, Mass. circa 1982

 *Rilertown*

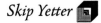

PROLOGUE

APRIL 20, 1975

N*o one responded to the girl's screams as she died.*

A pillow muffled her cries of anguish as the man pressed hard on the back of her neck, lustily gyrating from behind. On her knees, she screamed for him to stop with panicked pleas inaudible beyond the bedroom. She flailed her arms, suffocating, losing consciousness.

Absorbed in his efforts, the man failed to realize that hers were acts of desperation, not enthusiasm for his sexual performance. He increased his pace, panting loudly and pressing harder, his guttural grunts carrying into the next room. The headboard banged against the wall in rhythmic response to his thrusts.

"Hey, save some for the rest of us, huh?" came a voice through the partially open door, where three other men sat around a coffee table strewn with empty beer cans, a half empty bottle of bourbon and an ashtray overflowing with cigarette butts and cigar ashes. A deck of cards lay scattered at the center of the table, set aside in favor of the booze and nicotine and the promise of sex in the adjacent room.

The cheap hotel room was sparsely appointed, a two-room suite perfect for a party for the four men and the young woman they'd hired for the evening. Two hours earlier, the reservation clerk had raised an eyebrow but said little to the attractive young woman when she paid cash for the room. He diverted his eyes when she cast a shy glance his way and continued.

Soon she was joined by four men. She spoke briefly with the one who had summoned her earlier in the day and exchanged shy, quiet courtesies with the others. Money changed hands, and she took a quick shower. Then she went to work.

She faced two or three hours of distasteful sex for which she would pocket a hundred bucks. Then it would be back to the dorm for a long, hot shower to wash the mens' stench down the drain and resume her life.

Hooking was an expedient choice for her, a stunning 20-year-old foreign exchange student from India with soft skin the color of cocoa who was paying her own way through a four-year university degree. She lived a dual life; by day, an eager, promising student of profound beauty and superior intelligence; by night, a call girl, an object for emotionless sex with men she despised yet who provided the means to continue her studies. Despite her conservative upbringing and strong sense of morality, she did what she had her entire life — survive.

The grunting, panting and banging of the headboard ceased from behind the partially closed door. One of the other men calculated it was his turn.

"One more for the road," he chuckled, fresh drink in one hand and cigar in the other. He stuck the toe of his brilliantly polished Florsheim into the door and wedged it open. His friend lay spent, face down next to the naked girl, who remained on her knees as if at prayer. Her partner shook her gently, then harder. He recoiled when she slumped on her side, still.

"Oh, shit," said the man, leaping from the bed and reaching for his boxer shorts. "I think we have a problem here."

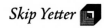
PART 1

*Rilertown*

SMALL-TOWN BOY IS NEW P-R SCRIBE

MAY 17, 1978

T he building looked more like an airplane hangar than a newspaper office. A sprawling monstrosity of textured concrete, glass and steel, the offices of the *Rilertown Post-Recorder* clung to the side of a small hill on the outskirts of the city. Its perch afforded a panoramic view of the distressed urban clutch of factories, rowhouses and pothole-pocked streets that crouched below. Detached from the residue of 50,000 lives immersed in a small city maelstrom, *The Post-Recorder* hovered over on the city as a guard tower over a prison.

Jake parked his car in the open space farthest from the front door, drawing upon his father's advice to always leave parking spaces closest to the door available for customers. He assessed himself in the rearview mirror, licked his palm and smoothed an errant spike of brown hair that erupted like an antenna from the peak of his head. He scowled at the new pimple on his chin and considered squeezing it, then decided an evolving blemish would be less obvious than an oozing hillock of red. Adjusting his tie — a woven, square-bottomed cravat of a color somewhere between ruby and black he had found at the bottom of a suitcase — he hauled himself out of the car for his first day of work.

He tugged open the enormous glass exterior door and stood in the foyer, scanning the staff photos posted at the entrance. Placed there to put a friendly public face on one of Rilertown's most loved and loathed institutions, a massive headline over the photos proclaimed in a classic, elegant font, "These are the men and women of the *Rilertown Post-Recorder.*"

Jake scanned the faces, recognizing Dan "Les" Moore, the managing editor who interviewed and hired him three weeks earlier. He also recognized Michael Zamboni, the irritable editor he'd been warned was a force to be reckoned with, yet a worthy teacher for a young reporter just starting out.

Bill Surety, news editor at *The Silvertown Eagle,* where Jake had completed his internship a year earlier had said, "Zamoboni's a prick; mean and hostile, but you can learn a lot from him. He's smart and knows his shit" as he counseled the young man on the art of finding a job. Smirking: "Just like me."

He gazed at the other faces, some smiling, others presenting themselves with intimidating stares. The men all wore ties, some of them with formal white shirts. The women all wore print blouses — save one, who appeared stone-faced, with a high-collared, ruffled grey blouson, her dark eyes expressionless and cold.

"Gladys McAvoy," Jake read aloud. "Human Resources Administrator."

Jake took stock of his clothes. He swatted lint from his pants, worn grey corduroys that fell an inch short of covering his scuffed brown shoes. A checked short-sleeved shirt was a benign partner for the tie that completed the uniform he had carefully selected to launch his career.

"You look like Robert Redford in *All the President's Men*," his sleepy-eyed girlfriend had told him as he prepared for work.

Appropriately suited in the uniform of aspiring journalists of the era, Jake nervously fingered the retractable pen in his shirt pocket and tugged at the right side of a double glass door. It resisted his efforts, and he self-consciously looked up to see if he'd been observed. He tried the left door, which joined in the conspiracy to exclude him by merely bouncing against the door jamb.

Jake noticed two things: the small "push" sign posted near both door handles, and the pleasant-looking blonde who stood behind the reception desk, stifling a laugh and feverishly waving at him to push his way inside.

He adjusted his tie as he approached the desk, noticing a sign that read "Reception/Classified." Jake wondered: *a dual-purpose department, or a closely guarded secret?*

"Hi, can I help you?" said the young woman, whose electric smile revealed an incandescent set of pearlies that must have set her parents back a pretty penny.

"I'm Jake Ketcher. First day. I'm here for a job ... I mean ... I have a job. I'm supposed to start today."

The woman studied Jake. He was good looking, with a slightly athletic build, a bohemian touch and an easy, yet self-conscious manner. His awkwardness was appealing, she thought. He was nervous, and cute — with broad shoulders and an eager, earnest smile framed by shining brown hair that complemented his eyes. *Deep hazel,* she mused, permitting a lingering gaze. *No. Just brown. Really, really gorgeous brown.*

Definite potential in this one.

Jake tugged at his collar, feeling faint beads of perspiration around his neckline. Failing to gain simple access to the building was a helluva way to make an impression, and now this girl was looking at him as a dog would eyeball a steak through the butcher's window.

"I'm Dolores. Dolores Strabaszinski," said Dolores Strabaszinski, hurrying through a locked half-door to her right created to keep the public from invading "Reception/Classified." Dolores stuck out her right hand. Jake stared, transfixed. From behind the counter she had appeared exceptionally pretty, with her perfect teeth, shining blonde hair and impossibly blue eyes.

In full view, she presented an altogether different appearance.

Genetics had bestowed Dolores with the upper body of a supermodel and the nether regions of a middle linebacker. Jake started in spite of himself. Dolores was built like an iceberg. He averted his eyes from her generous rump that stretched the fabric of her jeans close to the point of failure as she led him across the room.

"That's reception and classified advertising," she said over her shoulder, nodding to the desk behind her, "and here's display advertising." To her left stood two rows of unoccupied desks. Some were covered in papers, others starkly bare, either awaited a new hire or signaled the sudden disappearance of an ad rep who failed to make quota. A chin-high row of white metal file cabinets ran the length of the building with a narrow corridor between the cabinets and the innermost row of desks, creating a five-foot tall steel moat between the advertising and news departments.

Dolores led Jake past the ad department and into the newsroom.

Jake stopped and drank in the sight. Thirty-six desks arranged in pods of four stretched in three rows from the center of the building to the offices at the rear. All of them — save one — were buried beneath mountains of paper and consumed by the chaotic tumult of a typical newsroom.

White walls angled high to a domed ceiling 30 feet above. Rows of fluorescent light fixtures ran over the desks, suspended 10 feet from the ceiling from electrical conduit. The high ceiling helped absorb the newsroom clamor, with its steady thrum of typewriters, voices and telephones.

Nearby, a reporter answered his phone, abruptly declared his last name and then, expertly cradling the phone ear to shoulder in one fluid motion, reached for a spiral notebook. People ambled from the reporters' ranks to the editor's pit, a crudely arranged mosh of metal, computer terminals and no-nonsense humanity in the form of the six trusted individuals who wove together the printed fabric of *The Post-Recorder* five afternoons every week and once on Saturday morning.

Jake fell instantly, deeply in love.

"Your desk is over here, in the toy department," said Dolores, her eyes gleaming as she led him to the empty desk across the room. "Oops. Sorry. I mean the sports department.

"That's Dick Busby, sports editor — your boss. Well, one of 'em. We all seem to have a lot of bosses around here, so join the club."

Dolores cast a nervous look back toward reception/classified, a bird unsafely away from her nest.

"Gotta go. Phones are ringing and customers are getting restless," Dolores breezed, gesturing with her chin at two people standing at the reception desk who were impatiently ringing a tiny bell, demanding service. Indicating Busby, a paunchy, youngish man on the phone sitting at a nearby desk, Dolores predicted, "He'll be with you in a minute," then spun on her heels and made tracks for home.

Pen in hand, Busby scratched on a notebook while listening intently. He grunted, "Got it. Thanks." and was off the phone. Suddenly aware of Jake's presence, he rose and extended his hand.

"Ketcher, right? Howdy." He feverishly pumped Jake's hand. "Busby, Dick, but call me BD. Sports editor. Pleezed tuh meetcha." BD tugged at his sansabelt slacks to recover turf from what appeared to be a losing battle with midriff bulge. An impressive potbelly, the product of countless evenings of beer, kielbasa and boiled potatoes, was winning the war and forcing his belt below his navel.

"Dolores ask you out yet? She's usually quick to pounce. The girl has slept her way through scads of reporters. It's a thing for her, carving up the new meat literally the moment they walk in the door," he quipped, then noted the embarrassed look on Jake's reddening face. "Ah, sorry. You'll get used to it."

BD nodded to the desk behind his.

"That's yours. Settle in and in a few minutes I'll take you to meet the ME and get you to orientation."

Jake sat down at the desk and surveyed his new domain.

The sports department occupied the extreme East in the North-South orientation of *The P-R* newsroom, a buffer between journalists banging away on electric typewriters and the advertising department that toiled on the other side of the file cabinet moat.

Like the others, Jake's desk was simple, sterile, and well used. A high-backed chair on wheels rested on a piece of translucent plastic roughly the size of his car, placed on the floor to permit fluid movement of the chair while protecting the sky blue carpet's worn warp. The desk was set in an L shape, a faux wood grain desktop with four feet of workspace populated only by a beige telephone, a spiral notebook and a retractable pen. *The P-R's* elaborate logo was proudly emblazoned on both.

"Welcome gifts," BD grinned.

Jake stared at the phone, perplexed. The receiver rested on the cradle with an evil-looking hook attached to the side: a phone cradle. "That thing'll save your neck. Takes some getting used to, but trust me … it's the best thing since women's sports." BD turned his back and resumed scribbling on his notepad.

The short leg of the "L" part of the desk was situated to his right, attached at a slightly lower level to make typing a possibility without dislocating a shoulder. A sky blue IBM Selectric II typewriter rested front and center with a stack of 8½ x 11 white bond paper to its right — implements of war, tools of destruction, palettes and paints for an aspiring practitioner of journalism's art.

His new home, to his young and idealistis eye: a robin's egg blue-colored roomful of intellectually lethal pundits — armed and dangerous, probing reporters and talented writers with keen eyes for detail, and demanding editors of incalculable brilliance. Woe to the crooks, incompetent businessmen and corrupt politicians whose misbehavior should catch the attention of this lot.

It was perfect.

An enormous, mustachioed man with wild, curly hair sat immediately to his right in front of a computer terminal that resembled a small TV console perched on a stainless steel pedestal. Jake looked at the man, eventually attracting his attention. The man stared back, unblinking, a furry sphinx in polyester.

"Hey, TP, meet Jake Ketcher," BD said, waking to the call for introductions. The large man slowly extended his hand while speaking in a tone so soft and low it was nearly inaudible. The hand was the size of a catcher's mitt. Jake's paw disappeared in it as they shook.

"Tom Polocinski," he said in a voice slightly above a wheeze. "Call me TP — like toilet paper." Something resembling a grin crawled from beneath the man's mustache then disappeared. TP quickly removed his hand and returned to work, pounding at the keyboard in a passionate display of activity. On his own again, Jake rummaged through his desk, taking inventory:

Spiral notebooks.

A box of pens.

A couple of red felt highlighting markers.

A stapler and paper clips.

Lots and lots of cookie crumbs and sugar packets.

"Time for orientation. C'mon," BD said, rising to his feet and gesturing toward the back of the room "I'll introduce you to everybody else later."

BD led Jake through the gauntlet of desks to the centermost office at the back of the room. On the way he explained the use of initials in the newsroom.

"You'll label your stories with a slug — your initials. So you're JK. I'm BD. He's TP. So it goes. Easier than having to remember names," BD said, approaching an attractive young woman behind the desk set before the row of offices to the rear of the room.

"Jennifer Waring," BD said. "Personal assistant to ME Dan Moore, whom I think you've met, and publisher Wick Dunn. They're waiting for us," BD said to Jennifer, who motioned the pair into the office behind her.

"She doesn't say a lot," BD said with a wink. "Wick likes it that way. Take the calls, book the lunches, and pack a bag for a long weekend. It's how he rolls."

A sign on the open door read "Wick Dunn, Publisher." BD gave a cursory rap then, without waiting for a response, led Jake inside.

The office was enormous, with walnut paneled walls and soft incandescent light that contrasted with the blinding fluorescent glare of the newsroom. Two sofas rested at perpendicular angles against the wall across from the desk. Two armchairs — one occupied — rested front and center before a desk the size of a pool table topped with a rich green felt blotter equally as plush. Photos covered most of the walls. Each included the beaming face of the mountain of a man in trousers and vest who rose from behind the desk and reached toward Jake with an enormous paw and a bellowing laugh that filled the room.

"Wick Dunn … haw, haw, haw! Welcome. This is Dan Moore," Dunn said, nodding to the man who sat before him, his steepled fingers partially blocking the unblinking stare beneath his bushy eyebrows.

Jake shook Dunn's hand and turned to Moore. "Thanks, Mr. Dunn, and hi, Mr. Moore. Nice to see you again."

"Oh, Jesus," BD said from his spot near the door. "Lose the 'mister' shit, willya? It'll go to their heads. Deadline's in three hours; gotta go." He left, closing the door behind him.

Moore turned to study Jake as Dunn settled back into his chair and prattled on about the newspaper's history of ownership, civic pride and journalistic achievement. The publisher rose, tugged his slumping trousers onto his expansive waist, and waved Jake to his side.

"See here ... these are photos of me with every contemporary US president, except for Nixon. Never could stand that asshole. Watergate couldn't have happened to a nicer guy. Great golfer, but I think his parents had the right idea by naming him Dick. Haw, haw, haw ...."

"Yeah, Wick loves photos of himself with important people. Trouble is Grover Cleveland wasn't available for a photo shoot when Wick graduated from college," Moore spoke at last.

"Les prefers his photos with noteworthy ballet dancers and interior designers," Dunn retorted, earning a scowl from the managing editor.

Jake marveled enviably at the banter between the two and recalled BD's verbal jousts. Mild insubordination seemed the norm. *Apparently that's the way we do things around here,* he noted, tucking the lesson away for future reference.

National press honors, Associated Press reporting awards, New England Newspaper Association Awards ... Dunn took Jake through each of the framed certificates in excruciating detail, as if ensuring the tradition of journalistic excellence should begin with an exhaustive historical review. Jake noted that the last award was dated 1970 — eight years earlier.

He paused, framing a question about the dry spell, but decided to hold his tongue when the publisher urged him along. Jake hoped the tour was near its end.

But Dunn wasn't finished — not by a longshot. He moved to the end of the wall, festooned with a disorderly collection of base-ball team photos.

"Eleven years in the running — 11 years," Dunn proudly proclaimed. *"The Post-Recorder* has dominated the Rilertown Industrial Softball League with 11 consecutive titles. Last year we swept the Series in three games with two shutouts. Great pitching and defense — that's what makes a winner."

Moore groaned.

"Kid's a reporter, Wick, not a softball player."

"You play the game, son?" Dunn asked Jake, ignoring Moore.

"Yup. Little League, Pony League," Jake responded.

"Positions?"

"Pitched a bit, mostly outfield. Right field. I'm known to have a bit of a cannon attached to my shoulder," Jake beamed, ignoring the fact that he had been banished from the starting rotation after beaning two teammates in pre-season tryouts with high rising fastballs. His coach rightly concluded that right field was a safer position for a kid known to unleash lethal unguided missiles with his right arm.

Dunn clapped him on the back.

"See?" he said to Moore. "Perfect! Well, welcome to the team. Both teams, actually! Season's half way over now, but maybe we can squeeze you onto the roster. Hell, I know the coach. It's me! Haw, haw...."

"Now, Les here is going to take you to meet with our office manager and get you into orientation. Then you get to work. No sense gathering mothballs on your first day. Leave that to me. It's almost lunchtime, too. Haw, haw, haw!"

Jake scowled, perplexed. Dunn noticed.

"Got a question, son? Speak up. A silent reporter's a useless reporter."

"You called him Les, Mr. Dunn. His name's Dan. What's with that?"

"It's what Wick would call newsroom humor," Moore replied, unsmiling. "I'm regarded as something of a dilettante around here, not as compelled by news as I am by information about arts and culture — ephemeral notions to most of these cretins. As far as Wick's pet moron — your other boss, Michael Zamboni — is concerned, I'm 'Les' not 'Moore,' and of course the rest of the newsroom lemmings have caught onto the joke. Feel free. I'm immune to it. You may get used to it, though damned if I ever will."

"Pay no attention to him," Dunn grinned, hand on Jakes' back as he pushed him toward the door. Moore rose to follow. "He and

Zamboni have been waging war on each other for years. That's why I keep them at opposite ends of the building — Les out of the newsroom and Zamboni out of budget land; that's what I say. Well, seeya. We'll grab lunch someday to get to know each other better."

Safely outside the publisher's office and back into the bustling newsroom, Jake stared at Moore. The air seemed more refreshing outside the publisher's office, nourishing salvation for lungs that felt starved of oxygen after a stint in Dunn's verbal wind tunnel.

"He's a bit overwhelming. Great guy. Completely committed to the newspaper his family founded, but I'm afraid he's clueless as to what running a newspaper actually entails. He takes care of the politicians, business leaders and religious zealots who line up to curry favor with *The P-R*'s editorial board. We're in charge of the news, and that's why you're here."

He smiled.

"Oh, and softball, of course."

The smile disappeared.

"Someone's gotta fill the newshole — feed the beast — and that's our job."

Jake followed Moore to a door in the corner of the building. Within was a cavernous conference room with 30 chairs around an oblong wood veneer table that rested on more dark blue carpet. Sunlight streamed from a bank of windows that stretched high against the ceiling and fell on a conservatively dressed middle-aged woman seated at the far end of the table. Two neat stacks of paper rested in front of her on the table, and an ornate black fountain pen lay across them as if holding them in place. Jake half expected the woman to slowly levitate, given her austere presence and the reverential tone of the scene. The woman — a clerical force in command at the management altar — was one cassock short of priesthood. She exuded a frigid, unlikeable air.

"Gladys McAvoy, meet Jake Ketcher," Moore said. "Gladys is our office manager, and she'll be taking you through orientation. If you have any questions, she's a good start. Knock on my door when you're done." Moore exited, closing the door behind him.

Gladys cleared her throat.

"Actually, I am Human Resources Administrator," she said icily. "He never can seem to get my title right."

She motioned Jake to a chair to her left and slid a stack of papers before him as he settled. She wasted no time.

"Employee manual.

"Employment registration form, which you must complete and sign before you leave this room.

"An electronic pass for the back door. Keep this on you at all times while you are in the office. If you lose it, you will be charged $10 to replace it.

"A press badge form which you must sign before you leave this room. We will take your photo later this morning. You shall have your badge in 48 hours. Also keep this with you at all times while you are in the building for the purpose of security.

"Questions?" she asked without giving Jake a chance to respond. "Good."

She slid stack #2 his way.

"An employee roster, updated through last week, which means there have been two or three changes since then, nothing you need to concern yourself with. People come and go here. It rarely matters. I think of this place as a haven for migrant field work that attracts people with journalism degrees."

She sniffed as though sensing a sour odor in the room, and pushed more papers toward him.

"A parking lot map with designated areas for advertising, news and executive, which is where I and other senior managers park," she sniffed once again, adjusting the neatly tied white bow around her neck and seeming to rise a bit more in her seat.

Jake instantly disliked her, sensing in her the haughtiness of a spinster kindergarten teacher with the attitude of a jail guard. Gladys picked up on Jake's disapproval and quickly moved to stake out her turf. She regarded him as she would a piece of gum stuck to her sole.

"Reporters come and go here. Most think they're out to make some sort of big difference in this city I've called home my entire life. Most think they're smart, and that they have all the answers. Most aren't, don't, and most fail. Many are drunks, drug users or simply stupid and incompetent."

She squared her shoulders, on a roll.

"As a policy, *The Post-Recorder* doesn't tolerate alcohol or drug abuse, and professional ethics and conduct matter a great deal to us. You will read the manual carefully before you leave this room, placing your initials on each page and signing the last. And you'll closely adhere to the contents therein…." She paused, rising even slightly higher. "… or we'll be meeting again under slightly less pleasant circumstances, and then you will be gone.

"You are here to gather and generate news for *The Post-Recorder*. Your daily work is under the guidance of the news editor, sports editor and managing editor, but your conduct is under my exclusive purview. I am always watching and listening, and I miss little. You will do well to remember that.

"Questions?" she again breezed perfunctorily, though she was clearly not interested in providing answers.

"Yeah," Jake thought to himself. *"How far, exactly, is your head stuck up your ass?"* Choosing a more diplomatic route, he smiled and shook his head. "Seems pretty clear to me. Where do I take the forms when I've completed the homework?"

Gladys pounced. "Homework? Do I detect sarcasm? I surely hope we won't be having a problem with you, Mr. Ketcher, but let me assure you we have the means and experience to deal with it if that turns out to be the case."

The moment passed, and Gladys wrapped up her monolog with a dissertation about tax declaration forms. She finally got to the matter Jake cared most about.

"Pay is the first and third Wednesday of each month," she said. "Dolores distributes paychecks. See me immediately if you find any errors or discrepancies."

Gladys rose to her feet, closing her leather-bound folder with an emphatic bang. She adjusted her calf-length grey skirt and white cravat, donned the matching gray jacket carefully draped across the chair behind her, lifted her chin to point her nose to the ceiling, and marched out the door.

"What a bitch," Jake said aloud as the door closed behind her.

The room warmed instantly. Jake spent the next hour dutifully reading, initialing and signing. He finished, stacked the papers and sat for a few minutes, fingering the pimple on his chin and wondering what was next, before he remembered Moore's invitation to knock on his door when he was done.

The managing editor was studying a copy of *Women's Wear Daily* when Jake appeared in the doorway. Moore tossed the magazine into his bottom drawer and slammed it shut.

"Done? Great. Toss it all on my desk. I'll get it sorted out in a bit. "

Jake placed the papers on Moore's desk and took a seat.

"Gladys is quite a piece of work, huh? She's related to Wick through one of his marriages, so we're kinda stuck with her. Luckily that'll be the last you see of her until the annual Christmas party, unless you fuck up and we need to take you through progressive discipline." Moore grinned as he muttered the phrase "progressive discipline" making quote marks with his fingers and lowering his voice in a threatening tone, mocking the office manager's strict behavioral standards.

He picked up a pencil and began tapping one end on the desk, then nimbly flipped it around and tapped the other end as he spoke. Point. Eraser. Point. Eraser.

"She hasn't been laid in 20 years — which explains her hideous attitude," Moore said. "She talked Wick into the 'progressive discipline' policy after one of our reporters got drunk before a city council meeting and picked a fight with the chairman. We could have fired the guy, but secretly we applauded his efforts. The chairman's a jerk and a bully, so we decided to try to salvage the reporter."

Point. Eraser. Point. Eraser. Jake couldn't help but watch the pencil as he listened.

"Didn't work out. We fired him after the pressroom foreman caught him feeling up Dolores in ink storage early one evening. Seemed at first like a consenting adults thing, but turns out he was alternating his attention between Dolores' boobs and a pint of Jack Daniels. Playing once around the mattress while on the job is not specifically disallowed according to the employee manual, but drinking on the premises is, so out he went.

"As a result, Gladys insisted that we install a code of behavior — as if that would provide any restraints to a bunch of 20-something newshounds whose hormonal activity is exceeded only by their inquisitive minds and ability to consume alcoholic beverages. But Wick signed off on it, so here we are. We're stuck with Gladys and her rules of conduct."

Hearing the mildly disrespectful conflict between executive protocol and employee behavior illustrated in detail, Jake fell further in love with his chosen career path. Some rules were meant to be followed, others subtly broached, if not ignored outright.

"Th' hell 'd you do to your chin?" Moore asked, paying notice to the zit that Jake had been nervously squeezing.

Jake reddened.

Moore abruptly snapped the pencil in half and tossed it in a nearby wastebasket. He rose and motioned Jake to follow.

"Time for you to meet the rest of the inmates in the asylum and get to work."

The next half hour was a blur of handshakes and welcomes. They exchanged names and made introductions, interrupted by ringing telephones and summonses to the paper's "rim" and "slot," the collection of desks where editors lorded over their charges and whipped the day's paper into shape.

Most reporters seemed friendly enough but distracted, and two of them — Phil Buckley and Sarah Turnbull — promised to "catch up after deadline for a 'beer and bull' session."

Jake retreated to his desk in the sports department and was studying the Selectric's operating manual when he heard BD mutter, "Oh, shit. Incoming Zamboni." He directed Jake's attention to the row of file cabinets to his right that separated the sports department from advertising. Jake saw a head barely covered with wispy hair bobbing up and down as its owner made his way along the other side of cabinets, drawing close to the sports department.

"Hold onto your ass," BD warned. "This could be bad. It's never great when he's on his way back from a meeting with advertising, but this could be epic. I heard a bunch of yelling a while ago — Zamboni and the ad director, going at it again."

Rounding the corner, a scowling middle-aged man with searing black eyes and an appallingly bad complexion stepped into view. Clad in a white shirt rolled to the elbows, black vest and black trousers, he looked more mortician than news editor. His clenched teeth and commanding frown left a whitish mustache above his lips, dominating his face with something between a sneer and the look of a man who had just eaten rotten sausage.

Jake took note of the man's face, which was framed by a thin mop of unruly, dirty sand-colored hair seemingly cut by a blind man who then combed his work using an egg beater. Strands of hair flew in every direction, giving Zamboni a disheveled appearance despite his crisp, neatly pressed clothing. Deep, angry pockmarks peppered his forehead, nose, cheeks and jowls. He squinted through tiny slits. Specks of black irises surveyed Jake and BD.

The emotional battle of Zamboni's unhappy, tumultuous youth had been waged on the landscape between his hairline and chin, leaving deep, reddened, conjoined craters. He looked like an angry sock puppet, but his eyes shone with imposing, steely aggression that made his appearance not at all comical.

Michael Zamboni was shorter than BD by a foot and a good four inches shy of Jake's 5′ 9″ frame, yet he loomed ominously as he approached.

He cast furtive looks at Jake, then at BD.

"This Ketcher?" As though Jake was a sofa on display and Zamboni was shopping for furniture.

"Yup," BD responded.

"Huh," retorted Zamboni, turning to Jake. He studied him for an uncomfortable, unblinking moment. His mouth eased into a slight smile.

He growled: "Nice zit."

Then he turned and stomped off toward the editor's pit.

RILERTOWN:

A CITY IN RAPID DECAY

It took Jake an hour to drive the two miles from the office to his apartment.

He was lost moments after leaving the newspaper's driveway. Ahead lay the foothills of the small mountain range that protected Rilertown from the brutal north winds that battered the city during the long winter months. He was clearly, mindlessly and hopelessly headed in the wrong direction.

Realizing his mistake, he doubled back and zig-zagged his way through the city's major arteries and side streets, staring with uninterrupted awe at the specter of turn-of-the century grandeur gone very, very wrong.

Rilertown was a city long past its glory and in rapid, obvious decay.

Crammed between a small mountain range to the west and the unpronounceable Oksaguganuatee River to the east (locals referred to it as the Tee River, owing to their commitment to monosyllabic vocabularies and reluctance to indulge the region's rich Native American history), Rilertown rested comfortably between the region's two immovable natural objects. One of the first cities in the United States designed for industrial greatness, Rilertown was criss-crossed by a series of polluted canals that once powered the city's paper and textile mills with pure, fish-rich waters. Row upon row of five- and six-story brick buildings lined the waterways, crumbling monuments to happier, more prosperous days that now offered direct views of putrid, malodorous canals strewn with garbage.

In better times, the canals drove the city's 19th century industrial success, which fell into the greedy and ill-prepared laps of a gang of uneducated second-generation immigrants. Born of Irish and French-Canadian heritage, these brawling, ruthless fools drank themselves into generations-long stupors of waste, mismanagement and nepotism. They consumed profits as fast as they were generated — nearly as fast as the beer and whiskey that filled their bellies and pickled what brains they had. Lacking foresight, business acumen and perspective, they ran their businesses with little regard for competition, changing economic realities or the future.

As 19th century prosperity evaporated, 20th century blight flourished. Chronic inattention led to the city's demise as industry fled from the region like canal rats from the tenements during annual spring floods. Block-long brick rowhouses built to house workers crumbled and cracked. The city's streets, carefully paved in grids that mirrored Manhattan by men who envisioned a rich mecca that would make New York the weaker sister, boasted potholes big enough to swallow a child on a bicycle — which, according to Moore, had actually happened one day to a nine-year-old boy pedaling home with a quart of milk under his arm. Failing to pay adequate attention, he disappeared on his bike into an enormous sinkhole that emerged after a particularly strong spring freshet.

Ever the opportunist, the city's mayor responded by announcing Rilertown's first-ever Bicycle Safety Week. Word on the street was that the kid received a serious beating from his mother's boyfriend for dropping the milk.

Jake assessed the city as he drove. Streets laid on a rectangular grid held rows of brick tenements in place, confining their urban sprawl in tracts of land that seemed too small to restrain them from oozing beyond their physical confines. Bricks from the crumbling buildings rested in dusty piles. Some found their way onto the streets' surfaces, having bounced there on their own. Others were deposited by one of the angry youths who routinely waged war on unsuspecting passersby.

People sat in distressed furniture along the streets. Sofas, armchairs and stools provided roosts for the unemployed, drunk, drug addicted or lazy to pass the days and wait for something to happen.

The city's canals did their best to control the landscape, bringing order to the chaos of narrow streets clogged with rusty cars, children and trouble. Water has a way of mitigating human behavior, and the canals played vital roles in keeping humanity from taking over every square foot of available space.

Spanish language signs abounded. Jake took note of the disproportionate number of Hispanics walking the streets in this part of the city — disproportionate as in *all of them.* Not a white face was to be seen except behind the wheels of shiny cars that whizzed through stop signs and blew through red lights to avoid the threats of the barrio.

Jake felt out of place, lost, and far away from the white bread comfort of his hometown that rested quietly only 25 miles to the north.

He meandered through the city, determined to acquire a sense of the turf that was now partly his, along High Street past the gothic grey looming edifice of City Hall, and past the Hall of Justice that clung to the back of City Hall like a remora to a shark. He signaled and turned south back into The Flats, slowing with his mouth agape as the face of extreme poverty and urban stress revealed itself.

Young men glared at him as he crawled past, scowling in contempt at the gringo who was out of his element, on ice so thin a feather would crash through. Groups of men in fresh jeans and brilliant white tank tops congregated at a major intersection ahead, posing serious threats to motorists forced to stop at the red lights. Jake turned right at the lights rather than stop at the intersection, choosing escape over the possibility of confrontation.

Recognizing the church near where he lived, Jake fled north back to the relative safety of the city's carefully delineated white neighborhoods.

Like many urban centers, Rilertown had stubbornly ceded space to the sprawl of poverty. The city's neighborhoods, Elmwood, The Highlands, Mountain View and Golden Acres, remained strongholds of the city's white middle class. City Center, Downtown and the notorious Flats had long been given up by the founding population as hopeless enclaves for the poor.

The nicer neighborhoods occupied the crest of a small rise that looked down on the rest of the city.

Stunned by the desperation of the city's poor, Jake was once again lost when he spotted a familiar street sign. He executed a sloppy turn, got flipped off by a young man driving a rusty Dodge, and, minutes, later, eased his complaining Ford Fairlane to the curb in front of his apartment building.

He and his girlfriend Sabrina had found the apartment two weeks earlier after a day of wandering the city. They quickly determined which neighborhoods would be safe and drove around, knocking on doors and walking through a dozen or so uninhabitable hovels before they got lucky.

They had seen the "Apartment for Rent" sign in the ground floor window of the house as they drove along. Jake pulled to the curb and knocked on the door once, twice and then a third time with a loud bang. Moments later a wizened elderly man reeking of booze and sporting five days' growth of gray beard stuck his face through the crack in the door restrained by a safety chain.

He studied Jake.

"You Puerto Rican?" he asked in a thick, eastern European accent.

"No, a reporter," Jake responded. "I work for *The Post-Recorder*. You renting an apartment?"

After several more uncomfortable seconds of scrutiny, the man unfastened the chain and waved them inside. A quick tour of the tiny, second floor apartment cemented the couple's choice for their new home. They moved their scant belongings in over the next few days and set about finding their way to the essentials: grocery store, laundromat, neighborhood bar, the best place to park a car that would reduce the likelihood of vandalism or theft.

The apartment occupied an awkward part of the city. One side of the street rested in Elmwood, and though barely on the edge of relative affluence, the quality and care of homes was noticeable. The other side — where Jake's landlord had plunked down his life's savings to buy a small, two-story Cape a decade earlier — was slowly being consumed by the lower city's blight. Two or three more years, and the fight would be lost as poverty crept across the street and continued into neighborhoods that had previously been spared the inevitable sprawl.

They invested all of Jake's savings — nearly $500 — in the form of first and last months' rent and one-month security deposit. 160 bucks a month — plus utilities — seemed like a financial mountain for them to climb, particularly given Jake's meager salary and Sabrina's uncertain personal financial prospects.

Jake had been hoping for nine grand a year but had accepted "the standard *Post-Recorder* starting salary of $8,000" after a poorly executed round of negotiations. That the annual salary translated to $666 per month wasn't lost on the young man. He wasn't big on Satanic numerology but believed in the significance of signs along life's path.

He asked around about rents and costs of living, did the math, and decided that he and Sabrina would be able to get by.

Sabrina was his smoking hot, unevenly tempered and reasonably talented girlfriend. A former competitive salsa dancer in

New York, once past her dancing and man-hunting prime Sabrina had moved into the uncertain world of self-employed salsa instruction. She was a frequent featured teacher at senior centers and dance salons wherever she'd lived, which was mostly between the Jersey shore and Canadian border as she'd bounced from relationship to relationship and job to job as the years dragged on.

She met Jake while he was attending Blendhurst University, a private college in western New York that boasted one of the country's best journalism schools. Jake applied to Blendhurst on a drunken bet with a classmate at the junior college he attended after high school. He'd landed at the junior college much to the relief and surprise of his doting but doubting parents, both of whom had him destined for a career with the Silvertown Department of Public Works. To his parents, kids like Jake seemed better suited to keeping Silvertown's streets clean than defending liberty as a representative of the Fourth Estate.

Ever the contrarian, Jake shrugged off the passive disapproval, packed his bags and embarked on a personal journey that offered excitement, change and anything but the abject stagnancy that his hometown guaranteed.

He first took refuge at a tiny junior college well out of Boston's intimidating intellectual zone but safely buffered from the decadent temptations of hardscrabble southeastern Massachusetts. He spent the ensuing two years learning about literature, Marxist principles and environmental policy while also learning to roll a joint with one hand. He bounced from class to bar and through a series of unfulfilling yet sexually satisfying relationships, adrift in a sea of misguided youthful intentions as the country struggled with its president's role in a noteworthy break-in at a Washington hotel.

Nearing the end of his "junior college vacation," as his sister liked to tease, Jake faced the unhappy prospect of either continuing his higher education or going to work. He chose the former, but, sporting a grade point average more respectable of a major league catcher than someone destined for educational greatness, found few options.

Miraculously, Blendhurst's admissions staff saw something promising in Jake and accepted him. He departed for the frozen land of buffalo wings and cheap beer to study journalism as taught by respected ex-news professionals who had found refuge in a life of academia.

Jake's insatiable curiosity, sarcastic outlook and intolerance for bullshit made him a natural for journalism. He quickly established himself as one of the favored insiders in his classes then augmented his reporting instincts and writing skills with a remarkable ability to consume beer. Soon, he was a regular at the campus haunts with his favorite professors, his night classes often cut short in lieu of ensuring prime seats at one of the countless campus watering holes.

Campus journalism during the 1970s published diluted versions of the fiery invective that had defined university rags a decade earlier. Like the old dog that still had plenty of bark but was plagued by teeth that broke at the first nibble, Blendhurst's campus daily, *The Daily Blendhurst* and its alternative sister, *The Student Association Report,* fired desultory, routine shots across the bows of the conservative university, the New York state assembly, and at whatever president happened to be calling 1600 Pennsylvania Avenue home.

The SA Report was a lean yet viable training ground for would-be anarchists. The paper, which was overseen by a disinterested advisor more intent on bullying the staff than sharing valuable expertise, somehow taught good reporting skills despite its awkward management and diluted mission. *The SA Report* provided an abundance of free range and plenty of fodder for the aspiring professional journalists, and they helped the school churn out legions of corduroy-clad Woodward wannabes that satisfied the nation's demand for people to work ridiculously long hours for miserable pay.

Jake worked his way into a staff role at *The SA Report,* earning a regular dumping ground for his turgid prose as well as a monthly stipend to feed his habits of pizza, cigarettes, pot and beer. He soon became features editor. That gave him access to student association funds, which he happily deployed in a series of "personal education and growth" articles that included a tour of the local brewery, a series of sky diving lessons that resulted in the death of one of his fellow students and thus drew his skydiving career to an abrupt close, and, again on a drunken bet with a buddy, lessons in salsa dancing.

"You're taking dance lessons?" chided one of his pals over 32-ounce Utica Clubs one evening.

"Yup," mused Jake, his glazed eyes revealing the comfortable aftereffects of the joint he had smoked on his way to the bar. "Dry spell in the romance department. I need new lands to explore."

"Looking for love off the Blendhurst campus is as likely to get you robbed or stabbed as laid," his friend countered, signaling the bartender for another round and reaching for a handful of peanuts.

But Jake, committed and undeterred, drove his black Fairlane off the campus and into the arms of salsa and the woman of his immediate future.

Sabrina happened to be teaching salsa at the community center as part of the city's Thursday Night Thrills series. Jake was instantly attracted to the loquacious, raven-haired beauty with the narrow waist and fabulous bottom who slithered, slid and wiggled around the dance floor, confounding the septuagenarians in the group but setting Jake's libido on fire.

Sabrina took equal interest in the good looking young guy who kept staring at her as he went through the salsa basics with his dance partner, a sixty-something grandmother who beamed as the "handsome young man" steered her around the dance floor while constantly looking over his shoulder at the instructor. Jake was gifted with broad shoulders and powerful legs that stretched the fabric of his jeans around his thighs. Yeah, he was a little thick around the waist, but man, those eyes. She was always a sucker for guys with legs and eyes, particularly if the legs were muscular and the eyes dark and searing, as were Jake's.

Framed by his dark brown hair and easy smile, Jake's eyes had proven valuable assets over the years. They quickly became expert at appreciating Sabrina's backside, and she noticed his lingering gazes. The first class was followed with a cup of coffee at the nearby Denny's ("I don't drink," Sabrina had said, refusing Jake's offer to go for a beer or glass of wine. "I cannot.") That puzzled the lad, whose regular consumption of beer bordered on religious zeal. But no matter, he was in hot pursuit and confident he could weave his magic as easily over a cup of joe as through the glorious bubbles in a glass of Utica Club.

They saw each other weekly after that, at first sharing a Grand Slam at Denny's as the hours whirled past. Soon they changed venues to Sabrina's miserable apartment overlooking the city bus station, where the relationship evolved.

Sabrina proved an athletic, imaginative and endlessly enthusiastic lover, which is why Jake failed to notice something amiss during one night of sex that reached gymnastic proportions. They were locked in coital embrace, bathing each other in sweat and panting loudly as their gyrations reached epochal levels. Jake breathed a particularly provocative query into Sabrina's sweaty ear and waited for the guttural "yes, yes" he had heard many times. When no response was forthcoming, he paused momentarily above her writhing nakedness, then dismounted, alarmed, when he realized that Sabrina was not immersed in pleasure, but experiencing what in the ensuing hours he would learn was a grand mal epileptic seizure.

At the hospital emergency room, the doctor explained that Sabrina's internal electronics made petit mal and grand mal seizures predictable occurrences in her life — and these were more likely with the presence of stress, alcohol and monthly menses. This knowledge spiked a protective instinct in Jake that rocketed past unhealthy. He worried about her constantly, and was thus vulnerable to Sabrina's cunning manipulation. She realized that her beau could be swayed to her wants with so much as a drift-ing glance, shudder or falsified pronunciation that, "I'm feeling a bit weird."

Sabrina's "condition" dominated Jake's life and psyche. He monitored her wellbeing by hovering when near, and through regular telephone calls when not. Being apart from her caused him considerable anxiety. His protective instincts combined with genuine love to create a textbook codependent quagmire.

Now, taking the steps to their apartment two at a time, Jake turned the key and noisily made his way in to find Sabrina.

"Don't sneak up on me," she had warned repeatedly. *"It might scare me and start a seizure."* So Jake developed a practice of loudly bouncing about their shared space so as not to upset her personal apple cart. He often got yelled at for "being as graceful as a water buffalo" as he slammed and stomped around the apartment, but he thought it better to endure periodic verbal abuse than risk inducing a seizure.

This led to a life of interminable psychological instability for the lad, who did his best to hold it all together while Sabrina became more and more disingenuous, calculating and needy as their relationship cured.

Sabrina was predictably tucked into the corner of the couple's sole piece of decent living room furniture, a wood-framed loveseat covered with a fireproof fabric whose pattern would have served well as drapes in any grandmother's sitting room. She was sipping a glass of ice tea and smoking a joint. ("Helps me stay calm and prevents seizures," she loved to explain.)

"What's for dinner?" she asked, foregoing any questions about Jake's first day at work.

"I thought we'd grab a pizza. And hey, what a weird first day. I'll tell you all about it. Come on." Sabrina sucked noisily on the joint, failing to offer any to Jake, as she slipped on her shoes and joined him at the door.

Soon they were tucked in a dark booth at a bar that doubled as a pizza joint about 10 minutes' walk from their apartment. Sabrina halfheartedly picked mushrooms from a slice of pizza while Jake chased down three slices with two cold Rolling Rocks.

"So, tell me about it," she said. "Any nice people? What will you be working on? Any good looking women?" He answered her questions, encouraged by her sudden interest. Jaked eased into a happy place he rarely visited, chatting and painting vivid verbal pictures of his new place of employment.

Sabrina scowled, avoided eye contact and occasionally glanced around the room, obviously bored and impatient, as Jake happily prattled on.

At last she spoke again, and got to her primary interest.

"So when do you get paid?"

Money was a divisive issue. As a reporter, Jake was committed to a career of poverty with little chance of significant improvement. Sabrina's lot as a temporary fill-in part time dance instructor made her financial profile even dicier, and the combined meager income caused constant friction.

"Two weeks. I get paid every two weeks. I signed up for max deductions so we won't owe taxes at the end of the year."

Bad move.

"Well, that's brilliant, just perfect. So the government keeps your money all year long while we go without, then they give back a fraction of it *if and when* they get around to it."

Pizza slice in hand, Jake stared at his girlfriend as a man on death row would regard his executioner.

"Hold on, Sabrina," he protested, "that's not it at all …"

Shaking her head: "Good thing you didn't go into banking or finance."

Despite her deeply held belief in Jake's reporting potential, such barbed comments fed on Jake's insecurity and sense of unworthiness. Sabrina compensated for her lack of formal education and general knowledge by doling out liberal doses of edgy, bitchy verbal abuse on her lovestruck boyfriend.

She loved him deeply despite her intemperate behavior. The combination of father figure, white knight, searing lover and tolerant boy friend appealed to Sabrina. She also thought of him as the sexiest man around. Sabrina's fawning physical adoration projected a sense of longing that filled a void in Jake, so he tolerated her abuse and chose to accentuate Sabrina's positive qualities. He rarely fought back in earnest.

Occasionally, though, he would remind her that she was the unproductive lay-about in the relationship, and that the job market could also produce steady income for her, if she'd only write a resume and get out of bed before 10 a.m. to look for work.

"I can't get a regular *job* job," she said. "It causes me stress. And that, well, you know ...." Her voice would trail off, leaving Jake's active imagination to visualize her writhing on the floor, wracked by an immense grand mal seizure as the pressures of a 40-hour work week short-circuited her synapses and plunged both of them into physical and mental hell.

Sabrina's threats of seizures always had immediate an effect on Jake. So did her caustic remarks.

He lost his appetite, dropped the pizza slice onto the plate and tossed back the rest of his beer. He stared at the wall. Money — more precisely the absence thereof — was the major reason why Sabrina had rejected each of his heartfelt propositions for marriage. The last time he proposed, several weeks earlier during a bathroom and burger break at an Arby's on the New York State Thruway during the six-hour drive from Blendhurst to Rilertown,

Sabrina broke tradition from her usual passive "it's not the right time for us," and became aggressive.

"You just don't get it, do you?" she attacked, her voice steeped in bitterness and conveying a sense that the world — and, more specifically, Jake — owed her. "So I'll make this as clear as I can for you. You aren't gonna have me, not completely, until you do something with your life that makes me go "ooh!" and gets me all hot.

"I'm not your girl, not if you think you can get me to sign onto a life with you that doesn't give me guarantees … I mean real, hard cash guarantees … that you're gonna take care of me. That's what makes me hot. And that's what you need to focus on.

"So far," she said, finishing her burger, rolling the greasy wrapper and paper napkin into a ball and tossing it toward a nearby rubbish bin — missing the barrel by a foot, ignoring the terrible shot yet rising to leave — "you ain't even close."

Jake hadn't broached the subject of marriage since.

What was it about this unpredictable, frustrating and often difficult woman he found so irresistibly attractive?

Aside from evoking his protective instincts, Sabrina brought out a lot of good in Jake. She reminded him of his certain, bright future. She pointed out how much smarter he was than a) his peers, b) his teachers and future bosses and c) most politicians, business leaders and religious figures. She told him, repeatedly, that having talent required that he do something with it.

He never found it odd that Sabrina routinely failed to include herself in the list of Jake's intellectual inferiors, instead choosing to view her sweeping condemnations of all others as emotional support he badly needed.

Part of this carefully woven ruse was true.

More than his parents, his sister and even his beloved godmother, Sabrina believed that Jake was bound for greatness; a modern Mencken with talent and vast potential who lacked the tragic profile that consumed HL and scores like him. With plenty of experience kowtowing to losers throughout her wandering life, she set standards and goals for Jake that were well beyond what he would set for himself, and she challenged him every day to strive for more.

Jake loved Sabrina's unique blend of abrasiveness, and he favorably weighed the positives of her dogged support of his goals against her insecure vulnerability and stubborn independence. He took enormous pride in knowing the soft, gentle and vulnerable truth behind the exterior that Sabrina projected to the world. He knew her personal history in great, saddening detail. Her unhappy, conflict-saturated upbringing left him with deep respect, in awe that she had emerged intact from a horrible string of bad luck, awful choices and unfortunate circumstances as a remarkable survivor.

He viewed Sabrina's assaultive conduct as sadly defensive; her caustic, often scathing attacks as pre-emptive strikes intended to retain her sense of self and sanity. He saw through her veneer, and deep into the soft, vulnerable woman who was simply never taught how to be a good daughter or friend, let alone partner or wife. His delusion allowed him to believe she would emerge one day, like a bear from winter's hibernation, and wrap him in all the love and attention he craved. Till then, he was committed to taking her criticism, accepting the great sex and spiritless partnership, and making the best of the situation. Far less than perfect became a perfectly acceptable option as far as their relationship was concerned.

Sabrina did her best to hide her vulnerability. Jake took it upon himself not to teach her the ropes — far be it for him, the son of a tire shop owner and a former nurse, to assume such responsibility — but to help her learn for herself how best to become a woman who one day might be his wife. Allowing himself to further wander into lands of fantastic speculation, he foresaw a day when the two might have children and create a family.

Now, however, there remained the task of hanging onto Sabrina as she floundered in the muck of daily pressures: money, career, family (his; hers were either dead, disenfranchised or disinterested), and what on earth she was going to do with herself. *Funny how one's self-criticism is often reassigned as others' failings,* he reflected, again softening to Sabrina and her weird commitment to expecting less of herself yet much, much more from him.

The conversation about money imposed a chill between them. Jake paid the bill and headed for the door, trailing Sabrina, who sulked the entire walk back to their apartment and purposefully strode five feet in front of him. Once home, she slipped off her shoes and eased back into her fixed spot on the loveseat, flicked on the television, and began to roll a joint.

Jake stared at her from the hallway, torn between heading to bed or sharing the weed with her and trying to shift her mood into the possibility of romance. Feeling his gaze, she lifted her eyes to his, scowled, shook her head and turned back to the television.

Disappointed, Jake headed to bed. He dreamt of a blonde woman with the face of Gladys McAvoy yet with sky-blue eyes, enormous boobs and an enormous, quivering butt, chasing him around *The Post-Recorder* newsroom, trying to sit on him.

APRIL 20, 1975

H*e stood in the doorway, frozen in fear as he struggled to absorb the scene before him.*

Within the hotel's dimly lit bedroom, a portly, shirtless man scrambled into his trousers, his boxer shorts bunching into the crack of his ample posterior as he struggled to dress.

On the bed, a young woman rested on her side, naked, quiet — dead.

In the suite's living room behind the man in the doorway, two other men rushed about in response to the urgent cries and flurry of activity.

What a fucking nightmare, *he thought, his breath catching in his throat as he contemplated the enormity of the problem.* How could this happen?

"She . . . she just choked and then went still," babbled the fat man, forcing an arm into his white shirt. "How the fuck was I to know she couldn't breathe? You have to get me out of here."

Three clients and a dead hooker in a cheap hotel room means major trouble — for them, and for me — worse for me. Gotta clean up this scene and protect these guys from their own stupidity and greed.

They cannot be involved, *the man mused. I* have to protect them.

He began a mental checklist of what must be done to cleanse the room and extricate the men from what had begun as a party but was now a murder scene.

There would be police, and reporters, and an investigation.

The worst part would come much later. The money guys ... the rich, powerful and ruthless men whose business interests created this mess, made the rules very clear: We'll pay for the booze, the golf, the meals and the hookers ... all costs of doing business. Your job is to advance our interests, make the locals happy, and keep us from view.

Be very clear about this. We are ghosts, and our involvement must not be revealed under any circumstances. If we wind up in the news, we go away. If we find ourselves trouble finds us, well, then ... *you* go away.

He glanced at the dead girl and indulged in a moment of sadness — but not for the wasted potential of a beautiful young woman who had breathed her last. He felt for himself, and for the situation he now had to navigate to save the clients who had fucked it all up and risked all he had worked to achieve.

I can handle this, *the man reasoned.* This is not the real threat — not the hotel staff or the cops. I can manage them.

The real *concern was with the nameless, faceless men who operated from a safe distance, the men who drank sambucca-laced coffee and smoked expensive Cuban cigars in back-alley offices while controlling business deals involving millions every day, men who cherished their privacy above all else. Men of fat wallets, uncompromising, unforgiving will and violent disposition who demanded anonymity and who exacted brutal punishment of anyone who failed to produce results. Their credo: Do it our way, or die.*

How to resolve this situation? Think, then act. Fast.

The man barked orders at the three others and worked to purge the scene of their presence. Anything they had touched was tossed into plastic bags for removal or wiped down to erase fingerprint traces. Completing the sweep, he ushered the three flustered men out the door into their waiting cars and tossed the final bag of evidence into the trunk of his own car. He returned to the room to take one final tour as three sedans sped from the parking lot.

Every detail must be attended to. No trace must be left. There's a way out of this mess, but I have to be thorough. There can be no evidence, *other than a dead girl lying naked in a $20 hotel room on a chilly April night.*

What a fucking nightmare.

SPLIT-SHIFT

Jake's job as split-shift news/sports reporter meant he worked 7 to 11 each morning and 7 to 11 at night. His colleagues sarcastically called him "Mr. Convenience."

He served as general assignment news reporter each morning. At night, he donned the hat of a sports writer on the graveyard shift. Such a multi-disciplined job with the most bizarre hours in the newsroom was designed for the young, hopeful, naïve and exploitable. Jake qualified on all fronts, so he accepted the role with commitment, enthusiasm and genuine happiness.

A few weeks into his new job, Jake was spicing up an AP story about drought in the region with quotes from a member of the state university's Agriculture and Farm Services Department faculty. The middle-aged woman had been up to her earlobes reading reports about chinch bug infestations and new methods of preventing asparagus fungus when Jake called. Her excitement was obvious; an interview for a newspaper story meant a break from the day's tedium. She loaded him up with technical quotes using terms that sent him scrambling for the dictionary, and seemed sad to end the conversation when he thanked her and hung up.

Jake was pounding away at his IBM when he was engulfed by an enormous shadow.

"And what story is our intrepid young scrivener concocting today?"

Wick Dunn.

Jake spun on his chair's wheels and rose to greet the publisher.

"Hey, Wick. How are you?"

"Fine. Hungry. Thinking of lunch in an hour or so, and thinking it's time we finally broke bread together and got to know one another. Noon OK?"

"Sure. I'm filing this in a few minutes and should be clear. Gotta check with Mike, though, but I'm sure it'll be OK."

Jake re-wrote the lead on the story and hammered the rest of it out in short order. He centered the typewriter carriage and typed the computer code for "end": -30-.[1] He scanned the pages into the OCR, cleaned up the typos and grammatical errors on a computer terminal near his desk, and filed the story with a copy editor for proofreading. He popped his head into Zamboni's

1. 30- is news writers' jargon for "end," in the days of hot type placed at the end of a story to signify its finality for typesetters.

office to make sure the story was acceptable and that it was OK to leave for lunch.

Zamboni grunted his assent, so shortly after 12:00 Jake followed Wick out the back door to the black Lincoln Continental Mark V parked in the space closest to the building. Wick's car was everything he was not: sleek, lean, polished, svelte and black. It was also enormous, mirroring Wick's most obvious physical attribute, and it glistened in the mid-day sun: a car of presidential qualities befitting a man of power.

Jake slid into the passenger seat while Wick fired up the engine, reversed from the parking space, and stomped on the gas pedal. He slid around two 45-degrees turns from the parking lot to the exit and out onto the service road leading to the city center.

"V8 … 402 cubic inches … four barrel carb … this baby weighs almost 5,000 pounds but jumps to top speed pretty quickly." Wick filled most of the car's front seat, his sausage fingers gripping the steering wheel at 10 and 2. His knees thrust into the dash and his mammoth chest nearly rested on the steering wheel as his voice boomed off the windshield and rolled over Jake like thunder across the western Massachusetts hills. Wick tapped the brakes as he approached a traffic signal changing from green to yellow. He ran the red light with a chuckle, spun the wheel and flew onto the city's High Street, then abruptly cut onto a side street and caromed into a reserved parking space conspicuously labeled "WD."

Moments later they slid into his private booth at The Purple Cow, a cozy 40-seat restaurant not far from City Hall that was a favorite among Rilertown's power brokers. The Cow owed its popularity to a reliable menu, gargantuan portions, liberal pours in the drinks that streamed forth from the well-stocked bar at lunchtime, and Wick's omnipresence as majority owner. Everyone who was anyone in Rilertown knew Wick. For the publisher to stop by your table as you dined with someone slightly more powerful than you, greet you by name and slap you on the back as he headed on his way, meant a certain surge in your political stock in the local power broker market.

A waiter appeared, placing a drink before Wick.

"Dewar's and a drop," he said to Jake, hoisting the glass to his lips and savoring a long pull before setting it down. He wiped his mustache with the back of his hand. "Senseless to ruin good Scotch with too much water. You want?"

"No, thanks," Jake said. "I have to work this afternoon," instantly realizing his mistake.

So did Wick.

"Haw, haw, haw … good one! Yeah, me too! Right after nap time!"

Jake looked with horror at the menu and its obscene prices, then realized that lunch would be on Wick. So it was sliced tenderloin and mashed for Wick and chicken Marsala for Jake, with an iced tea. They chatted as they waited for the food to arrive.

The waiter poured water for Jake.

"None for you?" he asked Wick.

"Never touch the stuff unless it's been washed in whiskey. Fish fuck in water.

"You know, our families have history," Wick said, shifting gears. "My dad and your grandmother were contemporaries, friends — not sure just how friendly, but they were close in their younger days...." he added with a wink.

Jake was well aware of the families' overlapping history. In addition to *The P-R*, the Dunns' Newcastle Newspaper Group owned *The Silvertown Eagle* — Jake's hometown paper where he had completed an internship only months before — and several other papers around the region. The Dunns were as well known in Silvertown as they were in Rilertown, firmly ensconced among the region's wealthy elite. In contrast to Jake's family, the Dunns lived public lives befitting their status: summers on Martha's Vineyard, skiing at the family compound in Smuggler's Notch, winter escapes on St. Barts.

"So, tell me about yourself, Jake. You look like a fit guy. You work out?"

"Uh, yeah. I work out at the Y, play racquetball and volleyball, lift a bit. I have a buddy who works there as boxing coach, and we play volleyball together. Then there's softball."

"Ever try Nautilus?" Wick inquired, taking another deep draught of his drink. "I just joined a club in Hazelton and I'm there three times a week. Gorgeous women. Makes you stronger. Builds endurance. Improves your fucking! Just ask Jennifer! Haw, haw, haw …"

Wick steered the conversation to his upcoming trip to the family's bungalow in St. Barts. "Great place. Walk around naked all day. Taking Jennifer in a couple weeks. Girl looks great at work; better in an evening gown … gonna be stunning lying naked by the pool."

Jake swallowed, overwhelmed and slightly nauseated by Wick's monolog.

"So what about you?" Wick encouraged as the waiter plunked a platter in front of him with enough meat and potatoes to feed a family of six.

Jake had heard enough about Wick's spending proclivity and sexual habits, so he launched into his own story. He took his time as he did his best to capture a family history that while humble and meager in comparison to Wick's history of entitled childhood of boarding school, prestigious Ivy League degree and ready-made executive position, was marked by hard work fueled by strong values of honesty, integrity and commitment.

Jacob Cameron Ketcher was the second child to brighten the Ketchers' lives. Jake the younger arrived on the scene three years after first child Mary and ended the couple's interests in further procreation.

"Two and through," was among his dad's favorite sayings. "Fun part's over. Now we get to pay for them."

"I was a pretty inquisitive kid," Jake opened, taking a sip of iced tea. He was second-guessing his decision to not order a beer. "I was a momma's boy ... pretty close to my mom, and grew up cooking with her.

"My dad was kind of present, but kind of not. He worked a lot, so that left me at home with my mom and sister."

Wick carefully unwrapped several pats of butter and placed them in a neat row on the table in front of him. He sliced a mammoth roll in half, then meticulously spread a thick coat of butter across one, then the other. He stuffed half of the roll in his mouth and chewed earnestly, his cheeks puffed, straining to contain the wheat and fat, as he listened to Jake's details of his young life.

Ceaselessly loquacious and perpetually in motion, Jake was often criticized by his teachers for "jittering, nattering and jabbering." After a few years of criticism, Jake developed an edge to his sweet disposition and a temper to go along with it. He would hold his tongue at home out of respect and honor for his parents, then tear into authority figures who, in his mind, had crossed the line.

"Once when I was 9, having endured one too many public humiliations at the hand of my strict fourth-grade teacher, I got fed up with her bullshit and let her have it. For my outspokenness, I earned the distinction of serving Bell School's first-ever class suspension.

"That's when I learned to swim against the tide," Jake told Wick. "Things got worse when the teacher called me to the front of the class after the suspension and asked me if I was *'ready to act like a normal human being and rejoin the class.'* I think I shocked her with my answer:

"I'm not sure. Let me think about it."

He was banished for another two weeks, consigned to a corner in the lunchroom, where he sat by himself for hours on end, fidgeting, reading and daydreaming.

"I think that's when I figured out I was never going to hold a 'normal' job," he told Wick. "Square peg, round hole thing, you know. And I always hated authority. Whoever's in charge instantly earns my distrust."

"Like parents, teachers and publishers?" Wick asked, spewing breadcrumbs as he spoke. Jake realized his error and changed courses, a bit red in the face. Unfazed by the verbal jab, Wick reached for another roll and pat of butter. He nodded for Jake to continue.

Jake droned on through years of Cub Scouts, Boy Scouts, Little League, Pony League, middle school football, and summers at the Ketcher family cabin on a lake nestled into the hills about 30 minutes drive from Silvertown. With plenty of time on his hands, the young boy had pursued interests in reading and writing.

"I was a fat kid when I was little," Jake told Wick. "My first newspaper job was as an advice columnist for my sixth grade newspaper. I went under the name of 'Dear Flabby.' It was supposed to be anonymous, but everybody knew it was me."

Wick nodded, waved his hand in encouragement and chomped away. Jake picked at his food and talked on.

An unremarkable student, he had bungled his way through high school, where he'd played varsity football and tennis, while playing drums in a series of garage bands that played a couple of dances and one noteworthy gig at the county jail.

"They bused girls in from the local community college to dance with the inmates," he mused, remembering the awkward embraces shared by inmates and coeds — all under the glowering watch of the warden and his edgy staff.

Jake had dated off and on throughout middle school and high school. As an awkward, pimply-faced 15-year-old, he'd discovered the magic wonders of sex with a senior who would become his first serious girlfriend, much to his parents' despair. Cindy was from the other side of the tracks and envisioned a future with Jake that gave credence to his parents' concerns: after marrying right out of high school, he would get a job with the local Department of Public Works, and they'd spit out a couple of kids. They'd enjoy a couple of cold beers at the annual county fair each fall as life marched by and they grew old together, she spending evenings with her girlfriends sprawled on the worn living room furniture, he, with his buddies developing prodigious beer guts at a local tavern.

"One day she told me she was pregnant," Jake told Wick. "I found out from her sister that she was lying … trying to force me into a quick marriage … so I broke up with her. The last I saw her, she was lying on the road in front of my car, crying and screaming that if I was going to leave I was going to have to drive over her.

"I put it in reverse, backed away, and took off."

Wick laughed out loud.

"Tough kid, were you?"

"Not really," Jake responded. "Just a handful, I think. I had my own way of thinking. Still do."

The drama between Jake, Cindy and his parents was only one of the challenges in the Ketcher home during a troubled period that drove wedges between young people and their parents. The Ketchers were no different from countless other families across America.

The 60s — brought to the Ketchers' door by his older sister's experiences at college as the country struggled with its role in the war in Viet Nam — cast a long shadow over Jake's adolescence and spawned ideas that would shape his attitudes. Friends and family pitched in, helping direct Jake's energies toward positive outcomes as he battled with adolescence, his parents, and the challenging task of shaping his relationship with the world around him.

"I was a hybrid in high school," Jake told Wick. "Part Jock, part musician, part troublemaker for my parents, part smart kid, but also part dumbass."

Jake had listened in fascination to his sister's Grateful Dead, Cheech and Chong, and Jefferson Airplane albums, heard her talk about lectures at her college by Abbie Hoffman and the Student Democratic Society, and edged ever closer to the Woodstock-spawned culture of free love and experiences of all kinds.

"I think that's where I got my curiosity, my interest in asking questions," Jake said between bites of chicken Marsala. Wick was on his third Scotch, listening intently and asking an occasional question to encourage Jake. "From my sister's influence, and from my godmother, Sam."

"Hang on. Godmother? Sam?"

"Samantha — my dad's oldest and closest friend since they were in grade school."

Jake went on to describe Sam Benson, and her gentle, encouraging ways. A wise, soft-spoken woman who also served as his father's accountant, Sam had suggested that Jake write for the sixth grade newspaper. Sam gave Jake a copy of Langston Hughes and Arna Bontemps' "Boy of the Border" as a reward for winning the fifth-grade "Best Avid Reader" challenge, seizing an opportunity to nurture the boy's interest in books.

As Jake made his way through high school, it was Sam — much to his parents' delight — who successfully lobbied Jake not to buy a Harley and ride it to the west coast, but to explore a junior college stint after high school and then hope to transfer to a four-year university.

Sam helped Jake locate Stuart Junior College as a place where the young man might develop his mind while continuing to find his way. She made periodic visits to the campus to make sure Jake was attending classes, keeping out of trouble, and getting a haircut before his increasingly rare visits home so he would avoid conflict with the elder Jake, who preferred crew cuts to the "girlylocks styles these jackasses wear today."

Jake emerged from adolescence and young adulthood — a troubled period of unrest punctuated by anti-authority voices that granted unprecedented power to the youth of America while encouraging them to "tune in, turn on and drop out" — as a fairly smart young man with a "screw you" attitude toward anyone in "the system."

"Politicians, business, anyone in authority: They were all suspect," Jake told Wick, mopping up a dollop of Marsala sauce with a slice of bread and popping it into his mouth.

Jake signed on to the McGovern/Shriver campaign in 1972, pushing his Republican father to the brink of despair but adding fuel to Jake's fire as he embraced the counterculture and discovered his own voice. He also learned about commitment for a common purpose, rising early many mornings to play his guitar outside factories with his pal Jim and other McGovern campaign staff, serenading overnight shift workers on their way home with choruses of "All we are sayyyyyyyyiiiiinnng…is give George a chaannnnnnnnce."

There was Jake, on the front page of *The Silvertown Eagle,* his red, white and blue "Buck Owens Buckaroo" guitar slung over his neck, earnestly crooning away in pre-dawn promotion of a candidate running on an anti-war platform who would turn out to be one of the biggest campaign losers in US history. The photo memorialized one of the elder Jake's lowest moments of his parenting career.

Then came the Pentagon Papers, then Watergate, which ceded the national stage to Bob Woodward and Carl Bernstein in the crusade against Beltway power mongers and led to the 1976 movie "All the President's Men." The blockbuster starring Robert Redford and Dustin Hoffman spawned a generation of journalistic minnows suddenly committed to doing their part to "inflict the comfortable, and comfort the inflicted" while encouraging its acolytes to adopt the haughty swagger of the era's media. It also provided the male members of media with their uniform of the era: knitted tie, corduroy sports jacket, shoulder length hair — accouterments of rule-breaking anarchists with, thanks to the jacket and tie, one foot in convention to confuse the opposition.

Jake was quick to catch on: Look the job, be the job.

As a high school senior, Jake happily affixed a "Don't Blame Me: I'm from Massachusetts" bumper sticker next to his "McGovern/ Shriver" sticker on the rear end of his rusted 1966 Ford Falcon, happily expressing his freedom of political opinion as he bounced along the county's rutted roads with his pals, beer chilling in a cooler as they headed back to Massachusetts from across the Vermont border Friday nights.

Jake rode the tide of journalism school applicants that reached an all-time peak in 1975, transferring from Stuart and joining Blendhurst's Class of 1977 as he rolled up his sleeves and got serious about studying.

He landed an internship at TheSilvertown Eagle — *The P-R's* sister paper based in Jake's hometown — to bridge the summer before his final year at Blendhurst. There he refined his reporting skills by gathering information about bean suppers and apple harvest projections from Silvertown's farmers. He scratched his itch to cover hard news by scrambling to the scenes of fires, car accidents and other rescue missions by the town's police and fire departments.

He would bolt from *The Eagle's* newsroom, hot on the heels of the paper's staff photographer, Steve Baker, jotting notes at the scene of trauma while Baker snapped photos for the front page and state police. The police 'honorariums' paid considerably more than *The Eagle* did, Baker said, explaining his odd double life as newsman and police event recorder.

"Supplemental income," Baker explained, giving Jake a valuable lesson in newspaper economics. "Someone has to pay me fairly, and since it ain't gonna be the publisher, might as well be the state."

Jake gave serious pause when *The Eagle* offered him a full time job at the end of the summer, suggesting that he forego senior year and get straight to work, but better judgment — not to mention emphatic lobbying by his parents and Sam — prevailed and he turned the offer down, packed his car and headed back to Blendhurst to wrap up his studies.

As senior year wound down, Jake adjusted his priorities, making time to search for a job while drinking beer and smoking pot with friends in lieu of attending classes. Following the careful guidance of Bill Surety, his mentor at *The Eagle*, he landed three offers — another from the Silvertown management, one from a mid-sized paper not far from his hometown, and the third from *The P-R*. He had chosen Rilertown because it was a bigger city with more complex problems — richer turf for an aspiring investigative journalist.

He also relished a separation from his hometown and parents, partly because of their obvious skepticism of his relationship with Sabrina. Eager to get at it, he skipped graduation, packed his car, and he and Sabrina headed to Rilertown to set up shop and get to work.

Wick finished his meal and slowly twirled his drink, the amber liquid spiraling in the glass as he studied the diminishing ice cube.

He looked at Jake.

"So who are your heroes?"

"Well, Sam, for starters," Jake paused to smile at the thought of his affable, wise godmother. "In many ways she's been more a father than my own dad. I mean, my dad was always around, but rarely actually present, if you get what I mean. He was always at work. Always. Sam is an interesting blend of gender. Soft and gentle but direct and no-nonsense. She's the best, and she always has my back — always. She's been involved in anything of significance I've decided or done in my life. She's my number one fan.

"And as much as my dad loves me, he thinks I'm over my head pursuing a career in journalism."

Wick set his drink down.

"Over your head? Why?"

Jake sighed.

"He says 'guys like us' don't have professions. We're the 'worker bees', he likes to say, the guys who take care of the stuff of life for the people doing the serious work, so they can get at the more important business of making our country run.

"My father, as good an example of the American success story as I can think of, doesn't think I have the chops to be more than he is — a tire merchant. So, despite the fact that he's made a success of himself without a college education, and the fact that I have the education he was never able to get for himself, I sort of think he's just waiting for me to fail … not in a mean way, though. I know my dad would love nothing more than to be wrong as he waits for me to crash and burn. But I think he's convinced my failure is inevitable. That's why Sam's my number one hero. She believes in me in ways my dad simply can't. Or won't."

Wick stared at Jake, unblinking. An uncomfortable moment passed. He scratched his chin, took another swig of his drink and, elbows splayed across the table, leaned toward Jake.

"So here's the central question I want to ask you, young Jake: Do you suck?"

"Excuse me?" Jake responded, flustered.

"I said: Do. You. Suck?" Wick was expressionless.

"Zamboni thinks you do. He thinks that about every new reporter, that they're talentless wastes of oxygen we ought to fire and so we can look elsewhere.

"Les thinks otherwise. He says you have promise and have shown flashes of raw, brilliant talent. He is rather emphatic about it, but one is never quite sure whether Les is capable of assessing male reporters' talents without allowing his romantic interests to rule his better judgment.

"I am on the fence. As publisher, my vote is heavily weighted, of course, but I'm not so much interested in the quality of your work as I am with what you can bring to the table from a business perspective.

"I want to know if *The P-R* can get something of value from you — whether you are a mediocre reporter, content with filing boring copy for a few years before you get your teaching certificate and disappear into obscurity, or if you'll actually do something worthwhile, something that'll help sell papers, earn awards, give *The P-R* a competitive edge."

"Most reporters last two or three years, tops. We've had reporters burn out in less than a year. One went to the cop shop on his first day to pick up the police log and simply never returned. Then again, we've had veteran reporters break stories that have led to indictments of sitting mayors, unseated city councilmen, and changed the course of state and federal elections.

"They are rare, talented people who can dig, ask questions and write, while keeping it together, staying reasonably sober and focusing on the task at hand. They put the time in to learn what's necessary to do this job well. It's not easy, but it's simple. You just have to do the work, and the time."

He leaned back into his seat.

"So I want to know. Which are you, Jake? A guy with answers, or just another young boy with a load of question marks? Do you suck? Or not."

Jake was silent. The irony that the publisher of his paper was pressing him for the same sort of commitment and answers that Sabrina carped on about wasn't lost on him. His mind raced as he worked up the courage to respond. His answer descended upon him as would the lead to a breaking news story, in a flash of clarity and perfect candor.

"No, Wick. I do not suck. I'm young and inexperienced — a work in progress. I may not be what the paper wants or needs right now, but I know my potential. I promise you this: you give me time, and some guidance, and a chance at a major story or two, and I'll prove to you that I very much do not suck.

"I've excelled at everything I've done, and I will master this as well.

"I don't care that Zamboni thinks I suck, or that Les thinks I don't. Seems like you have an open mind. I'm a safe bet. I know what I can do, and so do the two other papers that offered me jobs out of college."

Wick cocked his head.

"Is that a threat, Jake? Sure sounds like one. Got a backup plan in the wings at one of our competitors?"

"Oh, geez. No, Wick; not at all. I only meant that *The P-R* wasn't alone in seeing enough promise in me to offer me a job.

"I want this job, Wick. Really, I do. I want to learn, to develop my skills as a reporter, and I think *The P-R* is the perfect place for me to start my career. Sorry, but I'm a writer, not a talker, and sometimes I don't do a great job at saying what I mean. But just you watch. I'll show you what I'm capable of, long as Zamboni and Les give me the opportunity. I'll prove to you that I not only do not suck, but that I'm actually pretty damned good."

Wick was nodding off, his bushy eyebrows weighing heavily on his eyelids as he fought to keep them open. His questioning stopped and he leaned on his elbows, dazed and ready for a nap.

Jake looked at the clock on the wall. 2 p.m. He had to be back at work in five hours. The night shift loomed.

"Maybe we should head back?" he suggested.

INSIDE *THE P-R*

Winter retreated from Rilertown, and then gave way to spring and summer as Jake passed his first anniversary at *The P-R*. The split shift began to wear on his patience and stamina as his interests drifted from sports and he focused on hard news reporting.

He spent mornings supplementing wire copy with local commentary so the paper could replace the "Associated Press" tag at the top of articles with a staff byline.

"Localizing wire copy sells papers and reminds me you jackasses aren't completely useless," Zamboni would growl.

Jake also picked up occasional breaking news assignments — fatal car crashes on I-85 or the Massachusetts Turnpike, both of which conveniently flowed near *The Post-Recorder*'s headquarters, or to cover one of the city's periodic tenement fires. These nasty blazes rarely resulted in serious injury or death. They were nearly always attributed to arson-for-profit by one of the dozen or so slumlords who owned most of Rilertown's congregate housing.

At night, Jake continued to slog away writing about local sports teams and figures, filing boring copy that did little to advance his career but sold papers. Despite being a life-long sports fan, he was beginning to resent working in the "toy department" and yearned for a full-time role in news. A city rife with poverty, social conflict and political intrigue resulting from its leaders' selfish mismanagement offered plenty of grist for "death, despair and cops" stories. Jake liked the idea of making a living reporting on this misery. Maybe hard work would provoke a change?

Jake sipped coffee at his desk while laboring to concoct a punchy lede[2] for a story about a truck fire that had closed Route 85 for three hours that morning. Struggling, he turned to Sarah Turnbull, the veteran school committee reporter who had become his friend and confidante. He often turned to Sarah for advice on sourcing a story, constructing a solid lede or for guidance on how to survive Sabrina's latest tirades.

"Write it like you're talking to your mother," Sarah advised, "but get at it. As they say, write it right; write it tight; but most importantly, write it tonight. In other words: stop screwing around and just write the damned thing."

Deadline loomed. Jake forged ahead.

---

2. A lead, or lede paragraph in literature is the opening paragraph of an article, essay, news story or book chapter. Often called the lead, it is the most crucial element to the inverted pyramid style of writing traditionally used in newspaper journalism.

> A 56-year old Vermont man is in serious condition
> at Rilertown Hospital after he fell asleep behind the
> wheel of a truck he was driving on Route 85 and
> crashed into an overpass support south of exit 57
> early this morning.

Awful. He ripped the paper out of the typewriter, bunched it into a crude ball and tossed it into the wastebasket.

> Police say lack of sleep and possible alcohol
> involvement was behind a crash on Route 85 early
> this morning that left a 56-year-old Vermont man in
> serious condition at Rilertown Hospital.

"Possible alcohol involvement?" Ick. Worse. He yanked the second take out of the typewriter, balled it and tossed it into the wastebasket, then sifted through the trash to find the rejected version. Jake smoothed it on the desk and began typing it onto a new page.

Lost in concentration, he failed to see Zamboni approaching. The news editor tossed a wire dispatch on his desk.

"Read this and get smart on the federal rail development program," he said. "You have a meeting with Congressman Williams at 11. I want 12 inches for today. We're holding for page one."

The wire dispatch revealed that Congress was about to approve a new transportation package that was the brainchild of US Rep. Wendell O. Williams, the district's long-sitting and

beloved representative in Washington. Jake's heart soared. This
meant a trip to the Congressman's office on the top floor of the
city's post office for a one-on-one interview. Then he would
scramble back to *The P-R* to file the story by 12:30. The editors
would look the story over, slap a headline on it and finish up the
front page in time for a 1 p.m. press start.

Page one byline, maybe. Serious story. Serious pressure. This
is what he yearned for.

He looked up at the clock. 9:15. *Gotta get at it.*

He finished the truck story and filed it into the city editor's
computer queue, then made his way into the paper's morgue
to research background on valley transportation initia-
tives. He scribbled a bunch of notes and hustled out the door
around 10:30.

Jake made his way to the post office and was greeted by the
congressman's aide, who ushered him through two heavy oak
doors into an expansive office. Congressman Williams sat behind
a desk the size of a small car, bookended by US and Massachusetts
flags in front of an enormous photo of himself shaking hands
with President Jimmy Carter: two men with beaming smiles from
opposing parties projecting seamless unity to the electorate. In
reality, neither would help the other from a burning building.

Posters from Williams' 18 consecutive winning campaigns deco-
rated one wall. Each prominently displayed his goofy campaign

slogan: "WOW! For the First!", a mildly effective yet obtuse marriage between Williams' initials and his iron grip on the First Congressional District seat.

Williams was scribbling on a piece of paper when he realized Jake was in the room. He rose, beaming, and rushed around his desk with outstretched hand.

"Jack!" he exclaimed, greeting Jake with the false familiarity of a grade school buddy but using the wrong name.

"Great to see you again! Have a seat. Coffee?"

Jake was unsure how to set the congressman straight on his identity and he was loath to point out that they had never met, so he politely declined coffee and became Jack for the duration of the interview. Besides, deadline loomed. He conducted the interview in a few minutes, scribbling colorful, self-ingratiating quotes from the great man in his notebook. Finishing, he shook hands with Williams, rushed from the building and wrote the story in his head as he drove back to *The P-R.*

He filed the story with five minutes to spare.

Zamboni believed that page one should be, "100% staff written, not regurgitated drivel from the wires. Leave that to *The Gazette*," he lectured acerbically, in spiteful reference to *The Post-Recorder's* obscenely successful competitor that liberally ran wire service copy to wrap about the abundance of advertisements it crammed into each of its three daily editions.

Ever the pleaser to Zamboni's demands, *The Post-Recorder*'s annoying wire editor would strip copy from the chattering AP terminal that detailed the latest development in the Iran-Iraq war, a surge in the US stock market or details on the developing national gasoline crisis and plunk it on Jake's desk with brusque instructions to "localize it."

As the lone "GA" — general assignment reporter — Jake "localized" his way through a mix of stories: tax policy debates in Washington, the oil crisis and the latest in the Iran-Iraq war. He learned about important issues along the way and developed a decent collection of sources. The local university became one of his "go-to" options when it came to finding someone to comment on complex subject matter, particularly foreign policy.

He would spend a couple of hours phoning contacts at the university's political science department, finding a professor between classes of "Political Problems of the Middle East" and "Behind the Battle of Algiers" and coaxing her into assessing the situation. Thus was every international conflict brought into specific and detailed local context for *The Post-Recorder*'s readers.

Jake tensed whenever the wire editor headed his way. Betsey (with en extra e) Firth was everything Jake was not: condescending, haughty and effete. Born of Boston bluebloods, she was educated at one of the pricey, upscale suburban Boston schools for the intellectually gifted members of the next generation. Betsey wore her superiority like a coat of armor. She relished life in the editor's pit, protected from the unwashed newsroom minions by the moat of her fellow higher beings.

Thin, angular, ghostly white and shapeless, she wore matronly calf-length skirts and high-necked blouses that made her look like a grey and white bleached stick. She dressed to cover as much of her womanhood as possible, though to her peers her efforts were laughable and needless. The distorted image of beauty, attractiveness and superiority that Betsey saw in the mirror was lost on most she encountered. She dismissed the cretins on the news staff with such words as "unevolved" and "inspired by mediocrity," often distributing photocopied stories of "truly brilliant pieces of writing" she had discovered by scrutinizing *The New York Times* and *The Boston Globe*. Betsey made it universally known that she had completed an internship on Boston's largest and best paper, as if her training in the big leagues somehow made her inexplicable banishment to Rilertown a temporary assignment she would soon leave behind.

She would rip a page from *The Globe,* loudly proclaiming "Oh! My! God!" in her inimitable slack-jawed Boston accent, repeating the exclamation every 30 seconds or so in an effort to attract someone's attention and sucker them into a conversation about the merits of a well-constructed declarative sentence.

To a person, *The P-R* reporting staff was wise to her ploys and immune to her lectures and false sense of superiority. She was a croissant among doughnuts.

Betsey's role as the most despised editor was underscored by the reporters' staunch refusal to refer to her by her initials. Everyone else on *The P-R* staff was JK, BD, TP and so forth, except for Zamboni, who was "Mike" on a good day, "Z" in collegial times, but mostly "asshole," the latter reference always made out of his earshot.

Betsey held a special place in the reporters' cynical hearts. As wire editor she had little authority over them; they were merciless in displaying their contempt. They insultingly referred to her behind her back as "The Floof." "The Floof" was a poor attempt at a portmanteau combining "floozy" and "aloof," and was attributed to a reporter whose tenure preceded Jake's by several years. The scribe — now long gone — had held Betsey in particularly low esteem and had come up with the nickname after a memorable night of shots, beers and cigarettes with reporter pals at his favorite watering hole.

The moniker stuck.

To her face, she remained Betsey Firth, not Betsey and never BF, the only whole-named person in the newsroom. A detached, insufferable elitist, she failed to recognize underlying contempt and interpreted the newsroom's chosen nickname as a sign of respect.

Part of the staff's immeasurable scorn was owed to Betsey's steamy affair with Zamboni. The tryst raged on as in Betsey's arms Zamboni found comfort and an appreciative audience for his impressive vocabulary, not to mention periodic respites from the rigors of running a newspaper and the demands of his wife and two whiny daughters.

Betsey simply liked sleeping with the boss.

The affair was pathetically transparent, and the couple provided endless entertainment to a newsroom that functioned like a pack of hyenas on the hunt.

Several days each week Zamboni and Betsey would surreptitiously eyeball each other as the lunch hour approached, always after the paper's edition was put to bed at 1 p.m. Press run underway, Betsey typically rose first from her desk, loudly banging the drawer shut after she removed her purse. That was a signal to Zamboni to let the lunchtime shenanigans begin. She would rattle about, clear her throat and proclaim something nonsensical as the final hint of her impending departure, and head out the door.

He typically followed seconds later, usually reaching the exit before the door had closed on Betsey's heels. The two would reappear in reverse order about an hour later, red faced and disheveled, often drifting into Zamboni's office, shutting the door, and then shouting at each other in muted tones. "What an asshole," Betsey would mutter as she would return to her desk in a ruse to distract her peers from the relationship battles. "He just cut tomorrow's international news by a full four columns."

Such efforts to steer focus from what really transpired behind closed doors failed to distract her audience, all of whom made their livings exposing bullshit proffered by politicians, business and religious leaders who eagerly served it up in support of their selfish objectives. Besides, Zamboni's office, though partially soundproofed to protect him from the clatter of the wire machines in the room next to his lair, featured an enormous window into the newsroom so he could keep tabs on his charges and choose his next abuse victim. This also provided a clear view of what went on *within* his office. Everyone could watch the lovers carry on. Often, they would lay odds and place beer bets as to who would be the winner of the day's battle of words and emotions.

Zamboni and Firth: two strong-willed, short-tempered verbal pugilists with academics' vocabularies and boxers' attitudes provided endless entertainment in the denouement of post-deadline release.

Filling in the unheard pieces of their arguments became a favorite newsroom gambit, and even the most boring, creativity-deprived wonk weighed in with reliable alacrity. Awards were handed out for whoever produced the spiciest submissions. Best entry earned free shots and beer at the next staff outing.

"God damn it, Betsey," Zamboni would begin. "Why the ...." lowering his voice to keep the gist of his entreaty private.

"...fuck don't you wear the lacy underwear I bought you last week," the Suburban editor offered from the nearby editor's pit.

That got it started.

"...ever make the hotel reservation," Sarah Turnbull chimed in, provoking a round of laughter.

Silence prevailed as the battle momentarily paused, and then surged on.

"Michael. You're really being unreasonable. It's not that I..." Firth would respond, also lowering her voice as she realized they had an audience.

"... can't handle banging a married man," came the offering from Phil Buckley, a reporter with a notoriously edgy wit.

"... hate your parents for not dealing with your acne while you were still an adolescent," Turnbull countered.

On and on it would go until Betsey gave up and emerged from Zamboni's office. As top dog in the newsroom, Zamboni controlled all the hydrants, and he defended his turf with rabid determination. Even his lover was susceptible to his big bark and imposing bite. Always the loser in such debates, Betsey would angrily return to her desk or bolt to the women's bathroom with a wad of soaked Kleenex clutched in her hand, furiously dabbing at the tears creating black streaks on her face as her mascara ran south.

Zamboni waged personal war as effectively as he enforced his strident rules in the newsroom.

He would stomp between the desks, angry, angling for an argument, muttering to himself in Polish, his first language, and occasionally in old English to show off his ever-expanding vocabulary or ruthless capacity to insult.

At times, for no apparent reason other than to show off and confound his charges, he would quote from the 16th century poem, *The Knightly Tale of Gologras and Gawain:*

> *"In the tyme of Arthur, as trew men me tald,*
> *The King turnit on ane tyde toward Tuskane,*
> *Hym to seik ovr the sey, that saiklese was sald,*
> *The syre that sendis all seill, suthly to sane."*

This left anyone within earshot befuddled and wondering whether the Boss's cheese had permanently slipped off his cracker, or whether he was making a deeply insightful analogy to a simmering work-related crisis.

At other times, he loaded on the multisyllabic gibberish in an obfuscatory fusillade of nonsense that sent everyone diving for cover.

"A retromingent, anfractuous, spiny-knobbed dickhead," he labeled the school board chairman. Positing searing, deeply personal criticism of the head of the local community college, he proclaimed, "The vast void between her ears is matched only by her profound lack of imagination. She is a pusillanimous prognosticator of her own predictable mediocrity."

"Which of you intellectually challenged Cro-Magnons is going to be the first in the history of this fine journal to actually meet a fucking deadline!" he would bellow from his office door. Or, sticking to simpler language, "Hey, Ketcher. If you make love to that story any longer you're going to get it pregnant."

Zamboni preached his special brand of "local-only, local-always news" with the fervor of a Jehovah's Witness proselytizer on his first house call of the day. Expressly "local" was the key advantage *The Post-Recorder* retained over *The Gazette*, the staff had been taught, and Zamboni advanced the paper's credo with determination that had long ago crossed the line of obsession.

A 24x7 newshound windup toy, Zamboni's tightly coiled spring was perpetually poised to release when his instincts kicked in and he sensed a story that would bring fame and notoriety to his beloved P-R. Zamboni's diminutive stature swelled when *The P-R* kicked *The Gazette's* butt, so he was all the more aggressive when he sensed an opportunity to beat *The Gazette* to a story. Every win, every scoop, and each exclusive provided a bit of satisfaction in his decades-long quest to punish the larger paper for declining to give him a job out of college several years earlier. He would "unleash the dogs" when he sensed opportunity, suppressing his conservative roots and profligately dispensing precious news-room budgetary resources with abandon.

Yet his instincts were nearly always right; *The Post-Recorder* had profited and improved under his stewardship. A year before Jake made his appearance on the scene, after decades of stalled circulation between 24,000 and 25,000, the Zamboni-infused *Post-Recorder* enjoyed a surge of readership growth. One year, the annual Audit Bureau of Circulation report came in at 30,013 copies "delivered and read daily," much to the delight of Zamboni, the parent company's board of directors, and the paper's profits-minded publisher.

Eclipsing the magical "30k circ" level justified a hefty increase in advertising rates — and, correlatively, quarterly profits that fed Dunn's hunger for food, booze, travel and young women. Dunn rewarded the staff for a job well done by cooking pork ribs and Polish sausage for all in the paper's parking lot, and serving up unlimited beer, coleslaw and potato salad to round out the feast.

Nearing the end of the beerfest and before everyone became too drunk to remember his stirring motivational oratory, Dunn mounted the bumper of a car and spoke passionately about "commitment, quality and money." He closed the celebration by handing a t shirt to each employee emblazoned with the paper's logo and "30k and more!" Most employees consigned their shirts to the backs of their cars, to gather dust among the newspapers, cardboard coffee cups and empty Doritos bags. Typical. The money went to management and ownership; staff got new dust rags. The odd celebration notwithstanding, crossing the 30k circulation barrier had been a significant accomplishment for the paper, the crowning moment in its unending competition with *The Hazelton Gazette*.

The *Gazette*'s circulation footprint dwarfed *The Post-Recorder*'s. As part of a massive national chain, *The Gazette* offered double the daily page count; was better staffed; and, as a morning, seven-day-a-week paper, was better positioned strategically to present fresh information — i.e., news — to its readers than its smaller yet determined rival in a smaller city 10 miles to the north. The *Gazette* reached more than 100,000 homes every morning, covering a circulation area that reached from Hazelton into all of Rilertown plus half a dozen additional communities whose upscale demographics offered marketing appeal to advertisers. So, in addition to winning the circulation war against *The Post-Recorder*'s 30,000 "evening readers, five days a week, and once on Saturday mornings," *The Gazette* was packed with ads from Sears, Kmart and other national chains whose marketing staff simply hung up when a rep from Rilertown made an obligatory ill-fated appeal.

In the advertising wars that powered newspapers' bottom lines, nothing signaled surrender like serving up news to a poor population of non-English-speaking working-class immigrants. Rilertown's white elite clung fiercely to its stranglehold on the city's property and profits, though, and since they still constituted the majority of the paper's paid circulation, they also represented *The Post-Recorder*'s lifeblood for readership and advertising dollars.

The Post-Recorder had a great reputation for insightful local news and investigative journalism born of talent, good luck and arrogance. Regional newspaper intelligentsia looked upon the paper as a great example of a quality small city daily, and the journalism school at the nearby state university provided a steady stream of reporters more than willing to work long hours for appallingly low pay. *The P-R* staff guarded its turf against *The Gazette* with the aggressiveness of a mother black bear over her cubs. P-R news scoops over *The Gazette* had become a cherished tradition that carried on generationally despite the constant turnover.

The Post-Recorder was the tick on the larger dog's butt, with its focused, harder-edged, insider reporting on news people in Rilertown cared deeply about; a gossipy, intrusive "Living Section" (which, oddly, included *The P-R*'s voluminous obituary listings) and an award-winning sports section that chronicled the panoply of athletic accomplishments within its circulation area.

Jake's nighttime role was to gather as much grist as possible for the next day's sports section. This beloved anchor of the paper offered up to 10 robust pages of results, features, photos, line scores and advertisements for tires, tools and personal escort services. The joke in the newsroom was that the tire and tool ads were there for readers; the escort services were for the sports scribes, themselves.

Every evening just before 7, Jake would ease back into the paper's parking lot to the rear of the building from an afternoon between shifts, parking in the executive spaces conveniently located near the back door. Such a brazen incursion against protected turf was safe after hours as the last executive would have long since scurried off to his or her favorite bar.

Jake would don his sports reporter hat, and for the next four hours dive headlong into gathering high school sports results, helping edit wire copy for the "National Sports Briefs" section, and enduring Polocinski's endless string of bad jokes, stomach churning puns and mindless mutterings.

One evening, TP appeared at Jake's desk, a mountainous apparition in polyester casting a shadow over the ream of wire service copy Jake was sifting through. He thrust a piece of paper at him. "BD wants a local lede on this — for tomorrow. Call the guy's family. Ten inches. No more."

Jake studied the paper, a press release from an obscure Division 3 university in central Ohio. "Prondecki named assistant head coach," claimed the headline. Jake read aloud. "Jared Prondecki of Rilertown, Mass., has been named assistant head coach in charge of tight ends for the women's football team at Chancetown College, Chancetown, Ohio, Athletic Director Irving Smith announced today."

Tight ends on the women's football team? "Poor bastard," Jake laughed to himself and got to work.

He scanned telephone numbers of the 32 Prondeckis listed in the Rilertown phone book and was about to start trying to locate the family and wrestle a comment out of them when BD swiveled toward him from his desk, an enormous grin on his face.

"Seriously, Jake. Tight ends? Women's football? TP went to Chancetown — was the PR assistant for the AD there, and he stole an endless supply of letterhead before graduating. Bam. Got him, TP. Nicely played."

Jake looked again at the press release and recognized the familiar font of TP's IBM Selectric II typewriter. The affable giant turned and stared at him from his desk, unblinking, a mild grin crawling from beneath his caterpillar of a mustache. The lead sports reporter, Billy Zatchnik, laughed at Jake from his nearby desk.

"Idiot."

Jake took it as a sign of acceptance that they had stopped the prank before he began to make calls, thus sparing him — and the paper — no small measure of embarrassment.

Jake tossed the fake release into his bottom drawer, in the same motion removing a 20 ounce jar of "Rose Hip Magic" hand cream. He removed the cap, applied a generous dollop on the back of his left hand, and feverishly began to rub his hands together to paint them front and back.

"Been meaning to ask you. What's with that?" said Zatchnik, turning in his chair and grabbing the jar from Jake's desk. "Rose Hip? Hand cream? Maybe YOU should be in charge of tight ends?" The entire P-R sports department — except the target of the prank — exploded with another belly laugh.

Personal attacks, exploited weaknesses and exposed peccadilloes were all part of the collegial magic of newsroom antics. No secret lasted long, and anyone's quirky, different or odd behavior would soon make the agenda at the weekly newsroom meeting, where people felt completely at home asking intrusive, embarrassing questions of one another as deftly as they did people from "the outside."

It's what they did. They performed, pontificated and pronounced with creativity and humor that, had it been transferable to the paper's broadsheet columns, would have either driven the paper's circulation past 40,000 or put it out of business.

The stunts provided comic relief to a staff that dutifully chronicled the day's unhappy events in inverted pyramid style. "Death, crooks and misery up front," Zamboni would intone, reminding everyone of page one priorities. So the staff eagerly seized any opportunity to provide a welcome giggle — often on deadline — as relief from the oppressive pressure of stirring Zamboni's recipe for news.

One day, a creative soul added a graphic to the United Way poster placed on the newsroom memo board to track the staff's contributions to the city's annual fund raising campaign. The blue line representing the paper's monetary commitment reached halfway to the top of the red line that was topped by a 72-point $10,000! goal. The graffitist had added a third line in black that stretched almost as high as the red: "Sid Reigner's monthly bar tab" it read, an only slightly exaggerated reference to the drinking habits of Rilertown's crude, irascible and devoutly racist alcoholic mayor.

Another time someone had a field day vandalizing the paper's daily report of the annual shad run, a weird statistic provided by the local water authority about how many fish had made their way up the fish ladder installed in the city's hydroelectric dam to prevent interruption of the endangered fish's spawning habits.

Locals loved to track the shad count during summer months. Rilertown insiders knew more about the year's shad run than anything, other than how the Red Sox were faring against the Yankees. The shad run was a leading topic for discussion and arguments in bars and coffee shops around the city. The paper religiously published a daily graphic on page one showing the number of shad counted in the ladder during the previous day's climb along with a second bar documenting how many fish had made the trip that year to date.

A miscreant added a third line to a copy of the graphic posted on a memo board after a pair of drunks got into a fistfight one night near the city's third level canal. The loser of the fight, a violent young man who was well known by the city's police department, had fallen unconscious into the canal and drowned. His body had washed up in the fish ladder, delaying the daily count while water authority workers waited for the coroner's office to show up and haul him out of the water.

The man's name appeared next to the third bar, scribbled on the chart posted front and center: "Yesterday's shad count: 385. Carlos Figueroa: 1. Year to date: Shad: 32,987 Humans: 1."

Jake loved the evening hours, especially the late nights when TP, BD and BZ all disappeared to the bars and cheap eateries, hauling their ample guts and butts out of their chairs in pursuit of cold beer and Polish sausage. Jake usually had the entire newsroom to himself. He dutifully banged away at the keyboard as the hours wore on. He made friends with the cleaners, in particular a young Hispanic woman who spoke halting English. She would linger by the young reporter's desk, often accepting his offer of awkward Spanglish banter and a dollop of hand cream.

Lucinda Rodriguez was soft-spoken and sweet. She seemed interested in what Jake was working on, no matter how mundane. She often asked questions about his work, family and life outside of *The P-R*, and seemed eager to share details of her own struggles as a member of the city's invisible minority. She was careful not to vacuum close to his desk when he was on the phone, noting that Jake was the only P-R staffer who didn't make a habit of screaming at her, mocking her accented English, for *"makeeng too much fuckeeng noise."*

Jake liked her. He welcomed the break, and cherished the chance to improve his Spanish. She sensed warmth in the young man who always smiled at her and tried to speak her language. As the nights and months passed, the two became friends. Jake made a point of pausing when Lucinda stopped by to empty his wastebasket.

The two would spend a few seconds chatting, teaching each other their native language, and gently rubbing hand cream into their palms as the clock marched toward midnight.

Young Reporter's

Career Changes Course

The arrival of fall brought high school football season. Jake's tormented workweek took a turn for the worse.

Saturdays, once an oasis of relaxation with Sabrina, evaporated in long hours spent at one game or another followed by lengthy stints in the office writing. In addition to chronicling the game he attended, Jake was also required to tally results by phone of another half dozen matchups and whip them all into a "Pigskin Roundup" column that was a Monday fixture for *The P-R*'s readers.

Tuesday became his other day off, reminding him of years working behind the counter of his family's tire business in Silvertown. He hated Tuesday/Sunday weekends then; now he loathed the schedule with renewed passion. But Jake approached this challenge as an opportunity to excel. He gave every boastful coach his full attention; every 1–8 team the adoration due an undefeated champion; and every strutting, self-absorbed high school quarterback six inches of copy to provide fame he desperately craved.

Jake perfected the art of writing about long-ended games. Since most readers knew the weekend's scores well before *The P-R* showed up on their doorsteps Monday afternoons, Jake focused on revealing the unsung heroes. He provided due coverage to the stars who led offense and defense for the day, but committed most of his time to kids no one talked about — mostly because they lacked significant talent or promise. Unheralded, moderately talented athletes were close to Jake's heart; he identified with their brief flickers of notoriety as their lives rocketed toward obscurity.

Most of these guys don't suck, either, Jake often mused, thinking back to his conversation with Wick over lunch months earlier. *They're doing the best they can, and they deserve a moment of glory.*

Jakes' high school years had been marked by lousy grades but varsity letters in football, basketball and tennis. Sports and girls, not academics, shaped the minds of most young men; he spent a disproportionate amount of time flexing his muscles rather than feeding his brain. Thanks to Sam and his family, he awakened in time to develop the latter and secure a path to a successful future, but he carried a soft spot within his heart for the young athletes he covered. He knew more than most that sports heroes' names are forgotten as soon as the crowds disperse.

Jake's balanced approach struck a chord with readers, and his column ranked high in the paper's quarterly readership survey. This rise in popularity — not to mention Jake's ability to reliably churn out reams of publishable copy — awoke P-R management to the fact that the kid actually had talent and might be more valuably deployed within the reporting ranks.

"Ketcher. Office," Zamboni bellowed to Jake one Monday morning. Jake stood and headed south toward Zamboni's lair.

"Nope. There," Zamboni said, directing Jake north to Moore's office at the end of the newsroom.

Being summoned to the managing editor's office normally meant one of two things: something good, or something really, really bad. As a relatively new staffer, Jake lacked the experience to predict the outcome. He assumed the worst and began to sweat.

Zamboni picked up on his angst.

"Relax. If I were going to fire you, I'd do it right here so I could enjoy the moment to its fullest."

Settling into the corduroy sofa that took up most of the space against Moore's office wall, Jake fidgeted while Zamboni shut the door and perched on the edge of Moore's desk. Zamboni took immense pleasure in irritating Moore at every opportunity. Invading his personal space, however, was an unusually bold move that warranted a response.

Moore roughly shoved his brass nameplate against Zamboni's hip. "This is my work surface, not a resting spot for your ass." The editor glared at him but moved to a side chair, and Moore nodded at him to get on with the show. Score one for the managing editor.

"Something's come up," Zamboni began, and Jake shifted to the edge of the sofa. "RT's leaving, so we need to fill his GA slot," he said. He was referring to the paper's general assignment reporter, Rich Tennenbaum, a P-R fixture with the abnormally long tenure of six years who got most of the best assignments covering issues outside the beat reporters' domains.

Beat reporters were assigned to specific departments. City Hall, police and fire and education reporters doggedly tracked civil servants and their minions while chronicling events and decisions that impacted readership. Tennenbaum got the plum stuff: National politics, environmental issues, major court cases and an occasional investigative assignment. The job was highly sought by the papers' 35 full-time reporters who languished in relatively less important jobs reporting on mundane details.

"It's yours if you want it," Moore chimed in. "It'd mean no more split shift, no more sports, but we'd wait to the end of football season so you can finish up with Pigskin Roundup and teach someone else to take it over. Oh … Monday to Friday, too."

Jake was stunned. He'd been at the paper just over two years and was already being promoted?

Jackpot!

"It's the same money," Moore apologized.

"Poof" went the euphoria.

He scowled. *Some promotion. Sabrina will have a field day with this. Time to man up.*

"Geez, Les, and Mike ... it's a great offer, but same money? You'd think there'd be at least a little raise, wouldn't you?"

Moore and Zamboni exchanged glances.

"Can't do it now, kid," Zamboni said, once again encroaching on Moore's turf by taking charge of the money matters.

Moore countered.

"We'll take a look at your performance on your anniversary, in (he shuffled what apparently were Jake's personnel records in front of him) ... uh, in May."

Jake had received two $10-a-week raises on each of his previous anniversaries, perfunctory bumps in compensation that, after taxes, barely changed his net paycheck. A promotion was different. This was his chance for "big money," maybe $50, $75 a week more.

But this?

Seven more months of a new job with tremendous responsibility, more work, but no more money, taking over for a guy who probably made at least a hundred bucks a week more than he did? This wasn't right. Jake massaged his temples and pondered his options.

"OK," he said, capitulating and thus sealing his fate for the evening's berate-fest at the hands of his girlfriend.

"What was that all about?" BD probed as Jake returned to his desk, disconsolate over his awful performance as a negotiator but happy to know his days as a split-shift sports scribe were numbered.

"I'm moving to GA as soon as football season's over," Jake offered enthusiastically. "Tennenbaum's outta here."

"Fuckshit," BD muttered, using one of his favorite expressions. "Typical of those two dipwads to not bother to mention it to me first. Assmunchers."

He slammed his desk drawer shut and stormed the length of the floor, ignoring Jennifer's plea to wait until she could announce his presence. He entered Moore's office, slamming the door. The next 20 minutes were pure entertainment for the reporters. Work stopped as they grinned and made rude comments about the audible raging conflict.

Jake seized the moment to head to Tennenbaum's desk for a briefing and to plant an early stake in his new turf. RT — or, as he was known among the editors' ranks as OSD (One Strange Dude) — was a page one fixture at *The P-R*. A reportorial pitbull with legendary typing skills, OSD churned out copy like kielbasa streaming from a sausage machine. OSD's ability to fill space on deadline made him the editors' darling. His dogged pursuit of phantom stories rooted in complicated conspiracy theories that often yielded zero results — along with his thinly disguised contempt for all editors — made him a newsroom favorite.

He was weird, unpredictable and irascible — which made him enormously popular. Unapproachable for many save from downwind, he suffered from acute bromhidrosis, an unfortunate condition that gave OSD the fetid odor of rotting meat.

"Hey, RT," Jake said, deferentially approaching the veteran reporter but keeping a safe distance to avoid the smell. "Looks like I'm gonna take over for you once you're done. They didn't tell me when you're leaving ...."

"Today," RT responded, removing an enormous stack of files from his desk drawer. "Congratulations, I guess.

"I'm leaving these for you. They're stories I'm working on ... notes, clips, photos. Most of 'em are crap, but there're a couple you should pay attention to. Read the files, get up to speed, and keep your ears open. I've got a few minutes to brief you.

"You might want to scratch a few notes."

Jake eased into an open chair adjacent to RT's desk and was instantly overcome by a malodorous cloud.

He breathed through his mouth, produced a notebook and scribbled as RT spoke.

"There's a story in the works about city water quality ... somebody told me they're not filtering most of it, but just pumping it out of the Tee from above the dam ... you know, where everyone from the Flats goes to swim?

"I have some notes about a farmer in West Village who's been busted by the FDA for violating food safety standards. He raises pigs. Brother's a district court judge, and the farmer has been providing pigs for the annual summer judges' roasts for years, so hizzoner is all pissed off at the feds. That would be my choice to start with. Chance to tuck it to the feds while making a pal in the district courts. I'd think that would pay off down the road sometime.

"Another file's about the death of a hooker in a hotel in South Cranfield a few years ago. Cause of death was 'natural,' if you call having your head shoved into a pillow until you stop breathing a natural death. Official word was she suffered some sort of seizure and simply suffocated, but I think that's bullshit.

"I nosed around and had a couple sources willing to talk but couldn't get anything solid enough to pursue. There were rumors of some political heavyweights involved, but nothing specific — maybe a couple bigwigs in government. Maybe they were with girl before she died; maybe even with her when she died. Lot of talk, but nothing concrete. I worked it for a couple years, off and on, until Zamboni got sick of me wasting my time and ordered me off the story.

"He ordered you off the story?" Jaked probed. "Why?"

Tennenbaum shrugged. "Ask him; I dunno — probably because I wasn't meeting my daily quota of Pulitzer-quality prose. That, and because he's an insufferable asshole.

"My advice to you is to keep it active and open, and quietly nose around. Maybe you'll stumble over something solid you can run with. I'd also keep it to yourself, and do not mention it to fuck-face (nodding in the direction of Zamboni's office) under any circumstance. Last time I brought it up he threatened to kill me first and then fire me.

"Good luck, and have some fun."

RT shook Jake's hand and tossed the files into his desk drawer.

"I suppose this'll all be yours, so I'll just leave all the files. I'll clear out the top drawer so there's plenty of room for your hand cream."

RT grinned, clearly aware that reporters seated nearby were paying close attention and were smirking, celebrating his humiliation as a hand cream aficionado at the hands of a guy who smelled like the Rilertown landfill. Jake's appointment to the prestigious job — in which he leapfrogged other, more experienced reporters who coveted the gig — was not widely applauded. Newspaper newsrooms were littered with casualties from countless competitive minefields.

At the other end of the newsroom, BD was the first to emerge from the management smackdown, red-faced and scowling, followed by a smirking Zamboni. "Little man always gets what he wants," RT said loudly, indicating Zamboni. Moore quietly closed the door behind them and retreated to the sanctity of his office as BD and Zamboni separated to neutral corners.

Jake arrived at his desk just before BD. He breathed deeply, appreciating the sanctuary of fresh air as the sports editor approached, flushed and irritated.

"You're staying on until the end of November. Gotta cover the turkey day games," BD informed him, settling back at his desk. "Great. Now I have to find some new simp and teach him the ropes all over again. Fuckshit."

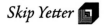

AUGUST, 1975

The scene haunted him relentlessly, a persistent demon feeding on remorse, thirsty for a compliant admission of guilt.

Nights were punctuated by recurring nightmares and gnawing stomach aches; days dominated by memories of an event that threatened all the man had worked to achieve, all he valued.

Snapshots of the evening interrupted the man's rare moments of peace: half empty booze bottles, an overflowing ashtray. Laughter, collegial banter, a card game. Two others with him in the living room waited their turn with the beautiful young woman who was entertaining the fourth in an adjacent bedroom.

It all felt like fun, like a secret party with no boundaries, rules or limits.

Anything goes.

Just bring your imagination.

It's all on the house.

Now, the smell of cigar smoke, beer or bourbon triggered memories that carved a hole through his temples and blazed like an inferno in his belly, a constant state of emotional unrest and searing physical pain, *listless, sleepless and edgy. He avoided cigars and booze, and physical contact of all kinds. Better to seek tranquility through avoidance than peace through self medication.*

Every time the phone rang, every unannounced visitor meant the possibility of a visit from police that would spell the end. There were many calls and many visitors, every day. The torment was endless.

He contemplated running, but where to? How far must a guilty man go to escape the truth?

So he remained.

At night, he would often lie awake, the hotel room scene playing over and over in an endless loop.

"I am half in the bag, enjoying a night out with a couple of pals, about to get laid, and then what? A dead girl in a cheap hotel room? Two other guys who, like me, cannot risk this kind of publicity, and a fourth guy who set this all up who was running around in a panic, trying to fix a situation that would be very difficult to obscure."

Remorse, guilt and regret are unfamiliar concepts, emotions that rarely visit the selfish, greedy takers of the world.

This was all new to him.

His mind did what minds do when humans do wrong.

It tortured him.

Lament.

Angst.

Evaluation and assessment.

Over and over.

Honesty that ranges freely in our minds and psyches yet rarely emerges into the realm of reality consumed him. He begged for release. All of this descended upon him as though a swarm of bats from hell, devouring him, clawing at his innermost fears.

In the thick, hot night he made promises to his God and his miserable, splintered soul that he would never do anything like this again if he could just please, please, please be granted the grace of a pardon from the crime, and a chance to get on with his life.

"I should never have been there, never should have taken the call, or accepted the first invitation. What the hell was I doing there?"

He thought of the first night, many months prior, with the same men, in the same room, and the same girl, long before it all went sour and she died in bed with a hungry, selfish soul eager to drink from the well of her youth and beauty.

The allure of power and soothing sex. The casual conversation among men of substance and authority in a venue that made them equal diners at the table of plenty: booze, smoke, conversation, and random, detached sex with a young woman. Her smooth, dark skin, lithe, perfect body, and long, sensuous black hair presented a package that, along with her obvious intelligence, normally would have made her an impossible object of the men's desires.

She was a rented vessel — just like me, he thought — someone to use at will and with mindless confidence, which men of power and money do so well, and with so little thought of consequence.

Just like me, he thought, sweat soaking his pillow and sheets as he lay as far from his wife as possible in the queen sized bed. Insomnia and sweat, symptoms of a guilt-tortured man who had done wrong.

He turned the pillow over, folded his arms beneath it and pressed his head to the dry side. He closed his eyes, but sleep would not come. The scenes repeated over and over.

So he quit the game, opened his eyes and searched the darkness for the promise of dawn and the opportunity to rise and move through the day as his quest continued for a peace that would not come.

I should never have been there.

HOME AND HEART

A bunch of flowers in hand, Jake gingerly approached Sabrina, hoping for a celebration and perhaps a roll in the hay to mark his meteoric ascension up the newspaper's ranks. She surprised him by not only having dinner ready, but by throwing her arms around him, planting a deep, wet, kiss, and delaying dinner while she took him on a slow tour of "Sabrina Island."

Two hours later, spent and sated by the amazing sex and mediocre meal, Jake eased back from the table and scraped at his beer's label. He smiled at Sabrina.

"I love you."

"Yeah, me, too," she replied with a sigh. "I just wish they'd pay you what you're worth…."

"Please, Sabrina," Jake interrupted. "Don't spoil this. It'll come — the money, I mean. This is a great opportunity. No one ever goes anywhere writing sports. This job gives me the choice assignments, front page stuff. Who knows where it'll lead?"

For once she relented, stacking the dishes and, with the remnants of the meal in one hand, she gently caressed the back of his neck with the other as she headed to the kitchen.

"I believe you, sugar," she said, "but it'd better not take too long. We're not getting any younger, you know."

She shifted gears.

"How did you like dinner?"

Sabrina was a horrible cook, lacking talent, taste and interest in much beyond dance and sex. Drawing upon her Latino/Jewish heritage, she turned out bizarre concoctions that defied description and digestion — like gefilte fish tacos, cold borscht with jalapeño salsa, and kugel with fresh mangoes, her standard, palatable dessert that Jake referenced when Sabrina came hunting for a compliment.

"The kugel was my favorite ... moist, really good, with the perfect amount of nutmeg, one of your best ever." It was a well-played sleight of hand, a deft dodge intended to stick to calm waters rather than risk the shoals of Sabrina's ego-driven temper by being honest.

She beamed. Jake stared at her lustfully, savoring the vision of her leaning in the doorway with her raven hair, gentle, sensual mouth, and the sloping curves of her lithe, athletic body.

Sabrina was the love child of a crazy Dominican seamstress, Angelica, and her customer, Jacob Goldfarb, who employed

Sabrina's mother first as his tailor and then to fulfill the sexual void created by his frigid wife. Jacob's wife, Thelma, not only acknowledged the affair but endorsed it, happily ceding her conjugal duties to a woman more suited to romantic pursuits.

It was all acceptable until Angelica announced she was pregnant. Then all hell broke loose, as the reality of having a bastard child join the weird threesome settled in. An awkward period of angst and negotiation followed, culminating in the couple's divorce. Rather than zero in on the opportunity, Angelica inexplicably chose to break off all contact with Jacob, and vowed to raise her child solo.

The word "solo" applied to Sabrina; not so much for Angelica.

Sabrina's infancy, youth and adolescence were punctuated by countless "customers" who came and went from her mother's life, and attentive, memorable weekends with her estranged father, who doted upon the girl and genuinely loved her. There was never any question about whose last name she would take, and Jacob was as proud of the young girl as a father could be.

He introduced her to Judaism, encouraging her to "pursue her faith" as a means of embracing her heritage. Jacob took the girl to temple, shared his vision of what it meant to be Jewish and once let her sit *shiva* with him after one of his sisters died. She demonstrated genuine interest in her bat mitzvah until she realized that the tradition required hard work and commitment. She wanted a party and a bunch of money, not a deeper understanding of the Torah.

So she quit.

Angelica saw the danger of an emerging adolescent beauty with time on her hands. She introduced the young girl to dance classes, as much a way to get the girl out of the house as out of genuine interest in her development. With Sabrina salsa-ing, and samba-ing the afternoons and evenings away, Angelica was free to cultivate a robust bevy of satisfied clients that kept her libido satisfied and her wallet full.

As Sabrina entered adolescence her obvious talent, emerging good looks and athletic ability pushed her to the top of each dance school she attended.

Mom's looming presence prevailed over dad's attempts at parenting from a distance, which waned as the years wore on, then stopped altogether when Jacob dropped dead of a heart attack while halfway through a "massage" at a dimly-lit parlor on the lower east side of Manhattan. Sabrina, then 17, hit the road. She joined a salsa revue dance troupe destined for an "East Coast Tour," meaning they played to a disinterested crowd of 50 in an American Legion Hall in Atlantic City before beating a hasty retreat to the familiar confines of Spanish Harlem.

Sabrina never dwelled on the fact that her father and boyfriend had the same first name, but Freud would have a field day interpreting the significance. The first time Jake pointed this out, she responded by denying sex for a week. From then on, Jake kept his amateur psychological assessments to himself.

Now, however, with the soft glow of sex and food conspiring to create a particularly soft moment in their relationship, it was all very, very good.

"I'm glad you liked the kugel. Did you like anything else I served you this evening?" she said with a coquettish grin, then spun and disappeared into the kitchen.

Moments like these reminded Jake how much he loved and cherished Sabrina, despite her many faults and the horrible way she treated him much of the time. He misjudged the moment as perfect for a fresh pitch on the idea of marriage.

"So, what do you say?" Jake shouted to her as she lowered the dishes into the sink. "I have a regular job that's taking me places. We're happy here. We have a nice home, and we're making some friends. Why don't we get married?"

Silence.

Sabrina returned to the doorway and tossed a dish towel over her shoulder, her mood shifting from sexy and warm to confrontational and icy.

"How many times do I have to tell you? Do something special — something worthwhile — something manly. Right now I just see a little boy in a sandbox — playing with his toys, making castles that will wash away when the rain comes. Regular job? Happy? Nice home and friends? You're fooling yourself by thinking you're building something worthwhile, and you've got the wrong woman if you think I'm buying into this bullshit.

"Yeah, little boy in a sandbox, I want a man who will make something out of concrete, not sand. More than that, though, I need you to make me excited, and sugar — this ain't gonna get the job done.

"Make me purr, sweetie, and then I'll consider marrying you. Till then, I'm keeping my options open."

The Promise of Fortune Valley

Rilertown was nestled in the center of Fortune Valley, so named in anticipation of the vast wealth that was expected to befall the risk-happy 17th century settlers who saw potential in the valley's fertile soil and supply of fresh water from the Oksaguganuatee River.

Around 1640, several wagonloads of mostly British settlers violently shoved aside the natives, forcing them north to Canada and west, and set up shop just an hour's ride on horseback from the developing city of Hazelton.

Formed during the wild geologic fluctuations of the Mesozoic Era, the valley — pierced down its middle by the mighty Oksaguganuatee — proved the perfect locale for humans and their commerce. Protected from nasty Canadian winter winds by two soaring mountain ranges (the Riler Range to the east; Mt. William Range to the west), the north-south valley offered shelter, great farmland, water for irrigation and transportation and proximity to consumer demands from other developing outposts further south.

Corn, wheat, barley and an abundance of vegetables sprung from the nutrient-rich soil with metronomic regularity each summer and early fall. Livestock flourished, fed by the rich corn raised in the farmer's fields. Farmers, too, grew fat on the food they raised and on the beer and spirits they created from the golden grains of their annual harvest.

Word spread quickly about the new land of opportunity in Hazelton, and within a few years the population soared from a couple dozen families to more than 20,000 souls throughout the sprawling, rapidly developing area. The evolving crowds convinced folks settled north of the hub to secede and set up their own town, uncreatively naming it Rilertown after the nearby mountain range. Many other communities followed suit and seceded from Hazelton, creating fierce rivalries over taxation, land rights and authority that continued for generations.

In contemporary times, the rivalries were rekindled during annual high school Thanksgiving Day football games. Locals donned headdresses and enthusiastically deployed tomahawk chops as they urged on their respective combatants, oddly embracing tired stereotypes eradicated by the revelers' forefathers who murdered and stole the natives' land to establish a toehold in the new world.

Industrialization awakened a bunch of wealthy opportunists to the chance for real money in the 1800s. A handful of Rilertown's evolving political and business elite reached across the state with their voter-rich tentacles and fat wallets, convincing the state legislature to invest public money in a series of canals that would divert the Oksaguganuatee to power their paper and textile mills. The western part of the state normally was ignored by Boston pols, but even in the rough and tumble 1800s, nothing bred legislative commitment and diversion of taxpayer dollars for private gain like a few greased palms and thousands of promised votes.

Rilertown prospered overnight. Mills and warehouses sprang from the canal banks like massive brick monuments to prosperity. Roads were widened and improved, secondary commerce flourished to support the burgeoning population, and the wealthy built enormous mansions in the city's preferred highlands.

All this growth created enormous demand for unskilled labor to exploit and expose to the considerable hazards of working in the era's unregulated, unsafe mills. The rich sent word north and soon welcomed hundreds of French Canadian families who had grown weary of Canada's stagnated economy and six-month winters. They flocked to Rilertown, bringing with them a rough, brawling, boozy culture perfectly suited to the challenges of industrial labor and sequestered community living.

Fiercely Catholic, they reproduced at an impressive rate that nonetheless fell short of the increasing demand for cheap labor. In the mid-1900s, the first Latino stumbled into a low wage job in Rilertown, bringing his family, a dog and two chickens with him to settle into a fifth-floor, unheated hovel in one of the city's tenements. Not long after collecting his first month's paycheck, the man sent word to family huddling in New York waiting for a break in their fortunes that there were jobs, apartments and plenty of open space just four hours to the north.

Hispanics flooded to Rilertown. They came in cars, on buses, and on the few trains that still carried passengers to Hazelton. Confused travelers were deposited along the tracks and left to find their way to their final destination in Rilertown. They set up home in the porous brick tenements that stretched for blocks in the neighborhood Rilertonians referred to as The Flats.

Some said the neighborhood was so named in reference to the British word for apartments. Others said it was to reflect the area's geography as the lowest point in the city's lower wards, where water pooled in vast swamps during the annual floods.

The Flats was the least appealing real estate in the valley, a repository of silt and sewage that greedy developers and captains of industry soon conspired to turn into the perfect place to house the poor, but it was home for the immigrant Hispanic workers, and they made the best of it. They faced each obstacle with stubborn resolve, deflected the ongoing racist attitudes with quiet determination and went about the business of making better lives for themselves and their growing families.

The French Canadians loathed these hard-working, family-centric, friendly people. Latinos brought their music, farm animals and spicy food to the city, starkly contrasting with their Irish jigs, snarling dogs and boiled meat and cabbage that until then had defined the city's social, culinary and entertainment fabric. The two groups had nothing in common except ability to produce large families, which over the years created a steady resupply of workers and combatants in ongoing turf wars.

Humans forced into close proximity with one another naturally become edgy. When you cram thousands of uneducated, poor people from conflicting cultures into a few city blocks to compete for living space and jobs, you create a social powder keg.

Tensions began and soon spread from the housing developments to the factories. Alarmed by the disruption in productivity, the bosses stepped in to put a stop to the arguments and periodic fistfights. They created a local boxing club to create an organized forum for hateful pugilists from respective camps to square off, and convinced the city to re-organize housing into segregated communities.

The populations separated like two warring siblings, glaring and snarling at each other but mostly keeping a respectful yet uncertain distance as they stopped fighting and went back to work. Business returned to Rilertown, and commerce enjoyed yet another surge. Bosses beamed, bought new cars, made their "honorarium" payments to local politicians and begrudgingly handed out paltry annual bonuses for the thousands of men, women and children who labored away in the mills.

The only element missing from this bustling hive of community growth and economic development was a newspaper to bind the community together. In 1874, Wick Dunn's grandfather, Joseph, wealthy patriarch and native son of Rilertown, plunked down a few thousand dollars generated by profits from two other papers he owned to launch the Rilertown *Post-Recorder*. *The P-R* was an instant financial success, providing crucial news to the population while providing friendly but cautious guidance to the rough and wild selfishness that flowed from City Hall like water along the Tee.

The paper made and broke generations of politicians — both wunderkinds and hacks — carefully choosing which candidates to endorse or lampoon. Support from *The P-R* was deemed crucial by anyone with an eye on making a career in local politics, so the paper's doorway located yards from City Hall was always full of middle-aged guys in three-piece suits who descended upon the paper to make their cases.

Joseph's son James took over when the elder Dunn concluded his life's journey on an ill-fated maiden voyage of a new ocean liner called the *Titanic,* ironically on tax day in 1912, the day the staunchly Republican patrician hated most each year. James exhausted whatever publishing talent remained in the family's bloodline during his years of passive management. When James died in 1962 of a cerebral hemorrhage brought on when he learned that his only son, Wick, had registered as a Democrat, Wick found himself in the publisher's chair and abandoned his quest to open a restaurant in New York's exciting Soho district.

Re-investable profits and a problematic lack of parking led the paper to relocate to the city's outskirts in 1968. The move was universally viewed as a blasphemous slap in the face by the city's powerful, who now faced the inconvenience of having to drive nearly 15 minutes to lobby the newspaper's leadership on turf that lay troublingly detached from the city center. But the paper's new headquarters — a sprawling, spider like, glass-encased compound perched on 20 acres of valuable real estate near the intersecting highways soon to come — provided room for growth and access to important suburban advertisers who sprung up in the 1960s and 70s.

Rumors of an interstate highway soon became fact. After *The P-R*'s editorial pages repeatedly endorsed the concept of Interstate 85 — located, coincidentally, on land just a few hundred yards from *The P-R*'s entrance seconds off what would become Exit 28 — the value of *The P-R*'s commercial plot magically increased tenfold.

Critics in the newsroom took regular cheap shots at Wick's disinterest in publishing but they respected his ability to mint money. In terms of business acumen and brass balls, Wick knew few equals.

Buildable real estate with great access to northern New England as well as to the riches of Connecticut and New York was still one of the region's most reliable assets. This meant the Dunn family would be wealthy for generations — at least on paper — regardless of whether they made money from their publishing pursuits or rode the paper into obscurity.

When the time came for Wick to ascend the family's publishing throne, he fell into the role with genuine enthusiasm. He hungered for the power, high salary and quarterly dividends that went with the job, but exhibited little interest in what appeared in *The P-R*'s news pages. He cared deeply about politics, though, and regularly weighed in on the editorial page with windy, ill-conceived opinions. Thus the paper maintained its rich history of sculpting the political landscape in Rilertown through the awkward efforts of its untalented young publisher, who, in addition to his other obvious shortcomings, was a Democrat.

By embracing the seditionist attitudes of his roguish friends and defiling the Nixon and Ford administrations at every opportunity, Wick abruptly reversed course on the Dunn family's doggedly

Republican history. This caused no small measure of discord within the walnut-wainscoted halls of the Dunn family homes and gave the young publisher immense pleasure.

"Makes for fascinating Christmas dinners," Wick loved to drunkenly joke to his pals as they celebrated the artform of using their growing political power to torment the elder custodians of familial fortune and fame.

Despite causing the paper's abrupt shift in political leanings, Wick had the sense to hire professional journalists who knew what they were doing and could consistently create a fairly high quality newspaper.

Zamboni and Moore formed an odd leadership, working in tandem to produce consistent, high quality journalism. They had a reputation of warring with one another while taking risks, bucking convention and exposing injustice, corruption and greed. Embracing the guiding principle of "Comfort the Inflicted; Inflict the Comfortable," they won awards, made friends in the liberal halls of the local university, and created powerful enemies from City Hall to the dimly lit rooms of the Hibernian Hall club in central Rilertown and into the mysterious confines of Boston's political establishment.

Their relationship with one another was best described as mutually contemptuous.

Zamboni correctly suspected that Moore was gay, and, like

countless faith-based homophobes of the era, seized every opportunity to sashay, lisp and mock his business-oriented counterpart, though usually well out of Moore's hearing and sight.

Moore was a native of Rilertown, well liked and respected, who carried himself with the understated demeanor of a man who had learned truths the locals simply could not understand.

His parents had married in their late teens, bore one child, and lived frugal, quietly religious lives. Moore's father, Gus, was pressroom foreman at *The P-R*, where he had worked since graduating Rilertown High School and quickly marrying Bertha. Born to German Catholic heritage and blessed with rich vocal talent, Gus's a cappella baritone rendition of "O Tannenbaum" was a cherished Christmas tradition at *The P-R*. Every year he would stand, hand over heart, before the enormous Christmas tree that maintenance erected in the newsroom. More than a few hardened reporters would wipe tears from their eyes by the time he finished.

Graduating high school and attending the local university, Moore had briefly answered God's call and joined the regional Catholic seminary. He dropped out when he realized that a life of celibacy was not for him, particularly if it meant giving up fantasies of young men in tight jeans. He moved to New York and got a master's degree in journalism from Columbia, where his lifestyle took an abrupt turn from the path of righteous tradition. He wound up back in Rilertown after Gus whispered in Wick's ear one day that the talented young journalist might be coerced to come home and take the vacant managing editor's slot, thus abandoning his boyfriends and perhaps returning to more normative ways.

Zamboni was many things Moore was not.

He was short, mean, unpredictable, impetuous, xenophobic and straight as a stretch of Nebraska highway (the likes of which he would never see, having no interest in venturing further than a few miles from home). Zamboni was a native of Binnfield, a nearby city about the size of Rilertown separated by the Oksaguganuatee yet a world of ethnic, religious and philosophical differences away.

Binnfield was 98% Polish and 100% Catholic. The few immigrants whose names ended other than in "ski", "icz" or the like earned acceptance into the community only because they, too, doggedly traipsed into one of the city's enormous churches for mass day after day and forked over 10% of their hard-earned pay in church-mandated tithings.

Zamboni's father was a hard-drinking, violent day laborer who alternated the direction of his anger between his wife and only child. His mother was a slight woman of Italian descent who, after finding herself unmarried and pregnant, tied the knot with Zamboni's dad despite repeated emotional appeals by her family to abandon the scowling, crude midget with whom she was consorting and raise the child on her own. Once locked into marriage, she abandoned her talent for preparing sumptuous northern Italian feasts to assuage Zamboni's father's daily demand for sausage, boiled potatoes and cabbage.

The younger Zamboni predictably became a product of his environment, compensating for his ongoing acne problem and diminutive stature by treating women with the same contemptuous disdain in which he inexplicably held his forgiving, doting mother. He learned anger, abuse and occasional violence from his stupid, talentless father, making poor choices about which side of the gene pool to tap to shape his own adult personality. Zamboni developed a talent for subjecting his targets to intense verbal and emotional abuse, discharging his impressive vocabulary in feverish tirades to compensate for his lack of height and horrid complexion. His wife, Betty, married him because no one else had offered, and the two somehow produced two daughters of forgettable intellect, spirit and talent.

Yet Zamboni and Moore had one common bond: their work. They lived, breathed and loved the practice of journalism — and they offered complementary skills; the odd couple of valley newspapering, one in three-piece pinstripes and conservative tie, the other in soft cottons and cravat. This odd duo created the perfect storm of intelligence, competitiveness, artistic flair and bravado. Learning to respect each other's talents while resenting and loathing each other personally, they carefully laid minefields that kept them separated. Moore stuck to strategy, budgeting, personnel matters and keeping Wick tethered to reality. Zamboni's job was to whip the staff into shape and produce a newspaper worth reading every day while beating the pants off competing media who struggled to keep up. He gave the paper its swagger and edge; Moore, its appreciation of arts, culture and society while keeping newsroom spending under control.

Outside of work, they were likely to disregard each other completely, often doing just that as they weighed produce next to one another in the Stop & Shop where both city's populations bought their weekly groceries.

The product of their partnership had been remarkable, and the paper was a regular at the podium during the annual press association annual awards dinners in Boston. Plaques memorializing honors in investigative reporting, news writing, best series, sports, lifestyle — even obituary writing, to the delight of the paper's Lifestyle editor — dotted Wick's office and spilled over onto the conference room walls.

Yet the paper had endured an unusual dry spell of awards as the 1970s headed for a close. Dunn thought this was yet another snub from the newspaper associations run by snooty eastern

Massachusetts paper owners. It concerned Zamboni and Moore, the former more than the latter, who made it his personal mission to return *The P-R* to the glory of journalism awards ceremonies.

MISFORTUNE CREATES OPPORTUNITY

"Ketcher," bellowed Zamboni from within his office.

Jake snapped to attention, grabbed a notebook and headed past the rows of reporter's desks, enduring Buckley's mocking "Uh, oh…Jakie's in trooooouuuuubbbble" and other caustic remarks from reporters who were in the office 7 a.m.

"Leave it open," Zamboni said from behind his desk as Jake entered the office and reached to close the door. "You won't be here long.

"Iggy's out sick," he said, referring to *The P-R*'s veteran City Hall and police reporter Zachary Ignotovich. "Actually, he's more than sick. He's apparently been on a bender for weeks, unbeknownst to me, of course. He wound up in the hospital last night. His family's taken him home now, but he's headed to detox to dry out and get his shit together. He'll be out at least a month, maybe more; don't know.

"You're in City Hall. Starting today. "

Zamboni shoved a sheaf of papers across his desk.

"City Council agenda for tonight. 7:30. Get up to speed and cover it." He looked up at Jake for the first time and grinned.

"Guess you'll have to call wifey and let her know hubby won't be home for dinner tonight, at least not long enough for supper and nookie."

Zamboni took pride in knowing intimate details of his staff's private lives, and he happily deployed this knowledge at every opportunity to keep them all on edge, wary and fearful.

"Mayor's press briefing this morning at 10. It's like pre-season for tonight's council meeting, so your attendance is mandatory as well. Get there early so the fucking *Gazette* doesn't get the prime seat; that's ours."

Everything was a competition to Zamboni, a stingy little man with tiny hands, gherkin-sized fingers, beady, perpetually blood-shot eyes and an overcompensating ego.

"Mike was goalie for his high school dart team," was the standing joke in the newsroom in spiteful reference to Zamboni's complexion. Bullies always got their due in the unforgiving newsroom jungle. "Either that or he was manager for the football team and they used his face to scrape their spikes clean after practice."

Jake excitedly grabbed the agenda and headed for his desk to read up and grab some background files before his maiden voyage to City Hall.

At 9:36 a.m., he was front and center in the mayor's conference room, occupying the preferred seat directly in front of the podium and studying press clippings related to the day's agenda. Five or six other seats quickly filled with reporters from the local radio and TV stations. One of them was Ben Davidoff, *The Gazette's* officious reporter of limited talent but remarkable staying power who, as always, showed up in a three-piece suit. He'd been with *The Gazette* since God was in diapers, or so it seemed, covering Rilertown with half-hearted interest as he desultorily churned out eight-inch stories with a writing style best described as terminally boring.

Jake had circled one of the agenda items that drew his interest. "Peregrine falcon update," it read, referring to the city's ongoing efforts to relocate a group of peregrine falcon nests atop Mt. Riler that represented one of the region's last natural nesting spots of the endangered species.

Moments later the room seemed to shrink as Sid Reigner blew in and strode to the podium. Reigner, the city's ill-tempered French-Canadian mayor, had bullied his way into office 15 years earlier and clung to the seat like a dog to a ham bone. Reigner's reputation as a fearsome jerk was enhanced by the .38-caliber snub nose revolver he carried wherever he went. The gun, he claimed, was protection against hateful members of the Hispanic community he routinely referred to off the record as "CooCooRicans."

Reigner had a Ph.D. in community development from a little-known Canadian correspondence school and required underlings to refer to him as "Dr. Sid." His charges preferred calling him "El Sid," though hizzoner bore little resemblance to Charlton Heston or any admirable qualities possessed by the lead character of the popular 1961 movie, *El Cid.*

Reigner was married to Bunny McFadden, daughter of Butch McFadden, who had logged 30 years and counting as chairman of the City Council. The marriage to Bunny "did the job," as Reigner loved to brag, creating a power consortium at the top of the city's ranks that political challengers found unassailable. Reigner was the consummate small city political hack — too stupid to work in the private sector, too untalented to qualify for broader office yet cagey, ruthless and politically astute enough to make the mayor's office his own for as long as he wished.

Rilertown was *his* town; City Hall *his* castle. Press briefings were the rare moments when outsiders were allowed in to ask annoying questions and try to unsettle the pear-shaped mayor. He regarded members of the Fourth Estate as vengeful interlopers and prepared for weekly briefings the same way he anticipated a colonoscopy.

He rarely wasted any time with the media minions, as he like to call them. Today, Reigner got straight to work.

"Good morning. Save your questions until the end. Item one…." For the next hour, Reigner droned on without pause, drawing on his ability to speak nonstop by deploying the rhythmic breathing of an operatic soprano. Wrapping up the last item — a review of plans for the annual St. Patrick's Day Parade — Reigner signaled that it was time for questions.

Jake raised his hand.

"Who are you?" Reigner asked.

"Ketcher. P-R. Filling in for Iggy, uh, Zachary. I'm wondering when we'll have details about the peregrine relocation schedule. You know, what'll happen to the birds, the habitat ..."

"You're new, kid, so we'll cut you some slack," Reigner interrupted. "We've covered that previously. Look it up. I'm the mayor, not your research assistant. Call and make an appointment with one of my staff if you want some background.

"Next?"

Jake slumped in his chair. His heart beat faster, and his face flushed. Davidoff was beaming at him, his abundant jowls jiggling as laughed quietly, celebrating Jake's humiliation. Jake scribbled in his notebook until the press conference mercifully ended, jotting notes of Reigner's responses to questions asked by others. Reigner slammed his day timer shut and strode from the room. Jake rose and headed for the door.

"Ketcher," came a voice from the front of the room. "Mayor wants to see you."

Reigner's chief of staff, Ted Price, an unlikeable flack whose primary job seemed to be driving Reigner from fundraiser to meeting and keeping him out of trouble while making full use of an abundant city car pool, led Jake to the mayor's vast office overlooking a canal. Reigner, seated at his desk, motioned Jake into a chair.

"I was probably a little rough on you out there, kid," Reigner grinned, trimming a cigar and reaching for a gold lighter on his desk. "Gotta keep you guys in line, though.

"But hey. No harm. I'm gonna help you out. What, you wanted info about the birds, right? Ted here will fill you in, but I'm gonna give you a tip to help us both get back on terma ferra."

Reigner was famous for liberally peppering his monologs with colorful malapropisms, many of which became important parts of the newsroom subculture vernacular.

"Can't see the forest through the leaves," he said of the city auditor.

"I'm an envisionary," he proclaimed of himself.

"My family is of tantamount importance," he announced in a re-election speech.

Today, however, he was in a giving mood.

"You know Ben Mills, right, from the insurance company TV wildlife show? Well, he's coming to Rilertown, and he's doing a piece on our bird relocation program day after tomorrow. Wanna take a hike with him? Ted'll set you up."

Reigner's intercom buzzed. He pressed a button, answering with an abrupt, "Yah?"

"Blake Thompson is on line one, Mr. Mayor," said his secretary. "He says it's important."

"Gotta take this," Reigner said, chuckling and rising to shake Jake's hand. He gestured him toward the door. "Golf partner. Very important stuff."

The name Blake Thompson sounded familiar to Jake, so he paused outside Reigner's office to jot the name in his notebook. He spent a few minutes scooping details about Mills' visit from Price, then scurried back to the newsroom to find the number for the local ABC affiliate. He tracked down Mills' PR staff at his New York office, confirming that, indeed, the popular octogenarian host of "Parliament Insurance's Wild Outdoors" would be filming the peregrines atop Mt. Riler in two days. Of course Mr. Ketcher was welcome to come along, interview Mills and write a favorable promotional piece.

Jake pounded out 10 quick inches on the story announcing Mills' imminent visit to Rilertown and forwarded it to the city editor for a look at the lead.

Rilertown's threatened peregrine falcon population
will be the star of an upcoming segment of television
host Ben Mills' popular Wild Outdoors show, *The
P-R* learned today.

Scanning it, she called Zamboni to her side. After a brief chat, they summoned Jake to the editor's pit.

"Where'd you get this?" Zamboni demanded.

"From the mayor," Jake offered.

Zamboni turned to the Betsey, who always paid close attention to what transpired in the pit, particularly if Zamboni was involved.

"Any sign of this on the wires, or in this morning's *Gazette*?"

"Nada," she answered, authoritatively. Competitive intel was her domain, and she was damned good at it.

"Page one," Zamboni instructed the city editor, Amy Amaczewski. "Bump the water main break to page 2. Run the falcon piece above the fold."

To Jake: "Nice work."

Jake stood before Amaczewski, stunned. This was hardly the kind of stuff that typically made the front page. Such a soft bit of fluff would stand out in contrast against the usual carnage on *The P-R*'s front page like a Mormon proselytizer cold-calling in The Flats. A water main break in downtown Rilertown that left hundreds of homes without water that morning moved to page 2 in lieu of a promotional piece about birds?

He made the mistake of asking why the story warranted such attention.

"Because he said so," Amaczewski deadpanned. "It's local. And it's ours. So it's running page one. Above the fold, like the man said.

"Besides, Wick's old man, who happens to remain as majority owner of this newspaper, has a soft spot in his heart for the natural world. For some reason, he still thinks Rilertown is a haven for wildlife. He's why we still run the shad count on page one every spring. Any wildlife — fish, coyotes, bear and, apparently birds — runs page one. Kind of an unwritten rule around here.

"Anything else?"

Jake returned to his desk to make some calls, get up to speed on the peregrine relocation program, then called Sabrina at home to ask her to look for his hiking boots.

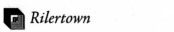

EXTRACURRICULAR ACTIVITY

After softball practice that night, Jake and a bunch of other P-R journos removed their baseball spikes and headed to La Bamba, a crossover pub that somehow managed to attract both Anglo and Latino customers without having every night end with a visit from the local authorities to break up fights.

La Bamba was a sports bar that religiously showed Red Sox, Patriots, Bruins and Celtics games on a dusty TV suspended from the wall while salsa music blared in deference to its Hispanic customers — sports in English; music in Spanish. This savvy gesture of détente kept everyone happy and the beer flowing.

Jake bellied up to the bar next to his buddy, centerfielder and Rilertown Department of Public Works employee Jorge Rodriguez "Cheecha" Morada. He looked at Morada's cold Bud and nodded to the bartender. "One just like this."

"Nice page one piece today," Morada said. "Real hard, breaking news, world-changing, even. Peregrine fucking falcons! Amazing!"

"Shove it," Jake countered, punching Morada on his shoulder and wincing in mock pain as his fist hit solid muscle.

"Shit, man; you lifting more than usual, or what? That's like punching a rock."

Morada flexed his torso, showing off his muscles beneath a light t-shirt.

"I tell, you, man, it's volleyball. You gringos run around playing all kind of passive shit: pool, ping pong, golf, bowling. If you played volleyball like me and my brothers, you'd be buff, too."

When he wasn't tending to Rilertown's roads, parks or other physical assets as a DPW manager, Morada spent long hours at the Rilertown YMCA, where he was number one hitter on a top-rated volleyball team and experienced coach of the Y's Golden Gloves boxing program. Jake and Cheecha had met one day after Jake had spent an hour flailing about on the Y's racquetball court and was soothing his muscles in the steam room. Morada was splayed on the bench across from him. The two struck up a conversation. Morada's easy manner and quick smile opened the door; their love of sports, beer and their women sealed the friendship.

Morada and his wife, Carmella, lived in a cramped apartment in the center of the city's conflicted poor zone with their six children and a pet goat named Choncho. Choncho, the only pet goat in a building illegally populated by numerous farm species that shared space with their owners, spent nights in the family's bath tub and days perched in front of the TV watching Spanish sitcoms and chewing its cud. Communal living took on new meaning in the barrio, where Morada ruled the streets with the quiet resolve that comes from strength, honor and respect.

A soft-spoken, friendly "everyman" who spoke lightly accented English, Morada seemed to know everyone — and everything — in the city. He quickly became one of Jake's most trusted sources, feeding him news tips about everything from inner city gang activity to the latest business deals in town.

"See that dude over there," said Morada, nodding at a table covered with empty beer bottles surrounded by six men. "The one with the girly pink Lacoste golf shirt. The jackass?"

The guy in pink was sitting next to a couple of local golf addicts Jake had gotten to know while covering the city's annual four-ball championships during his stint as part-time sports reporter.

"Blake Thompson — big golfer, big money, bigger asshole — a real man about town, big time player. Been around for awhile, but he's been relatively quiet, unless you're big into the golf scene. Guy's into some funky development investment stuff with city hall, too, or so I hear. Maybe he'd give you an interview, you know, give you something to unseat your grip on the migratory habits of local birds?"

Jake reflected on the phone call that had interrupted his brief encounter with Reigner earlier that day.

"Blake Thompson? What kind of investment stuff?" Jake pressed.

"Dunno, but I hear big. I don't know a helluva lot more, but here's a chick who might."

Morada's eyes drifted across the room, where a small-framed woman with straight chestnut hair and a white tank top under serious strain was making her way across the dance floor. She saw Morada and headed straight for him.

"Hey, Beebo," Morada said. "Meet my pal Jake Ketcher, P-R's finest scribe. He's the one who broke the big story about the eagles or whatever in today's paper."

Jake shot Morada a nasty look and shook the woman's hand, looking her over. She was trim and pretty, but her face and eyes showed the effects of having spent too many evenings at La Bamba.

"Beebo Burns," she said, sliding onto the open stool next to Jake. "You probably know my father. Top of the slag heap that constitutes the city's finest."

Jake knew Lester "JC" Burns, all right — not personally, but through his reputation and the cult of fear and loathing the chief of police had carefully nurtured over the years to keep his ample keister in the department's top chair. Burns was Rilertown's fat, mirror-sunglassed top cop. Stupid, ruthless and supremely racist, Burns was perfect for the job. He spent what the city gave him without asking for more, gave the mayor and city council a minimum of crap, maintained a civil tone with the patrolman's union and thus kept police raises in line with other municipal unions, and ruled the minority community with an iron fist. These highly evolved management skills kept him in favor in city hall, and thus in power.

Burns had cemented his legend as a hopelessly ignorant racist by once greeting a new P-R reporter — a female Indian graduate student from the respected nearby university who had appeared before him sporting a bright red bindi and a thick accent — by saying, "Well, you're a weird looking fucker, you are. What are you, some sort of fuckin' Filipino or something?"

Jake had heard about Beebo, too. She had a reputation as a chronic boozer who once after a particularly hard night of drinking legendarily tried to bail a friend out of jail using a half-eaten chicken sandwich as collateral. Her friend, who had been arrested for drunk driving, spent the night in the hoosegow after the desk sergeant rebuffed Beebo's drunken reminders of just who she was. He also declined the remnants of her sandwich and sent her on her way to sober up somewhere else.

JC was instantly alerted to his daughter's misconduct and confronted Beebo in a nasty public dressing down, finally catching up with her when she was well into her third beer the next day at La Bamba. He blasted her, humiliating her in front of her friends. The two had rarely spoken since.

"What do you know about this jerk, Thompson?" Morada asked Beebo, who was making friends with a 24-ounce mug of beer the bartender had wordlessly placed before her.

"That schmuck?" she took a deep pull on the beer, wiped her mouth with the back of her hand and adjusted herself on the stool. "Connected to big bucks. He's got something cooking on Mt. Riler, I hear, working with some out of state heavyweights.

"Probably has something to do with your birds, too. Thompson has designs for some sort of resort and casino up there. He's been nosing around for years, looking to find a way to encourage New Yorkers to pull off the highway en route to their Vermont ski chalets and divert a few million into the pockets of him and his buddies."

Jake watched as Thompson rose from the table, smoothed his shirt around his sculpted torso and sauntered to the bar to replenish the group's drinks. He was tanned, fit, handsome and obviously of money. Thompson ordered beers for his buddies and a cognac for himself, earning a disdainful glare from the bartender. Drinking upscale in a dive like La Bamba was a bad idea unless you tipped extraordinarily well. Thompson, well versed in the art of flaunting his wealth, tossed a $20 on the bar and told the bartender to keep the change. He turned to survey the room while the bartender fetched the drinks.

Noticing Beebo nearby, he smiled, revealing two rows of glistening enamel. "Hey, Beebo. Nice to see you. Can I buy you and your pals a round?"

"I'm good, Blake," she said softly, shaking her head and declining the offer for free booze. "Better than ever, in fact."

Drinks in hand and smile in tow, Blake shrugged and returned to his golfing buddies to resume regaling one another with their stories of conquests both on and off the links.

Jake instantly disliked him.

The three sat for another hour, talking sports and life, and sipping beers. The rounds came and went as their tongues became looser and their speech mildly slurred. Talk returned to Thompson, who was well into his own drunken stupor at the table across the room.

Beebo leaned closer to Morada as she lowered her voice.

"Guy's such a piece of work; likes to make like he's the center of the universe. Truth is, he's just a middleman. Guy like him is useless without people in power who use him. I hear he's working on some big project with his buddies from down south."

"South?" Jake probed. "Florida?"

"Naw, New York," Beebo explained. "Big development project using money that comes from places it probably shouldn't. Takes connections to make something like that happen, though.

Blake has a big friend in City Hall. I hear Reigner's involved —
big time — and of course that jackass McFadden. Lord knows
Reigner couldn't figure his way to a corrupt deal without his pal
McFadden."

She stared at Jake, clearly sizing him up.

"There's a story for you. Follow the money — for the birds. I
like those birds. They're sweet.

"Besides, that's protected area up there, and the falcons — not
eagles, you dick (looking at Morada) — should be protected.
These guys want to knock them off and build a fucking casino."

"Wait," Jake began, his greenhorn excitement in overdrive.
"Where's this coming from? How do you know this stuff?"

"Who the hell is this guy?" she said, turning to Morada. "He
for real?"

Morada nodded. "He's good. You can trust him."

Jake blundered ahead.

"Talk to me — on the record. Give me something to work with."
She sighed.

"No. I will not 'talk to you on the record.' You fucking kidding
me? Not here, and not now. Wake up, sporto. These guys are
not to be fucked with, so whatever I tell you would have to be
at another time and in no way traceable back to my sorry ass.
Call it survivor's rules of engagement. Later? Sure, I'll tell you

what I know. I'm more than happy to help blow the whistle on that bastard.

"See, Thompson and me, we used to be an item. He's a complete and utter dick, but he's rich, always buys the drinks, and is great in the sack. At least he was until he moved onto some other chick, some hooker he liked to brag about, as if renting a hooker required talent or in some way demonstrated his unequalled value to women."

Beebo acknowledged Jake's shock.

"Yeah, unbelieveable, huh? A hooker, and he was proud of it. That's when I bailed. Even I have standards — and no way do I want some nasty disease brought home by my golf nut loverboy.

"You know pillow talk? Well, this guy's an open spigot of info once he's had his ashes hauled. And nothing makes a guy talk like a woman fawning over his abilities after a game of once around the mattress — 'specially if his ego's bigger than his Johnson."

Jake grabbed a fistful of bar napkins and a pen, shifting into work mode and getting ready to take notes as she talked. Beebo snarled at him.

"Knock it off. This is serious shit. Buy me lunch tomorrow and I'll talk to you, but not here. Not now. Not with that guy here. No way."

LUNCHTIME REVELATION

Jake shoved open La Bamba's door and stood in the dank darkness as his eyes adjusted to the low light. He looked around and spotted two off-duty patrolmen chomping on burgers at a nearby table. Seated at another table equidistant between the bar and jukebox, an elderly woman sipped a bowl of soup.

He smiled at the waitress *("Sit anywhere, sweetie")* and then heard "psst" from the back of the café. Beebo waved him into a corner booth near the kitchen's swinging door. Dark circles under her eyes belied a heavy session the night before. A fluffy black and white scarf encircled her neck and draped onto the table next to a half-empty glass of Coke.

"Morning sporto," she said. "You drinking? I'm easing into the day. Hair of the dog's unthinkable today, even for a seasoned vet like me."

Jake eased into the booth at an angle to Beebo.

She fidgeted nervously, wiping the droplets of water from the side of the Coke glass, then tugged at her fingers, snapping the knuckles one after another. The scarf settled around her neck, revealing the purplish tint of a nasty bruise.

"You really should go easy on those digits," Jake counseled. "You'll have arthritis before you're 30."

"I have a few bigger problems than arthritis," she countered, "but I didn't come here for a wellness consultation. I came because you promised to buy me lunch. So, buy. My order's in. You gonna eat, or would that impede your ability to grill me?"

Jake assessed the young woman. With sloped, defeated shoulders and a face that reflected night after night of drinking and smoking, she looked well beyond her 24 years. The fire in her eyes and sharpness of her tongue revealed an edgy persona fueled by loss, unhappiness and disappointment — and more than a little anger.

He studied the menu, signaled the waitress and ordered a burger, fries and Coke.

"Well, aren't we just two peas," Beebo commented, her voice laced with suggestive sarcasm. "We both like our meat plain and hot."

This was unfamiliar turf — an awkward interview with a reluctant, attractive source his age. Jake forged ahead. Her choice of words was loaded with double entendres. What she hitting on him?

"Mind if I take notes?" he asked, producing a spiral notebook. She nodded in assent.

"So tell me about Thompson — what you know about him, his business associates and this deal involving Mt. Riler and the falcons."

Beebo launched into a detailed narrative about her short but steamy affair with Thompson, whom she described as "some sort of business consultant. "He's really a matchmaker, the kind of guy who doesn't make anything, doesn't represent anything and isn't responsible for anything. But he knows people, and he knows how to bring people together who have mutual interests."

"Mutual interests? Like what?" Jake probed.

"Making money. Look, Jake, you're new to town, and you're obviously a bit of a bumpkin who doesn't know the score quite yet. You're from Silvertown, right? Well, welcome to the big city. Rilertown is made by men who built their wealth, power and nasty reputations by screwing other people. Everyone — my illustrious father included — made their way to the top by climbing over other people. It gets nasty, sometimes, and people get hurt."

"Like you?"

"Yeah, like me. I'm a casualty, sort of," Beebo said, adjusting the sleeves on her blouse and sitting up in the booth. Her scarf slid a little lower, and Jake got an eyeful of the vicious bruise.

"But not a victim. No, that ain't me — not by a longshot."

The waitress brought their burgers and refreshed their Cokes. Jake summoned the courage to ask about the bruise.

She sighed deeply, an exhalation that merged suffering and release.

"Part of the turf. It's what you get when you forget your place and cross powerful people. I'm fine, though, and it's not the first time I've ignored a warning."

"Warning about what?" Jake leaned forward. "And from who?"

"About knowing too much, and about talking to the wrong people. Last night after you left, Thompson caught up with me outside the lady's room. Had a little chat with me about my choice of friends and conversation topics. He overheard some of our discussion and wasn't thrilled about my 'lack of discretion.' I guess he thought I'd pay better attention if he massaged my throat a bit while we talked.

"Look, forget it. Let's just say it's one of the reasons why I'm here today. Not much I can do about this," fingering the bruise, "but it's motivation for a little payback."

Thompson already represented much of what Jake despised: flamboyant, arrogant; a small-time player profiting from political connections while he golfed, drank and slept around. But a woman abuser as well? Jake thought of his sister. She was about Beebo's age. Moments earlier Jake was just interested. Now he was focused, motivated — and angry.

Forget it, my ass, he thought.

Beebo shook her head when Jake pressed for more details about her brush with Thompson.

He placed his hand on her forearm.

"Look, Beebo. Nobody should get away with roughing up someone else. You don't need to take his abuse."

She smiled softly.

"So what? You're going to help me? Save me?"She took a deep pull on her Coke. "Or maybe you want to get to know me better?" Her coquettish smile didn't fit. "A little afternoon delight for the handsome new reporter in town?"

Jake shook his head.

"Look, Beebo, I'm in a relationship. So, no. No afternoon delight for me, thanks. Just trying to be a good guy — and get to the heart of a story. You want help, I'm here, but I'm here to listen and work. Nothing else. So, you gonna talk, or not?"

She sat back in her chair and assessed him. Tapped the side of the Coke glass.

"OK, I'll talk. But you're not using my name, right? Obviously I need to keep my looks intact for someone else."

For the next hour-and-a-half, Beebo shared what she knew about the development plans, the players and Thompson's role. Jake left the restaurant mid-afternoon, $20 lighter but with a notebook full of quotes, facts, dates and questions to ask and research to complete. He also left with Beebo's bruise fresh in his memory, residue of a violent warning that foretold further danger for the young woman — and perhaps for him as well.

THE ART OF THE STORY

Jake created a new split shift. Daytimes, he filed stories about car accidents and robberies. A couple of candidates for statewide office stopped at *The P-R* on their way through western Mass. on obligatory campaign swings to curry favor with voters, providing interesting profiles for Jake, along with the chance to ask probing, revealing questions. Then came a brief stint in Hazelton's Superior Court, covering a murder trial involving a young man from Rilertown.

Wrapping up the day's efforts, Jake would leave the office with the rest of the staff around 3:00. But unlike his counterparts who headed to bars and gyms, Jake headed home. He turned his tiny dining room table into a battle zone for the story about Thompson's development, creating a small mountain of papers, documents and notes that he warned Sabrina not to touch.

"I know where everything is, and if you mess around with it, it'll just add weeks or months to what I'm working on."

He kept the details of the story from her, making phone calls from the kitchen to keep out of her earshot. Her disinterest in his work kept them separate; she, curled up on the sofa watching television and smoking pot; he, at the dining table, sorting through papers, making notes and organizing the growing pile of information.

Jake briefed Zamboni and Moore every day or so. He made sure to feed them enticing tidbits to keep them asking questions and earn their support. As time passed, he filled in holes in the story, and pressed on for more damning confirmation of Thompson's exploits.

Jake was able to piece together Thompson's role as financial middleman for a string of construction projects along the East Coast. The golfer had a bit of reputation, working his way through New Jersey and the Connecticut shoreline on a rash of minor development projects, always as a deal maker but never as the money guy. City planners Jake spoke to had little good to say about Thompson, his silent partners, or their projects, which usually were multi-unit residential buildings. A planned entertainment complex would be his first large-scale project.

He built a list of sources like a pyramid, badgering his P-R colleagues for names and phone numbers of sources in the city who made careers of ratting out people more powerful than themselves in return for favors. In the unforgiving business of city politics, careers advanced by the failures of others as frequently as they did by one's own accomplishments.

People talked — sometimes brazenly on the record, but more often than not off the record with random, ill-supported opinions and theories that would never make it to print. City Hall staff knew the rules of press engagement; they uniformly deployed the phrase "off the record" whenever they gave up valuable or condemning information.

Building a story means stacking facts atop one another, cross referencing them, and finding someone of authority to verify and confirm information. Credence to the "nuggets" of a story, the salient, specific details upon which the story is built, comes from getting the right people to acknowledge each set of facts, sometimes in reaction to the wild rants of people who are in the know yet incapable of articulating a credible, authoritative answer to a direct question. It's a house built of toothpicks, a series of interrelated facts, allegations, suppositions and quotes carefully constructed to lean on one another. Care must be taken to connect each element to the next lest the entire house should collapse into a tangled mess of tiny, meaningless wooden shards.

Jake filled notebook after notebook with his awkward scrawl. He developed a system to help focus on key dates and facts, circling important quotes in red, underlining follow-up questions in thick black, and highlighting key dates with a yellow marker.

He included reference notations that related to the supporting documents that grew in massive stacks on his dining table.

Some afternoons he turned his attention to *The P-R*'s library, dubbed "the morgue." The brightly lit room was packed with microfiche and carefully clipped and dated news stories in floor-to-ceiling card files meticulously maintained by *The P-R*'s matronly librarian. He copied more files and added it all to the pile of information that made Sabrina grumble. It gave Jake enormous satisfaction to see the story came into focus.

After a month of intense labor, Jake had constructed the guts of a solid news story backed by unconfirmed hunches and second-generation "facts" — a story still in raw, unpublishable form, but it looked bad for Reigner, McFadden and of course Thompson. This preliminary reporting motivated him to dig deeper.

He reviewed what he had learned so far. A crib sheet gave form and structure to the evolving story. Late one night, he sat back and surveyed the outline, allowing his thoughts to settle around what he knew, what he suspected, and what he needed to confirm.

Jake felt enormous pride over what he had learned, coupled with worries about reactions from the powerful people implicated in the story. Young, inexperienced reporters don't take on connected developers and powerful politicians and escape unscathed.

He learned Thompson had paid cash bribes to the mayor, the city council chairman and to the head of the city's parks and recreation department. The Recreation Department maintained the Mt. Riler Reserve, home of the much ballyhooed peregrine falcon — six birds and their offspring that stood in the way of Thompson's quest to secure development rights to 10 prime acres atop the region's highest peak.

Months earlier, Jake's tour with TV host Ben Mills had yielded a nice, soft feature, and also provided valuable background on the preserved forest and craggy peak that constituted Mt. Riler, not to mention the collection of birds that enjoyed the projection of the US Department of Interior. The tour introduced Jake to the Rec and Park chief, who provided the first solid evidence of bribery when he casually admitted accepting cash from Thompson. Jake took a longshot and inquired how much Thompson had paid him to keep the deal quiet; the guy shocked him by simply answering the question: "$5,000, but you can't say I told you that. That's off the record."

Continuing their discussion over pizza and beer later that night, and with a promise from Jake to keep his name out of the story, the affable civil servant with room temperature IQ made reference to the bribe as "walking around money" that Thompson was using liberally to grease the city's wheels of progress. He was in

Reigner's office when Thompson came by with a briefcase that remained with Reigner after a one-minute meeting. "Reigner tossed me out of his office when Thompson arrived. He was in there for less than a minute, and when he left he told me to keep my fucking mouth shut and slipped me a $50," said the parks chief, reaching for the last piece of pepperoni pizza. "Pretty clear to me what was going on."

Following up, Jake learned that Thompson was a regular on the mayor's calendar. He also discovered that the mayor was preparing to announce development of "a major entertainment and ecological center complex" atop the reserve that would "bring valuable tax dollars and a burst of secondary economic prosperity to Rilertown." The plan, according to an eager young mayoral assistant who thought Jake was cute and therefore told him far more than she should have, was to highlight the reserve's biological diversity and sanctity as one of nature's original gifts while playing down the fact that half the mountain would be blown off to make way for an enormous casino/hotel and a four-lane access road — birds be damned.

Another source, an environmental activist Jake met while doing background research at the Mt. Riler Wildlife Sanctuary, told Jake during a lengthy walk around the sanctuary's reservoir that Thompson had paid off the local Audubon chapter, buying their silence with a generous gift earmarked to enhance the chapter's pet project, a "river otter repopulation center" located just above the entrance to the city's First Canal. Jake confirmed this and other details during an evening with one of Thompson's golfing buddies. Jake tracked down the pudgy 40-something-year-old on the 19th hole of the local country club while he was drowning his sorrows after missing a crucial birdie putt on the 17th earlier in the day. A $10 investment in two bourbon-and-cokes yielded important confirming detail as the guy spun on and on.

The golfer had a serious axe to grind with Thompson, owing to the fact that the latter's proclivity for lying about his score had resulted in a string of ill-deserved top-five finishes on the local golfing circuit, the latest an apparent theft of the Mt. Riler Cup at the expense of Jake's bourbon-saturated confidant. "Thompson loves to brag," the guy said, reaching for a fistful of peanuts as the TV behind him showed highlights of Jack Nicklaus' latest PGA victory. "Spend five hours in a golf cart with him on a Sunday and you'll get an earful from the twit."

"What's he in this for?" Jake pressed.

"You're kidding, right?" the guy sneered. "Thompson's a selfish prick. He's interested in precisely two things: money, and stuff he uses money to buy: influence, people, booze, chicks, whatever.

"He's tied into serious dough in New York, some of it dirty money — I think mob. He told me many times that the people he represents were going to make him a very wealthy man once he pulls off the deal. He never told me what the project was, but it's not too hard to figure out. Blake's no nature nut, so I figure the amount of time he spends on Mt. Riler probably doesn't concern his interest in birds, plants or weather. "

Jake left the country club with a notebook jammed with information, grateful he had never taken up golf. The sport seemed populated by world-class jackasses in horrible clothes — liars and cheats who drank heavily to give credence to their embellished stories of athletic prowess as they clapped one another on the back and called for another round.

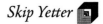

OCTOBER, 1976

His *fingers gripped the message slip, then slowly closed into a fist, crumpling it into a tiny ball. He angrily tossed the paper into a wastebasket beneath his desk. This was the latest in an endless string of messages bearing the same name and phone number, all imploring him to return his call, all from the spineless coward who, bathed in guilt, remorse and fear, imperiled all their futures by trying to make contact.*

He is not going away, and he simply doesn't get it. We cannot speak, and he risks it all by trying to make contact. What happened that night to that girl is history. It is unfortunate, but not intentional — just an accident. It will go away if we remain silent, have no contact with one another, and DON'T LEAVE A FUCKING PAPER TRAIL FOR SOMEONE TO FIND AND EXPLOIT.

Like phone messages.

His fingers drummed the desk as he contemplated his options.

How best to silence the weakest member of a select group that shared a horrible secret? What to do about a man whose refusal to simply be still could end their careers and place them in jail? Ordering him into silence him hadn't worked; neither had ignoring him. He thought about dispatching a minion to threaten him, but such an extreme measure would be risky in its own right. He massaged his temples as he fantasized about having the man eliminated.

Dead men don't talk, *he thought, frightening himself with the very thought of premeditated murder.*

He rejected the option. Every man has his limits.

How did I get myself into this mess?

Sigh.

This constant, needy pestering has to stop.

In an instant he decided upon the course of action, and picked up the phone. He pressed "4" on speed dial and was greeted by the familiar "yeah?" of the gruff voice at the other end of the line.

"We have a problem," he breathed into the phone. "A very big, loud and persistent problem."

THE CONFRONTATION

Zamboni was out of town at a press association meeting with Betsey (meaning the two were taking advantage of a rare opportunity to spend an entire night together), so after returning from the golf course, Jake called Moore at home to talk through the new developments.

Classical music was audible in the background as Moore answered the phone with his customary, "Speak to me."

Jake scowled. Two years dealing with snooty, affected and entitled interview subjects had made him suspicious of annoying affectations, but he liked Moore and had learned to laugh at his quirky habits.

"Hey, Les … Jake here … Calling with an update on the development story. I need to be out of the office tomorrow morning so I can look into some details."

Jake heard Moore cup the phone, and whisper "I'll be a minute," followed by a brief delay. Consort relegated to the background, Moore returned.

"OK. Tell me what's up."

Jake walked him through the details of the story, being careful to cover what questions remained and what he needed to do to "nail it down and write the thing."

"I have to get Thompson to talk," he told Moore. "If I can somehow get him to tip his hand, the whole thing crashes down on Reigner and McFadden."

That would be a challenge, Moore pointed out. Why would a guy wired for self-preservation talk to a reporter about the countless ways he had bribed public officials and broken numerous local, state and federal regulations?

"Look, Jake, you have zero right now — third party claims and accusations, but not much confirmed. We're not going to risk this kind of exposure for a bunch of speculative ramblings. No Thompson; no story. The question is, what's the best way to rattle this guy's cage so he squawks?"

"I reason with him," Jake offered.

"Oh, please."

"OK, I threaten him."

"That's like you taking a poke at Michael Spinks. He'd eat you alive."

Jake paused.

"I've got it; I lie to him."

Moore thought for a moment, his grin nearly audible over the phone.

"Good dog, Spot. Perfect. Best way to outfox a sleazeball is to out-talk him. Long as you can bullshit him into thinking you have far more than you do, well, it's the perfect way to appeal to Mr. Thompson's sense of justice and civic duty."

As further enticement, they decided to offer Thompson anonymity if he would confirm the details of what Jake had learned. Their primary targets were Reigner and McFadden, after all, two officials elected and trusted by Rilertown's public, not some moderately talented amateur golfer who dressed like a garden elf.

As much as Jake cherished the idea of Thompson taking the fall along with his elected pals, in the quid pro quo world of hier-archical preferences he realized it would suffice to nail the city's two top officials.

There would be only one shot for Jake to get Thompson to squawk, Moore predicted. He would have to be thorough, direct — and brutal; the only way to out-bully a bully is to appear to be the toughest guy in the room.

"You're going to have to hit him hard with what you know. Confront him with enough facts so you overwhelm him. Your goal is to make him stain his BVDs, make him see that he has no choice but to tell us what he knows to save his ass," Moore coached. "From what you've told me, it's clear this guy is a survivor. He'd toss his grandmother under the bus if he thought he'd get an advantage out of it, and I think he'll choose giving up Reigner and McFadden over making pals in the hoosegow for the next few years.

"Once you've dispensed with the recitation of facts, look him in the eye and tell him you have him by the short hairs. He plays ball; he walks. He doesn't; he's going down, and you'll see him after the Grand Jury convenes.

"And be sure to remind him that his friends in New York, the money guys behind the deal, won't take too kindly to a Grand Jury investigation looking into the money trail and their role in the financing."

The next morning Jake approached Thompson as he exited his upscale apartment building on his way to a practice round. Jake had memorized a list of facts to use in the confrontation. Thompson strode confidently to his gleaming back Mercedes-Benz coupe resplendent in his signature pink Lacoste shirt and contrasting green golf pants, looking like a six-foot tall lime-raspberry popsicle.

There was no room for finesse when dealing with a testosterone-powered egotist like Thompson, and Jake grinned at the prospect of the task at hand. He relished ruining the guy's day with a recitation of facts, and looked forward to watching Thompson's bravado disappear.

Adrenaline surged.

His pulse quickened.

Showtime.

He intercepted Thompson as he placed a hand on the Mercedes' door.

"Blake? Jake Ketcher, P-R. We met at La Bamba a few weeks ago, remember? I have a few questions for you. Actually, I have some information to share with you that I think you'll be interested in."

"Really?" Thompson opened the car door. "If you want an appointment, call my office and make a date. I'm late for golf."

"No, Blake. Now," Jake said, stepping closer. "I think you'll want to hear what I have to say."

Jake outlined what he suspected.

"I'm working on a story about an illegal development you are promoting on protected municipal property," Jake said. "I have a list of details I'd like your comment on."

Thompson's face drained of color. He looked around to see if anyone else was in the parking lot. *Better to continue this in private*, he thought to himself. He told Jake to follow him into his apartment.

Thompson was a product of the streets, a brawler-turned negotiator. Once safely inside and on familiar turf, he tried being tough. "You got nothing. If you did you'd just run it," he shrugged, a hard scowl punctuating his resolve. Jake looked into his eyes and saw fear and apprehension, not confidence and swagger. "You're fishing."

"Fishing? Hardly," Jake countered. Time for the body punch, a string of facts slightly embellished to make Thompson believe he knew more than he did.

"I have details of you paying bribes to elected and appointed officials, and of violating numerous laws. You think I need your comments to make this story? Wrong.

"You paid bribes to government officials to get the city to move a bunch of nesting peregrine falcons. You paid more bribes to fast-track permits to build a casino and hotel complex on the top of Mt. Riler, a protected reserve.

"I already have the story, Blake. Oh, we're running it, alright. Question is, do we toss this line in the water and reel in the fish one at a time, or do we trawl for the entire school? We have all the time in the world, and we just got a new shipment of ink and paper. You need to figure out how to avoid the net."

Thompson stared out the window. He changed tactics.

"Maybe I'll call my lawyer. Maybe we'll test the limits of what you know. Get an injunction."

Jake smiled.

"There's the phone. While you're making your call, I'll head to the payphone outside to call Wick Dunn and tell him to fire up the pit bulls at *The P-R*'s law firm — you know, the guys who handle libel, public access and freedom of information requests for every major East Coast newspaper? They love a long, winnable, expensive fight, especially when it's waged with an asshole like you."

"I'd rather take my chances standing by silently while my lawyer ties you guys up with injunction after injunction," Thompson countered, recovering a bit of bravado.

"This would be a first for you, right, Blake? Using legal tactics to attempt to tie up a newspaper? We do it all the time. We're as experienced at this stuff as you are with bullshit and two-foot putts. You might know your way around development laws, but you're out of your league on First Amendment and press rights issues.

"We'll run story after story while your lawyers file motions and send you bills."

Thompson leaned against the kitchen counter, pensive.

"I know people," he threatened, "people who make people change their minds, or, if need be, simply go away."

Jake felt a fine film of sweat develop beneath his collar. He had expected this and was prepared.

"So now you're resorting to threats, huh, Blake? You think that's going to scare me off this story? Think again. I have an entire news organization behind me. It's not just me. It's *The Post-Recorder*. And it's *The Post-Recorder*'s parent company. And the regional press association. And the national press association, as well. See? It's a whole, conspiratorial world of reporters, editors and publishers, all ganging up to make your life the living hell you deserve.

"And thanks for telling me that mob money is behind the development project. I'd thought it was some heavyweight investor, but your threat makes it pretty clear who's driving the bus. That's one detail I had yet to confirm.

"I'm going to let you in on a secret about reporting, Blake. There are all sorts of ways to get information: direct, indirect, on and off the record, for background. There's research, use of public records. It takes time, but with effort, concentration and help from people who are highly motivated to make someone else look bad, elements of a story like this come into focus pretty quickly.

"Loads of people are eager to tell what they know about you, Blake. You're not exactly a well-liked guy around town, you know, at least not outside of City Hall, and certainly not among people whose palms you haven't greased yet. One's enemies are always the most eager to talk.

"I have more than enough to run with this story," Jake lied. "As is. More is better, but not necessary.

"Your call. I can stay and listen, or leave and start writing."

Thompson turned the color of concrete, as though slowly being consumed by death. His head slumped against rounded shoulders; his arms folded defensively across his chest — a defeated man.

Jake went for the kill.

Once again he summarized his findings, this time with simple clarity. He wanted to impress Thompson with the scope of the story while concealing that none of it had been confirmed. He needed Thompson to verify the details, so he piled on fact after fact.

"So that's what I'm writing, and it's what the Grand Jury will hear as well," Jake ended.

Thompson — ever the pragmatist — concluded that he would encounter no better deal than to accept the paper's offer for anonymity. His investors were intolerant men of short temper and violent predisposition; he knew Jake's story had the potential to destroy far more than the development project. The money men from New York would have to be protected at all costs. They wouldn't take kindly to losing money over the project, but their reaction to a five-figure loss would pale by comparison to their rage and response if the issue went before a Grand Jury. If that were to happen, he might as well cut across the Canadian border and hide out on the tundra in Alberta for the rest of his life.

Better to own up and take my chances.

If he had to let Reigner and McFadden take the fall, so be it. Far better to be publicly lampooned and exiled from Rilertown than privately eviscerated and, perhaps, dead.

If he were to emerge from this disaster intact, he really had only one choice.

He spilled his guts.

Entering Zamboni's office with a memo that meticulously detailed the story, Jake was soon joined by Moore. The ME[3] shut the door behind him and took a seat facing Zamboni. Jake stood by the door, fidgeting.

Jake slid a copy of the memo in front of both of them. They quickly read it then exchanged glances, first with each other, then with Jake.

"Fuck me," Zamboni said.

"Well said," Moore chimed in.

"OK, details. Where'd you get this? Sources? I need grist," Zamboni pressed. Jake was prepared. For the next two hours, he endured a grilling that made Sabrina's interrogations seem like a meeting with Mr. Rogers. He answered their questions, often pausing to write notes and take their suggestions.

"Thompson paid bribes to Reigner, McFadden and a half dozen other players in the city," Jake said, sliding a piece of paper that

3. Managing Editor

listed amounts from $5,000 to $20,000 next to a list of names that began with the mayor and city council chairman.

"All cash. I need to find out how it got where it landed, but Thompson confirmed that he paid it all. Not for attribution, of course, but he confirmed every single bag of dough he schlepped into city hall."

He had more.

"Here's a list of stuff these assholes have done, and some of the laws they've violated," he said, offering the two another piece of paper.

"Prosecutable under RICO statutes, the Hobbs Act, even the FCPA." Jake was on a roll. Zamboni and Moore were impressed. *Pays to do your homework and prepare,* Jake thought.

They're on board, he mused as the meeting progressed. *Holy shit. We're going ahead with this.*

Not so fast.

Zamboni and Moore launched into a heated discussion that left Jake feeling like the third wheel on a blind date. They verbally ping-ponged back and forth while Jake idly stood by, mentally placing himself elsewhere while the two talked about him as though he weren't in the room.

"I don't think we take this big a risk with a kid barely out of J-school," Zamboni warned. "I mean, the friggin' mayor? *And* the city council chairman?"

"Look, he's got the details, and the story's solid. I say we let him take a run at the mayor and McFadden. Let him talk to them. Look what he got from this asshole Thompson," Moore defended.

"How's our libel insurance? Premiums up to date?" Zamboni countered sarcastically.

"*Times* v. Sullivan," battled Moore, reminding Zamboni of the federal law that provides journalists with broad latitude on the right to comment on public officials. "It's protected."

"Yeah? How about Thompson? He an elected official, too?" Zamboni seemed intent on derailing the story, but Moore, as managing editor was the more senior presence. One step closer to the paper's ultimate authority, he had the upper hand.

"Let's take it to Wick. It's his decision, ultimately. He needs to be involved. Now."

All eyes in the newsroom were on the three as they walked from Zamboni's office the length of the newsroom to the publisher's lair — a grim, purposeful parade that set off every reporter's instinct as the trio made their way.

Shocked by the enormity, scope and targets of the proposed story, the publisher — typically flummoxed by the details of news-gathering — opened the meeting by asking a series of increasingly banal questions. Some of his queries prompted lengthy philosophical arguments between Moore and Zamboni while Jake and Dunn sat as idle witnesses.

Fifteen minutes passed, and Jake had yet to make his case. This was not a great start.

"Walk him through it," prompted Zamboni, eager to get on with the discussion and stop the petty squabbles.

"OK," Jake said, flipping open his notebook and shifting to the edge of his chair. "Story's that this guy, Blake Thompson, big money developer representing investors from New York, paid off Reigner, McFadden and a bunch of other lower ranking public officials so he can ignore a bunch of laws. Corruption and ethics violations concerning bribes, environmental laws that protect Mt. Riler and the falcons..."

"Hang on," Wick interrupted. "Where did this story come from? I need some context, here."

Jake walked him through the genesis of the story: The hike with Ben Mills to the falcons' nesting place, Beebo's tips, his reporting with the Rec and Park chief, and his confrontation with Thompson.

"OK, so I get the thrust of the story — bribes for political favors — but what proof do you have?" Wick asked.

Jake glanced nervously at Zamboni and Moore.

"Well, I have architect's drafts of the casino complex ..."

"Of the *money,* fer Chrissake," growled Zamboni.

"Just what Thompson told me he paid," Jake muttered.

"Nothing concrete? Bank receipts? Canceled checks?" Wick was giving it his best to sound like an active player in the talks.

"I don't think these guys are going to leave a paper trail that obvious," Moore defended. "But Thompson spilled his guts to Jake. Tell him."

"Well, Wick, Thompson told me he gave $20,000 in cash each to Reigner and McFadden to push the project through the city channels, and another $5,000 to the Rec and Park chief so he'd look the other way while surveyors from out of state were sizing up the land. There were other payments, too, less, smaller, but still illegal."

Worry lines furrowed Wick's brow.

"You got a deposit receipt? Passbook entry? Any proof at all? Or just the word of a crooked golfer with mob connections? Not the most reputable or reliable of sources, is he?"

Wick had a point, but Jake pressed on.

"The Rec and Park guy, Reigner and McFadden conspired to relocate the falcons — even to bring Mills here to do the TV segment to make them look like environmentalists rather than greedy developers planning an illegal project on public, protected land."

"That's why Reigner sent Jimmy Olsen here into the wilds with Ben Mills and his TV entourage," Zamboni chimed in. "He used us to direct attention away from the development," he told the publisher. "Doesn't that piss you off just a little bit?"

"We figure there are about 10 violations of local, state and federal law here, including a couple of RICO[4] charges," chimed in Moore, "since it involves bribery and interstate commerce. The money guys are New York."

Wick's eyebrows shot toward the ceiling. Federal laws. Bribery. New York mob money. His temples began to pulse. He was in the news business to gladhand and exercise his expense account, not to raise hell, investigate public officials and cause an upheaval that might impact advertising revenue.

"The DA and AG will be all over this," Moore added as if reading Dunn's mind. He added that they were planning a follow-up story to obtain reactions from the District Attorney as well as the state Attorney General.

"Look, Wick," Moore said, leaning across the publisher's desk. "We run the story, and the AG subpoenas Reigner, McFadden and the rest to track the money. You're right, it would be better with some hard evidence that money changed hands, but I think we're solid with what we have."

As the meeting wore on, Dunn, emboldened by Moore's assurances that the paper was protected from legal recourse by First Amendment and other laws — not to mention the practice of

4. the Federal Racketeer Influenced and Corrupt Organization Act

sound journalism — was leaning toward giving the story the green light.

The final push came when Jake made a casual reference to the plight of the peregrine falcons. "You know, Ben Mills told me this is one of the last natural nesting habitats of the peregrines," Jake said, referring to the TV host's helpful lesson in falcon behavior offered over brown bag lunches on the top of Mt. Riler weeks earlier. "Relocating them isn't an option. Peregrines have been known to nest atop buildings in New York, for cryin' out loud, but their young don't make it.

"Taking away this habitat might spell the end of them in New England."

That did it. Wick Dunn was a lot of things: boozer, womanizer, chronic over-eater, political insider and deft manager of a generous income and a family trust fund. But like his father, he was also a life member of the Audubon Society, a well-heeled, active conservationist, and avid bird watcher.

"OK, guys, I've heard enough," Wick said, noting the setting sun out his window and checking his watch. Happy hour was well under way at the Yankee Doodler, his favorite after-work haunt. "We're going with it. Call the lawyers and give 'em a heads' up. And you," turning to Jake. "Good job. Be careful, though, and go cautiously with Reigner and McFadden. These guys don't like being messed with, and you're a little out of your range. Watch your ass."

It was nearly 7 p.m. when Jake finally left the building, his face flushed, head pounding and mind reeling. He'd gotten what he wanted: permission and support to proceed. Now, he had to face Reigner and McFadden, confront them with what he had learned, and then get to work writing the biggest story of his young but rapidly accelerating career.

CITY LEADERS UNDER FIRE

Over the next two days Jake endured a series of confrontational, abusive and at times threatening meetings and telephone conversations with Reigner and McFadden. Both not only denied any wrongdoing but denied having specific knowledge of Blake Thompson, his casino project, or even the plight of the peregrine falcons.

"You are kicking the wrong sleeping dog, son," Reigner warned from across his desk as he listened in quiet fury to the list of charges that challenged his self control. "This is not going to end well for you. It's a template in a teapot."

"Piss off. Call my office for an appointment," McFadden growled over the phone when, after numerous failed attempts to catch him in his office, Jake finally reached him at home during a station break in a Sox game. Jake made the appointment for the next day. He showed up at McFadden's office at the appointed time and recoiled but recovered nicely when he found the council chairman cozily perched on his office sofa next to his lawyer. Jake smirked at the contrasting sight: a crude Weeble in worn tweed with ample gut and rounded shoulders, and a slender, distinguished pin-striped wall of defense with squared shoulders and a strong chin.

Jake asked the questions while the lawyer declined comment for his client and tried his best to restrain the scowling politician. McFadden occupied more than his share of the sofa, his knees splayed and hands resting on a mahogany walking stick.

"What are your business dealings with Mr. Blake Thompson?"

A brief conference, lawyer to client, preceded, "My client has no specific knowledge of the person you make reference to."

"So you're saying you do not know Thompson … you wouldn't recognize him? And you've never met with him or spoken to him?"

"My client meets with and talks to hundreds of people each week," came the bland retort. McFadden grinned.

"You received $20,000 in cash from Thompson. What was the purpose of that payment, and where was it deposited?"

McFadden scowled. Another brief conference followed.

"My client has no knowledge of such payments, and we challenge you to provide evidence of the payment as well as its origin and alleged date and time of payment. Should you make any public allegation of such payment we will act accordingly and strongly defend my client's image and integrity. You, personally, as well as *The Post-Recorder*, will be named in any lawsuits as defendants."

Wick, Moore and Zamboni had prepared him to expect threats. Jake was unfazed.

"Huh. Integrity. Fat chance," Jake muttered.

McFadden exploded off the sofa, cane clutched in white-knuck-led fury as he brandished it threateningly.

"You pusillanimous twit!" he screamed, "You think you can march in here, make these outrageous, unfounded allegations, screw with me? You don't scare me, you little shithead …" The lawyer counseled McFadden's outburst into remission, coaxing him back onto the sofa. The councilman glared at Jake, his face the color of an overripe plum.

Jake pressed on, firing question after question but receiving nothing from McFadden and pablum from the lawyer.

McFadden sat with his hands on his knees, legs splayed beneath his expansive belly, an angry human bowling ball with blood-shot eyes, pencil mustache and hairs erupting from his nostrils. Quiet since his initial outburst, McFadden again lost control as Jake concluded the interview, snapped his notebook closed and stood to leave.

"You little shit. You think you have something here? You got nothing. Nothing. I'll eat you for a mid-morning snack, you sanc-timonious shithead."

Smiling sweetly at the gyrating man whose face seemed prepared to explode, Jake re-opened his notebook and carefully jotted the extent of McFadden's diatribe, if not for publication, then perhaps for sheer entertainment value.

"Sorry, can you spell 'sanctimonious'? And I think you might go easy on the snacks. You've looked more svelte, and you should keep an eye on your blood pressure."

Jake smiled as the veteran politician again struggled angrily to his feet. He got the feeling that had the lawyer not been present punches might have been thrown. "Thanks for your time, Mr. Chairman. Counselor," he added to the lawyer, departing with a swagger and the distinct feeling that a small slice of authority had just shifted from Rilertown power brokers to a young reporter who was about to break the story of his life.

He left City Hall with a ton of confirmed hunches but nothing more tangible than he had expected: emphatic denials, some bluffs, a ton of chest-thumping and a few mild threats — all predictable responses from a pair who had controlled Rilertown since Jake was in diapers.

What he hadn't expected, though, was the specter of the elaborate freeform artistry performed on his car parked in the far corner of the City Hall lot; swirls, gouges and circles where someone had scratched the paint with either a key, knife or screwdriver. The Fairlane rested low on its haunches due to the four flat tires that rendered the scarred vehicle undriveable. Jake grimly assessed the damage, then turned and glanced back at McFadden's office window that overlooked the parking lot. The shadow of a head moved behind the curtain as Jake turned to look up, and the draperies fell back into place. Jake turned back to the car, and sighed deeply: "Fucker."

Then it was off to a nearby coffee shop to call a tow truck and make arrangements to get his car back on the road. He hoped Moore would approve the repairs as a business expense.

Zamboni and Moore carefully planned the story's publication, deciding to break it on the next Tuesday before that night's City Council meeting. That would leave time for follow-up stories throughout the week, keeping Reigner, McFadden, Thompson and the other guilty parties on the defensive while giving Jake ample time to find additional sources to pour gasoline on the immolation of the two public, powerful personas. Reigner and McFadden, meanwhile, would likely hide from other media, duck constituent calls and dedicate their free time as well as the entire coming weekend to devising some sort of a response.

Jake drafted the piece on Friday, and he, Zamboni and Moore put it through repeated exhaustive reviews over the weekend. They spent a couple of hours with the newspaper's lawyer on Monday, taking her through the story's evolution and facts, one by one. Exhausted, Jake left *The P-R* office at nearly 1 a.m. Tuesday morning, due back to work in a few hours.

He made the trip home in record time through the slumbering city. There was no traffic to speak of, and even the traffic lights approvingly flashed their permission for him to proceed uninterrupted. He quietly made his way to the second-floor apartment, slipping off his shoes so he could ease into bed without waking Sabrina. Then he noticed the note on the dining room table.

"Come to bed, my wonderful star reporter," it read, "and wake me up when you do."

So he did.

"Mayor, Council Head in Development Scandal" screamed the 72-point banner headline across *The P-R*'s Tuesday edition, accompanied by a subhead which read, "Bribes Clear Way for Entertainment Complex on Mt. Riler," and, importantly, a byline that read, "By Jake Ketcher, P-R staff reporter."

The city erupted.

Calls for investigations into political misconduct were trumped by demands for both men's immediate resignations as various civic associations and political opponents' camps eagerly fed upon the opportunity. Reigner and McFadden became chum in shark-infested waters.

Their PR machines clicked into action, desperately struggling to keep up with calls from furious constituents and "gravely concerned" campaign contributors. Their "no comment" deflections in the story hadn't helped their cause. Neither had Jake's careful annotation of the federal, state and local laws the two had allegedly violated in support of the project. Thompson's thorough explanation of the deal was related in detail from behind the cloak of an "an informed participant in the negotiations who, fearing retribution, requested anonymity for this news report," Jake wrote.

The state's Attorney General, whom Jake reached for comment and who had agreed to a lengthy interview for a second-day story, took considerable interest in each of the troika's involvement, thus pulling Thompson further into the vortex of a story that knew no bounds and — much to his consternation — seemed capable of placing him behind bars.

He called Jake the day the story broke, distraught and panicked.

"I'm a dead man," Thompson whined. "You gotta protect me."

Jake responded in print.

"AG Joins Development Probe" pronounced the Wednesday banner headline. The follow-up story included commentary from the District Attorney, whose nose was out of joint from being upstaged by the Attorney General, his media-savvy superior who had statewide power and influence. Thursday's story continued the assault, but with a new twist, "State, Local Legal Trouble for Development Trio?" with a new detail in a sidebar that tossed an unhappy wrench into what otherwise had been a week of uninterrupted triumph for Jake and *The P-R*: "Developer Missing after AG Launches Probe."

Thompson had done what many crooks do when they get their hands caught in the proverbial cookie jar: he bolted. Overnight, Thompson had cleared out from his penthouse apartment, leaving town in his coupe with a few clothes and his passport. Since he hadn't been formally charged, detained or restricted from leaving the county, his departure from Boston's Logan Airport to Bangkok hadn't raised an eyebrow.

This was great news for Reigner and McFadden, who still had questions to answer but slowly began to recover. Though Jake hadn't named Thompson as the origin of the graft, the developer's allegations remained the story's foundation. Without him around for the AG and DA to grill, the story lost momentum.

The AG and DA turned to *The P-R* for evidence of the bribes, and Wick's demands for proof suddenly took on new, important relevance. The story began to unravel, withering under scrutiny and calls for concrete proof as a sand castle before a rising tide.

Sensing opportunity, Reigner and McFadden shifted into high gear. They filtered out word that they had turned away

Thompson's repeated attempts to influence their roles as the city's leaders and compromise their philosophical objections to "ruining Mt. Riler, one of Rilertown's most enduring physical assets." They repeatedly challenged *The P-R* to produce hard evidence of wrongdoing.

Letters to the editor were still 10-1 in opposition of the city's leadership duo. Meanwhile, the Attorney General issued a warrant for Thompson's arrest as "a person of interest in an ongoing corruption investigation." Once Massachusetts's troopers and federal marshals found Thompson and brought him back for questioning, it would be all over for the Reigner/McFadden era in Rilertown politics. A mid-storm calm fell over the story as Jake waited for the next development to surface.

After four straight days of leading the paper, Jake took Sabrina out to a celebratory dinner at their favorite pizza place. Earlier that day the Associated Press had picked up Jake's latest update, adding another layer of sweet icing on his professional cake as his byline made the regional, then national wire feeds.

"From the Associated Press," read the byline, "Jake Ketcher, *Rilertown Post-Recorder*."

Sabrina beamed at her beau as they happily munched their way through a large mushroom and pepperoni, and she uncharacteristically joined in the fun by sipping a glass of red wine while Jake contentedly quaffed four beers.

Sabrina smiled at Jake and reached across the table.

"You did it, babe. I'm so unbelievably proud of you. Truly. This is what we've been waiting for."

Jake paused in mid-bite, the last slice of pizza halfway between table and mouth.

"Yeah, this is it," she said, slipping off a shoe and nuzzling his calf with a bare toe up his pant leg. "This is what I've been looking for. I have always known you had it in you. And this is what makes me want to be with you — permanently."

She paused, smiling gently.

"You heard me. This is what I've been waiting for. Let's get married."

Jake dropped the pizza slice and seized her hands.

"You mean it? Really?"

She nodded, grinning through tears like droplets of radiant joy.

"You bet. Let's do it."

The two exchanged soft smiles that melted beneath the fire in their eyes. He looked for the waitress, who had inconveniently disappeared.

'I'll pay the check," he said, sliding the keys to the car across the table to her waiting hand. "I've had too much to drink. Why don't you pull the car to the front door so we can get home and celebrate."

Sabrina smiled as Jake came around the table, met her waiting hand on her shoulder and gave it a soft squeeze. He bent, kissed her on the right ear lobe and whispered in her ear: "Get the car, Mrs. Ketcher, and be quick about it. We have unfinished business." He hurried to find the waitress and pay the tab, glancing over his shoulder as the door closed behind Sabrina. He rapped on the counter to attract someone's attention, impatient to join his wife-to-be as she made her way from the restaurant to their car parked in a vacant lot across the street.

Sabrina Maria Goldfarb had taken many steps in her life.

Most of them comprised the 53 million or so strides that a woman typically takes over the course of 28 years. Many of Sabrina's steps had been purposeful, complicated footsteps on the dance floor. Others had been philosophical strides, taking her in new directions, toward new opportunities, or away from troubling challenges.

But no step in Sabrina's life proved as meaningful as the one that took her from the curb into the path of Sally Wheeler's 1968 Volvo. The distracted young woman was popping a cassette into the tape deck on her dashboard and failed to see Sabrina.

Sally would forever replay the event in slow motion.

Her gaze attracted by sudden movement at the front of her car.

A bump and shudder as vehicle collided with human.

A tangle of arms and legs as the woman's body rose from bumper to hood and into the windshield, clothing askew and, in the awful confusion of the moment, head indistinguishable from feet.

A terrible crack as Sabrina's head collided with shatterproof glass, creating a spider's web of fissures that obstructed Sally's view as she slammed on the brakes and twisted the steering wheel toward the curb, coming to a halt at an angle steps from the restaurant's door.

Sally's hands rose to her face, then to her eyes, as if to block the image. Her screams fled from the car's open window into the still night air as Sabrina's body rolled from the hood and onto the road. She came to a rest there awkwardly, a twisted version of her athletic self, half in the road, half on the sidewalk.

There, crushed by the impact and mercifully unconscious, Sabrina breathed her last.

SURVIVING THE LOSS

Jake somnambulated through the next few weeks as the devastation of Sabrina's death entombed him in misery.

The young driver was charged with vehicular homicide, but the charge was later reduced to driving to endanger and, months later, she got off with a six-month license suspension. There would be no criminal charges, and the event would be expunged from her record once her probation ended.

Jake's reporter buddies kept him vaguely aware of the case in its early going, but he quickly lost interest, as he did with everything, except breathing.

There was no Jake. No world. No friends. No car that killed Sabrina, or one to take him back into his former life. No P-R. No food. No booze. No past, future or present. There was no meaning, no sense, and certainly no justice.

Breathing was the one constant, evidence that he was still alive and part of the world that otherwise seemed a kaleidoscopic, horribly abstract version of what previously had seemed a fairly decent place to live. Breathing required no effort, no thought. No planning, no intention. In and out, in and out. Chest rise, and fall. Air in, and out.

I am still here.

She is not.

Still not.

Still...

Not...

Here.

Every day, the truth of Sabrina's absence plunged Jake deeper into the muck of despair and loneliness. A young man who based his perception of truth on empirical data and fact, Jake was lost in a world of abstract concepts: life, uncontrollable emotions, and death.

Seeking refuge, he disappeared into the loving embrace of his parents and into his childhood bedroom on the second floor of his parents' house in Silvertown. A cramped room of simple design, it offered a dresser, a bedside table with an ancient AM/FM radio, a reading light, and a single bed. Stuffed animals from Jake's childhood leaned against the wall. They waited patiently with glass eyes eternally open to give or receive comfort in case the boy who once rested within the room should awaken in the dreaded dark, fearing something under the bed, or a sound from outside the window, or, worse, the ghost of a beautiful young dancer named Sabrina.

A wallpapered panorama of colonial-era soldiers marched ceaselessly across the room's walls, in tight formations of three, displayed in careful precise repetition every six inches — the perfect place for a young boy, or a teenager, or a young man visiting from college during spring break — a room that reeked of the past.

This was a room for a child, not a man of Jake's age.

Unless, of course, he was grieving.

Jake spent day upon day on the bed, his ability to cry long since exhausted, staring at the mottled ceiling but seeing nothing but Sabrina's face. The wallpaper soldiers kept him in silent company, always marching right to left, eyes locked on the horizon in clear sight of a secret promise that only they understood, and in righteous pursuit of all that is good, fair and just.

Food, drink, conversation and human company were of little interest to him, and all of it, plus the rain, wind, sunshine and even an early season snowstorm, seemed part of the jumbled up suckiness of Jake's New World.

He entered Jake's New World when he left the pizza shop and saw Sabrina's shoe on the side of the road. It was the right-footed partner of her favorite pair, a ruby pump, now abraded and scarred and lying on High Street under a flickering amber streetlight, surrounded by cigarette butts and empty fast food containers. Alarmed, he shifted his gaze to the Volvo that had stopped at an odd angle in the road, its engine running and young female driver half out of the driver's side having what appeared to be an emotional meltdown as she flailed her arms, screaming, and rushed to the front of the car.

At the side of the road rested a crumpled heap that looked like a disheveled mound of clothes someone had discarded, or perhaps lost on their way home from the nearby laundromat. Illuminated by the car's headlights and the streetlight overhead, the mound of clothing was Sabrina curled in fetal defeat. The scene took on a surreal tint; a snapshot of insufferable misery on a gritty city street.

Then came police and an ambulance, and helpful arms that eased him to a seated position on the sidewalk as the young man inconsolably, hatefully, and, screaming and crying with rage, pain and anguish, entered Jake's New World.

In the following days he perfunctorily endured a small but emotional memorial service in Rilertown that served his family and friends more than him or Sabrina.

This is how we do it, friends told him. This is how we mourn, how we say goodbye.

Jake and Sabrina were not religious, so when Moore offered to say a few words Jake dispassionately assented.

At the service, Jake's mom, dad and sister sat dutifully to his right with fixed jaws and moist eyes as Moore stiffly conducted the rite. Sarah Turnbull, Phil Buckley and Jake's other pals from the paper showed up, as did Cheecha, Carmella and their six kids. Beebo made an appearance, too, staring briefly at Jake as the tears streamed beneath her RayBans, down her cheeks and into the corners of her trembling mouth.

Jake foggily acknowledged the presence of each of his friends and colleagues, but his head snapped up in shock when Lucinda Rodriguez approached him. The night cleaner at *The P-R* held both his hands in hers, tears streaming down her face, "Oh, you poor, poor, man … I am so very, very sorry."

She held him, taking him in her arms in a maternal embrace that shifted the pain that had enveloped him for days from his chest, to his face, to his temples and then … away. The horrid ache departed only briefly, but sweetly, gracefully, permitting him a brief respite from the awful, irreconcilable feeling of profound loss and penetrating sadness.

He held Lucinda's gaze briefly, holding her by her arms, then, too, let her go as the awful pain came roaring back.

Sabrina's mother didn't bother making the trip from New York, but a few of her students showed up to cry and, after Moore had concluded his talk, paid their respects by gently touching the photo of Sabrina that rested on a small table in the center of the room, surrounded by rubrum lilies, her favorite. Their obligations fulfilled, they moved to Jake, pressed their soggy cheeks against his, and then headed for the door and back into the sunshine of their normal lives.

In addition to attending the service in somber allegiance, Zamboni, Moore and Dunn all had been great, gently reassuring Jake. "Take whatever time you need," said Moore. "Just go. Don't worry. We'll be here, and everything else can wait."

Glum, wordless and thin, he headed back to bed in his darkened room in his parents' home with marching wallpaper soldiers and photos of New York Giants linebacker Sam Huff above his bed.

His mother lovingly prepared what food he endured. His paychecks continued, but since he spent little he paid no mind to finance, responsibilities or costs. His sister, Mary, deposited his checks, paid his rent and expenses, and made sure his car insurance remained current. She placed the checks before him and he endorsed them, pen grasped in a sweaty grip, his unseeing eyes ringed with red and framed by the dark black circles born of tortured, sleepless nights.

Mary accompanied her brother on walks through the wooded forests that surrounded Silvertown. They would stroll for hours, sometimes arm in arm or hand in hand, often separated by yards of distance and miles of sadness.

After several weeks of walking, talking and mostly just being together, Mary gingerly approached the subject of how her brother might find a way to live in Jake's New World. "So, you think at all about going back to Rilertown?" she ventured.

Jake sighed deeply. He stopped, picked up a twig from the forest floor and turned it in his hands, studying it as if looking for a secret within. The late fall sun kissed his back with a gift of warmth yet did little to penetrate his frozen soul.

"I can't even think about it. I mean, back to the apartment, to her stuff, to our home? So full of her, but so empty? And work?

"Really. Who gives a shit? Not me."

They walked another two hours and chatted. Mary had the sense to let Jake move at his own pace.

"He'll get there," she assured her worried parents. "He just needs time."

Jake's dad was a simple, blue collar businessman who spoke with few words but acted with boundless magnanimity — particularly where his beloved family was concerned. Jacob The Elder had the same first name as his son, but had wisely given him a different middle name to protect the boy from the horrors of being called Junior throughout his life. Now, recognizing his son's cravings for quiet company, he sat idly with Jake for hours on end, sometimes watching television, occasionally engaging his son in a game of cribbage, mostly just being together.

One day he put down his cards and fixed his grey eyes on Jake's.

"You know, you are always welcome here, with us," he said, placing his hand on Jake's arm.

"I know. I'm here, dad," Jake said, dropping his cards, shoulders slumped.

"No, I mean, you could move back. Join the business with me. Come home for good."

Jake's dad had never pressed the idea of joining the family's tire business with his literary-minded son, instead ponying up his hard-earned money to pay for tuition, room and board while Jake honed his skills in junior college and journalism school.

After Jake's graduation his father celebrated his son's success. He was the first to call with congratulations when Jake's first byline appeared in *The P-R*, somehow aware of the milestone despite the fact that Silvertown was well out of Rilertown's circulation area. He made the hour-long drive after a typical 10-hour day to take Jake out for a beer to celebrate the first story in the Reigner/McFadden investigation, patting him on the back and buying another round before hauling himself back into his 1964 Dodge for the trip home.

Now, however, seemed the time to suggest a change for his son.

"It's a good life. You might even like it," he smiled gently.

Jake sighed.

"Dad. I love you and mom so much, and I'm so grateful for what you've done for me. Always. Yeah, always. But I'm not done. There's too much unfinished. You understand? I don't know …."" He quit the card game as his father abandoned the idea of him joining the family business.

On a Friday morning three days later, Jake announced his decision to his parents over breakfast.

"I'm calling Les today," he began, "and heading back to work on Monday. Mary's coming with me over the weekend to help me clean out the apartment, and then I'm gonna get back at it. It's what I have to do, what I want to do. Besides, it's what Sabrina would expect of me."

The three sat in respectful silence, forks suspended over scrambled eggs and toast. Perfection and truth sometimes descend in unheralded clarity, arriving in digestible doses that humans don't act on or engage with, but simply absorb and accept.

They ate their eggs. And they accepted what would come next.

NEW ROLE FOR VETERAN REPORTER

Jake pulled into the parking lot shortly after six, deciding it would be best to get to the office before the others. The thought of entering a gauntlet of pity turned his stomach and left him reconsidering whether returning to work this soon was such a great idea.

He strolled into the darkened hallway, past the lunchroom and library, and into the edge of *The P-R*'s fluorescent world. Even at this ungodly hour the newsroom was alight with radiant brilliance and faint odors of ink, sweat and overheated electronics. Betsey Firth was there, stripping dispatches from the wire and dashing to and from the wire room at her typical frenetic pace to keep up with the latest developments around the world.

He stopped at the newsroom entrance, surveying a once-familiar landscape that now felt foreign. Rows of desks, devoid of human beings and quiet under mountains of paper that rose everywhere like fibrous, living memorials to the underpinnings of newspapering, seemed to Jake like mocking, incongruous reminders of what on the surface seemed a normal workplace.

Jake entered without speaking to Betsey. Her head snapped up as he passed, and she tracked him from the editor's pit as he hung his coat in the closet, walked to his desk with an ancient, tortured gait and slid into his chair. Betsey rose and silently approached him.

"Hey, Jake," she said in a soothing tone that Jake found discomfiting. "Great to see you back. I'm so sorry about … about it all. Shit. Well, let me know if I can do anything for you. Really."

She patted him on the arm and hastily departed for the safety of the pit.

Was this how the whole day was going to go? Jake wasn't sure he could handle it. The shame of pity, of vulnerable exploitation of his loss, goddamn it, *his* loss, not theirs. It just didn't belong here, where all his friends were, where his work was. His loss couldn't coexist with his work. He fought back tears and resisted a powerful, pulsating voice that screamed in his head to grab his coat and go home. Instead, he reached into his top right-hand drawer for a reliable moment of grace and salvation in the familiar jar of Rose Hip hand cream.

A small bag lay where his hand cream usually rested. A tiny blue bow and a note card was attached. Jake looked around to see if Betsey was watching, but she had turned her interest to an update on the Dow's previous day's late trading that declared it a sure bet to eclipse 1,000 points later on in the day.

Jake opened the bag. A new jar of Rose Hip rested in the bottom. He opened the note, reading through tears that came in a flash flood of emotion and quickly dampened the bag.

"Dear Jake. Please that you accept this gift. I hope it remind you there is always comfort, always soothing, always possible make even the roughest skin once again soft, smooth and beautiful. Your friend, Lucinda."

Jake took the note with him into the men's room. He hurried into the stall furthest from the entrance and slumped behind the closed door. He locked his arms around his knees and sat on the toilet, clutched Lucinda's note to his chest and shed what he promised himself would be the day's last tears.

He rested there for a long moment, collecting his thoughts and considering his next move, when his gaze fell upon a word scratched in pencil on the door facing the toilet.

"Headrest," it read, conjuring an image of one of Jake's newsroom colleagues, hung over and mildly constipated, forehead pressed to the chipped blue paint of the toilet door as he struggled to purge himself before returning to work.

He smiled through his pain, the quirky-black sense of humor typical of newsroom wonks penetrating the fog. Kindred familiarity trumped searing anxiety as he contemplated the writer's self-deprecating humor.

"Time to get back to work," he said aloud, folding Lucinda's note and placing it in his wallet for safekeeping.

The rest of the day was awkward if not bizarre. Reporters stopped by on their way into work, clapped him on the back and then quickly moved to safer emotional ground, diving into the day's work. Sarah Turnbull hugged him, patted him on the shoulder and reminded him: "Available for coffee, walks and beers after work."

Buckley slugged him on the shoulder.

"Good to have you back."

Jake numbly rode the current of another Monday morning at *The P-R*, vaguely aware but barely engaged. Phones rang and were answered. The buzz in the newsroom rose as the staff swelled to full ranks around 8. Moore showed up around 8:15 and called Jake to his office.

He shocked Jake by wrapping him in a hug, then offered him a seat.

"Look, Jake, I'm glad you're back and all, really happy you're here. But take it easy. No need to push. Easy does it."

He fidgeted.

"We're gonna have you on rewrites for a couple of days — just to ease you back in."

Jake shook his head. "Thanks, Les, but we have follow-up on the Reigner/McFadden story, don't we?" Two weeks prior, Moore had sent a courier to Silvertown providing Jake with a file of stories and clips from other papers that had accumulated while Jake was away, all documenting a complicated legal and ethical case with unusual staying power. Jake had skimmed the file but was only remotely aware of its contents.

"We're gonna leave that with Zabriske for now," Moore said, referring to Dan Zabriske, the general assignment reporter who had taken over the story in Jake's absence. This was a stunning blow to his territorial rights. Jake reacted with benign acceptance, in doing so confirming for Les the wisdom of keeping Jake on a gentle course toward recovery.

Jake huddled at his desk for the rest of the day, and the next, and also the next, dispassionately accepting re-write assignments from Betsey and Zamboni, and turning out bland copy that was well below his normal quality and unworthy of his byline. Sympathetic editors nonetheless affixed his name to stories, gently applying what salve they could to Jake's deep and oozing emotional wounds.

On Thursday Zamboni hailed him from his office door. With a trained response that would have made Pavlov beam, Jake scooped up a notebook and headed for the editor's office. Inside, Zamboni made cursory eye contact while, as usual, getting straight to his objective.

"Human interest story. Woman at the front desk. Grab Spike (Tom "Spike" Johnson, *The P-R*'s affable but modestly talented photographer) and get some pix. For Lifestyle. Today."

"Do I get any idea what this is about?" Jake inquired, his curiosity raised as he imagined the possibilities:

Son, recently returning from the Peace Corps in Central America, discovers he brought with him a highly communicable disease?

Displeased with League of Women Voters chapter's efforts, housewife turned activist starts up a new political action organization for women?

Woman discovers early drawings in her deceased father's trunk that demonstrate that he, not German engineer Felix Wankel, invented the world's first rotary engine?

Zamboni smiled softly.

"Of course. No problem. Your interview subject, who is waiting somewhat impatiently for you at this very moment at the front desk, or so Dolores informs me, is a woman who this very morning plucked an abnormally large zucchini from her garden that bears an uncanny resemblance to her recently deceased father."

Jake stared at Zamboni, dumbfounded.

"You're joking, right?"

"Nope. Afraid not. You're the only one available, so you're it. Go get 'em, tiger."

In the world of serious journalists, nothing defines an occupational smackdown like being assigned to a human interest story. Soft, fluffy news has no place in the land of men and women accustomed to dealing blows to the balance of power — like turning a CEO into a janitor for the day.

For the next 30 minutes Jake sat in resigned humiliation at the small conference table at the side of the newsroom, in full view of the amused staff as he conducted the interview. Perched proudly on the woman's lap was her prized zucchini, a 14-inch vegetable with several green malformations that she insisted resembled two arms and a leg and a half. She beamed and commanded her hair into place while Spike snapped photos.

"See? My dad used to sit with his legs just like this all the time," she implored, showing Jake a Polaroid of an old man sprawled in a Barcalounger with a can of beer in his hand. She grinned and faced the camera when Spike tried to grab a candid shot.

The camera clicked and whirled while Spike ducked and focused. Mary with the zucchini, and without it. The zucchini by itself, propped against the light blue arm chair.

"How about one with all of you," prodded the copy desk chief as he headed past the trio en route to the men's room. "Ma'am, wouldn't you like a photo of you, your vegetable and our highly skilled reporter?"

Jake glowered as he stood with the woman and her zucchini, managing a faint grin when she placed the vegetable in his hands for a close-up. As the woman made her way for the door, possibly conceiving recipes to turn her prized vegetable into the evening's dinner, the newsroom collectively rose to a standing ovation.

"And thus signals the end of our intrepid reporter's unscheduled vacation!" bellowed Zamboni from his office doorway, laughing and pulling the door shut behind him.

The next morning, Jake made his way to Moore's office shortly after the managing editor arrived. He felt rejuvenated by producing what turned out to be an entertaining story about the woman and her zucchini that displayed nicely on the front of Lifestyle Section, as well as a good meal kindly prepared by his landlady that ironically included an abundance of zucchini. Four beers and a good night's sleep hadn't hurt, either.

"Hey, Les," Jake said, entering without knocking. He took a seat.

"Look, I want to thank you — all of you. I mean, it's great to be back, and yesterday, painful as it was to be saddled with a story about a vegetable, well, it made me want to get back in the thick of it.

"For real. I want my beat back. Zabriske's done a good job and all, but it's my story.

"I want it back. Now."

Moore studied him, fingers steepled.

"Let's talk it over this afternoon, the four of us."

Jake's internal alarm went off, sounding loudly in his head.

"Four of us? What four?" he asked.

"You, me, Zamboni and Wick, of course," Moore explained, fixing Jake with a friendly gaze that unsettled him. Attempts to pry more from Moore proved fruitless, so Jake strolled back to his desk and began sifting through a stack of AP copy Betsey had dumped there for him to edit into the day's front page "World Briefs." Jake fitted a sheaf of paper into his typewriter and started banging away.

At lunchtime Jake declined offers for sandwiches and beer. Instead, he picked up a pastrami on rye from Schwimmer's Delicatessen and set out for the local reservoir for an hour of sunshine, quiet, reflection and fat-laden deliciousness.

He watched a family of ducks splashing in the water under the mid-day sun, tossed bits of bread to the ducklings and grinned when they squabbled among themselves, competing for the scraps. He breathed deeply, felt the sun warm his back through his winter jacket and sweater and listened to the silence. Minutes crawled by, and his thoughts kept him quiet company.

Lunch over, he returned to the office. Zamboni saw him and headed him off before he could reach his desk.

"Wick's office," he said, coaxing Jake down the length of the newsroom and into the publisher's suite.

Dunn was seated behind his desk, clad in his customary vest and matching trousers but wearing an uncharacteristically glum frown. Moore sat to his right, and Jake was surprised to see Julie Brown, the company's lawyer, there as well. She rose, shook his hand and expressed her condolences before turning to Dunn and nodding.

Zamboni closed the door and sat in a chair furthest from Dunn's desk in a calculated move that foretold doom.

Les's meeting with "the four of us" had become "five," counting the lawyer.

Blindsided, Jake thought.

"Tough news, Jake," Dunn opened. "We wanted to meet with you right away to let you know."

Scripted meeting. Uh, oh.

Moore took over.

"Thompson was found dead late yesterday, probably suicide, but we won't know for awhile. He was in south Thailand, on a beach somewhere, and the cleaning woman found him in his bed."

Zamboni took his cue.

"Of course, that means the whole story is gone. Everything. No Thompson, no testimony, no evidence. The AG is dropping all charges. Mayor's holding a press conference right now, and both he and McFadden are demanding retractions and apologies from the paper."

The room contracted, then spun. Jake struggled to absorb the news.

This was all terrible, of course. But why was the lawyer there? Had he done something wrong?

"Look, Jake, this doesn't change a thing," Dunn reassured him. "You did great work, and you exposed a serious issue. And look, the development project is done — permanently derailed — so there's that — no casino, no hotel, and the birds keep their nesting places."

The four stared at Jake, assessing his reaction.

"Oh, by the way," Moore said, rising to his feet and handing Jake a folder imprinted with the Associated Press logo. "It's a letter of commendation to you and the paper, for breaking the story."

"You're up for Investigative Story of the Year," Dunn beamed, gesturing to the wall of honors as if to imply that Jake's work would soon join the rows of plaques that Dunn held in such high esteem. "This is quite an honor."

Jake stared at the floor for several minutes as the others watched him.

Slowly, he raised his head and stared out the window past Dunn, over the parking lot and on, envisioning the road to the reservoir and the duck family that was probably still splashing along the shoreline. He thought beyond the reservoir, to the street outside the High Street pizza shop, to Sabrina's ruby pump in the dirty road, and to the soldiers marching 1-2-3 on his child-hood bedroom wall. He thought about his parents and Sam, his sister; about truth and honesty versus deceit and lies.

Seconds felt like minutes.

He faced Moore.

"You lied to me," he said. "This is why you kept me off the story, and why you allowed Zabriske to turn out his typical soft crap as follow-ups. I wanted back on the story when I returned, but you kept me away from it. You killed this story even before Thompson died. You'd already decided. Too much heat from City Hall. You were protecting yourselves.

"That also explains how this scripted meeting of four became five. And since when do you invite a lawyer to a meeting like this, unless it's to cover your asses? What; you think I'm going to sue you, or maybe squawk publicly about *The P-R*'s lack of balls?"

"AP award? The birds keep their nests? Are you fucking kidding me?"

Jake nodded at the lawyer. "She's not here to provide counsel on the story; she's here to protect the paper, isn't she? — from me. You're hanging me out to dry, here. The shit's hitting the fan and the paper's turning tail. I'm all alone on this, aren't I?"

No one responded.

Wick studied his feet. Zamboni smirked. Moore looked ill.

"Holy shit. You're turning your backs on me — all of you … after all of this … all of … everything."

Jake paused, shook his head and stared at the floor. Reality arrived. He sighed, accepting his fate, then rose to leave.

Hand on the doorknob, he paused. Zamboni snickered softly. "Something else on your mind, star?"

A rush of memories, of allegiances and combatants past, of those who had stood by him and those who had abandoned him. *What does all this mean? Who really cares? And, what matters most?* All blazed through his mind in a moment's searing mosaic that at once left him unsettled and resolutely calm.

He opened the door, put one foot into the newsroom and then turned to face Zamboni, glaring at the pockfaced gnome with blazing eyes that spoke more than words could convey. But he spoke anyway.

"Fuck it. I quit."

PART 2

HOME AGAIN

Jake parked his car behind the building on Silvertown's Federal Street, pausing to listen as The Pretenders' "Back on the Chain Gang" finished playing on the radio.

"That's me," he mused, "Slogging away."

Shutting off the car, he stared at the building's cinderblock wall. He gazed to his right along the sidewalk that stretched along Federal Street to High Street and on into the foothills of western Massachusetts, which in turn led south though the valley toward Rilertown. He drifted away for a moment, lost in thought and memories — searing, hurtful memories of loss and separation, anxiety and profound sadness.

He sighed, then reached for the door handle.

Jake exited the car and strode around the side of the building, entering through the back door into the six-bay shop where the bulk of Ketcher's Tire business was transacted. He greeted the employees who were already busy with tire changes, brake jobs and muffler repairs, grease-streaked and filthy though the day had just begun. Then he headed to the office he shared with his father near the storefront showroom that looked down the barrel of Silvertown's commercial center.

Fall brought full daily calendars as customers prepared for winter. That meant endless tire changes, muffler upgrades and new sets of shock absorbers for Ketcher's customers who lived on one of the countless dirt roads that ringed the county's hills. Fall also brought the annual inventory of tires, batteries and the other stock that made Ketcher's a going concern. Jake had responsibility for the annual count, for the first time taking the responsibility off his father's tired shoulders.

Inventory was the latest task added to Jake's resume as tire shop manager in training, nearly a year after he left *The P-R* and returned to his hometown.

Easing into the tire business, Jake had filled in for workshop staff when someone was out sick or on vacation, or when the workload threatened to annoy one of their loyal customers to the point of tempting them to try the new chain tire store that had opened nearby. In the mornings, he learned the hands-on tricks of the trade. Afternoons and evenings were spent absorbing the business details from his father, who seemed to grow happier each day to have his son by his side.

Jake's arrival in Silvertown had been hailed by the family as a smart and worthwhile move that would ensure another

generation in the business started in the 1920s by Jake's grandfather. Evolving with the times, Ketcher's had morphed from
providing bridle, tack and wagon repair to offering maintenance
for the early automobile models that belched their fumes and
predictably broke down on Silvertown's rutted main streets —
a sturdy business run by generations of dependable Ketchers:
strong, reliable, solid people, pillars of the community, the kind
of people the Chamber of Commerce loved to highlight in their
promotions of "Silvertown: A great Place To Raise Your Family."

Taking over when Jake's grandfather moved into retirement,
Jake's dad injected the business with contemporary efficiency over
the years; adding an inventory, ordering and billing system along
with the enormous and expensive emissions control machine
required by the Massachusetts Department of Motor Vehicles
to make sure the county's cars were roadworthy. He diversified
the business to meet consumer demand and was rewarded with
steady growth and reasonable profits that remained constant even
during lean years in the local economy.

Children grown and gone, the elder Jake and his wife, Beth
lived quiet, satisfied lives in the house they had owned for over
40 years on a tree-lined street. Beth, a delightfully sweet and
kind woman, spent her days volunteering, caring for her ever-
expanding community of friends and admirers, and preparing
tasty meals to reward her husband for his hard work.

Joining his dad after his abrupt exit from *The P-R*, Jake became immersed in the hours of mindless labor while engaging his mind with business matters. He took over management of the books, payroll, and interaction with his godmother Sam, who was the firm's accountant. Sam had been a force in young Jake's life, joining the family on most holidays while indulging Jake and Mary with lavish gifts on their birthdays and impromptu dinner invitations for "Auntie Sam time."

A contented single woman with varied interests, Sam was also a bit of a kook. On election days she would dress up in a red, white and blue outfit, don a long white beard and wear a towering red white and blue stovepipe hat while parading up and down Main Street, loudly proclaiming, "Auntie Sam says vote today! Vote today!" People tended to laugh at Sam yet took her seriously, and her talent for affably lobbying for candidates and causes made her an effective public figure in Silvertown.

Sam made a good living as an accountant, providing advice, tax preparation services and a full range of accounting support for many of Silvertown's businesses. She employed six full-time junior accountants plus a couple of secretaries, one of whom was in charge of her primary non-work passion: her golf schedule.

Same made full use of the shortened New England golf season March through October, and her daily "summer" office hours rarely began before 1 p.m. in lieu of 18 holes and lunch with her buddies at the Silvertown Country Club. During three months each winter, she scratched her daily itch on one of the courses near her condo in Orlando. She alternated time on the links with trips to the post office, retrieving and dispensing enormous packages of documents, keeping up with what was happening in the office in the Bay State while keeping her handicap in single digits in the Sunshine State.

Sam had been in Orlando when Sabrina died, and she had missed the funeral and Jake's return to Silvertown. But she was on hand when Jake returned to the family business and homestead, once again stepping up as the steady, reliable foundation Jake had relied on all his life.

His dad's best friend from high school, Sam was best woman at Jake and Beth's wedding and a fixture at family events. Today, she had booked time for a financial update with her godson, foregoing an invitation for 18 holes with a friend. After her customary breakfast of coffee and Danish at a local working class coffee shop, she made her way onto Federal Street, eased her cranberry-colored Cadillac into an open parking spot in front of the shop, and headed inside.

"Jake the snake," she called to her godson, teasing him with the nickname she'd branded him with as an infant and had failed to encourage others to use. A kind, easy-going yet intelligent kid with a good heart, Jake defied the image, but that didn't sway Sam.

"How's my second favorite Silvertown business mogul," Sam said, easing into a chair before Jake's steel desk. "What's on the menu today? Tax prep? Inventory forms? Payroll review? Lunch?"

Jake loved these meetings with Sam. He always learned a lot, laughed even more and cherished time with his godmother. Sam knew technical aspects of the business that escaped Jake's father, so between the two Jake was acquiring a thorough knowledge that one day would give him the competence to run Ketcher's on his own.

Aside from Jake the elder, Sam was the person Jake admired and looked up to most. Jake's father, whom the young boy worshipped, lacked experience outside the tire business and Silvertown, so he fell a bit short in the mentoring department. That's where Sam stepped in. Sam's encouraging word had opened Jake's mind to journalism while he was still in high school, suggesting that he look into a role with the student newspaper and taking him a tour of the local daily newspaper that was published by one of Sam's golfing buddies.

Sam wrote a personal recommendation for Jake when he applied to Blendhurst, defying the odds and overcoming an awful high school transcript and an equally unimpressive junior college GPA by gaining acceptance in the widely respected school of communications graduating class of 1977.

It hadn't hurt that Sam was a graduate of Blendhurst, a regular financial supporter and a long-time member of the university's alumni mentor program.

Throughout his college years Jake had kept in touch with his mom and dad first, then Sam a close second. When Jake landed the job at *The P-R*, he made two phone calls in time-tested order; mom and dad, then Sam.

Sam and Jake huddled over a broad ledger with multiple columns, creating a template for the annual inventory. Ideas prompted jokes, one-liners spurred them on, and laughter turned what ought to have taken an hour into much longer.

"El Camino. 205/70-14," Jake read.

"No habla Espanol, senor-ee-tee," Sam giggled. Butchering Spanish was one of Sam's favorite gambits.

"You don't speak English particularly well, either," Jake jousted back, and on it went.

They worked for three hours until around 12:30, when Sam snapped her notebook shut and announced it was time for lunch. They headed out of the showroom together, jumped in Sam's car and within minutes slid into Sam's regular booth at Dan's Cafe.

Sam caught Dan's eye as the affable cook worked the grill and traded barbs with regulars at the counter, nodding when Sam raised two fingers, ordering two daily specials. Lunch at Dan's with Sam was one of Jake's favorite traditions. His dad had never been much of a "lunch out" kind of guy, instead showing up at Beth's back door each day shortly after 12:30. He'd have a quiet, quick sandwich with his wife, take care of what family business needed tending, cover the upcoming limited social calendar items with her and then head back to the tire shop, usually returning to work shortly after 1.

Jake, on the other hand, always took at least the full lunch hour, often with Sam, and always at Dan's. Daily specials were reliably delicious, fast and reasonably priced, and though Sam always picked up the tab, Jake on occasion was able to elbow his godmother out of the way and pay for lunch without completely messing up his monthly budget.

Sam rose from the table and headed for her regular bullshit session with Dan. This would take a while, Jake knew, so he stared out the window and let his mind drift.

He took stock of the previous months.

Jake had taken a pay cut to join the family business, and after barely making it on a reporter's salary it had taken some time to adjust to the lower pay even though he was living at home, and spending little. There was one fewer mouth to feed, but the fixed costs of his life had remained.

Moving into his parents' home, Jake was still paying off debts from Sabrina's memorial service as well as the hefty credit card balance she had left behind; money was tight. Eager to eliminate payments for lingerie, cosmetics and shoes as part of Sabrina's legacy, he figured he'd be clear in two more months. Then he would be able to find his own place. His parents had been accommodating, but a guy in his late 20s needs a little breathing room, particularly after what he'd been through.

Jake's life was simple and straightforward: work, family, more work, more family. He followed his father's hours, Monday through Friday, 8–6; Saturday 8–1. His parents religiously attended church services, but Jake always took a pass. Religion had no place in his mind or heart.

"God and I have no time for one another," he said when the issue of religion came up in conversation. He relaxed while his parents prayed, opting to sleep in or just enjoy the quiet.

Then came Sunday dinner with his parents, Mary, and Sam. It was usually the week's most elaborate meal, featuring roast beef, grilled steaks, barbecued chicken or his mom's delectable roast pork. Then Monday came, and the schedule would repeat.

He resisted his sister's invitations to join her and a girlfriend for a movie or a beer, preferring to spend evenings alone, reading, writing or thinking. He wasn't ready for even casual encounters, and certainly not for a date.

He missed Sabrina.

He missed reporting.

He missed Sarah, Phil and his other journalist friends, with their crude ways, sardonic wit and "screw you" attitudes.

He missed Rilertown.

He had nightmares: Sabrina's shoe, Reigner's smug grin, the gloating look on McFadden's swollen, purple face the last time Jake had seen him, triumphant, defiant and challenging the young reporter to "go head, you shitsucker, take another shot." Often, his nightmares placed him in *The P-R*'s office, Zamboni looming over him, Moore's voice in the background, Betsey whimpering in the editor's pit about the headline that just wouldn't fit.

He dreamed about the look on Thompson's face when he had confronted him outside his apartment building, and the contrasting emotions for the two men: for Thompson, defeat and despair; for Jake, elation and conquest. It was a defining moment in his young career, a jolt of adrenaline like victory to a quarterback, acquittal to a defense attorney, or heroin to a junkie.

"Once it's in your blood, it's there for good," Zamboni told him shortly after the story broke and the calls and letters started pouring in. "We love to win, and we win by getting the story. It's what we do. We have pit bulls' attitudes and crocodiles' jaws. Once we get pissed, we sink our teeth. And when we sink our teeth, we don't let go."

Jake forced his journalism career into a mental closet, locking the door and doing his best to keep that part of his history well away from his new life in Silvertown.

He avoided reading local newspapers — especially *The Silvertown Eagle,* the hometown rag where he had completed a summer internship years earlier. A lifetime of change had happened since he had wrapped up the internship, shaken hands with *The Eagle* staff and headed back to Blendhurst for his senior year.

Now and then he picked up a copy and read the stories with a reporter's critical eye, lamenting the bad writing and mentally plugging factual holes in stories that somehow had made it past a careless editor. He told himself that journalism was like an abusive relationship and that he was fortunate to be beyond all that. The lousy hours, awful pay and challenges of being wedged between those in power and those consuming information often made journalism a thankless task.

But how he loved it.

He loved it as a parent loves a child, with a soft, accepting acquiescence to all that is wrong with the profession, but with a devout, unwavering appreciation for its inherent value: To readers, to the political and business matrices that media keeps in check by acting as independent watchdogs, and even to advertisers. He loved it dearly, deeply, and, if he allowed himself to think like this, missed it desperately.

So he kept away from it.

His father devoured *The Eagle* in the evening and *The Hazelton Gazette* every morning. Jake cringed when he saw *The Gazette's* familiar masthead, evoking the competitive juices that fed

The P-R staff's daily efforts to create fresh, local news to beat *The Gazette* at its own game. He would decline the sports section when his dad offered it over breakfast, opting to buy the Boston Globe every day on his way to work to keep in touch with news and sports from New England and around the world.

His father was reading *The Gazette* one morning over breakfast, his arms splayed as he held the broadsheet open, front page facing Jake.

"Rilertown erupts in flames," screamed the banner headline, and Jake stared, transfixed. A photo taken from the softball field where Jake once roamed right field showed the lower Flats engulfed in fire. A burned-out car smoldered in the foreground.

"Dad, can I take a look at that?" He grabbed the paper and went numb as he read about the riots that had erupted after weeks of racial tension in Rilertown. "Mayor Issues Curfew, Considers Calling in National Guard," read the subhead. Jake absorbed the story's details, imagining himself back in *The P-R* newsroom as part of the coverage team.

He thought of his friends at the paper and in the community, particularly Cheecha. He hadn't spoken to him since leaving Rilertown, but Cheecha had been a true friend after Sabrina's death. Available, concerned and a great listener, he cemented his role as Jake's best friend as he found his way through the haze.

Cheecha was among the first to learn that Jake was leaving Rilertown. Once his apartment's contents were packed into Jake's car, the two had shared a quick beer at La Bamba, then Jake had hopped into his loaded car and driven to Silvertown. Looking back never seemed an option.

This was serious; a valued friend was at risk. Jake rose from the table and moved to the living room. Sitting in his father's armchair with the phone extension conveniently placed to his right, he called Cheecha.

The two spoke for less than 10 minutes. He and his family were fine, he said, but the city was a mess. He was doing his best to keep calm in the Hispanic community, but it was tough. Police had gotten tough, arresting people on sight if they ventured out after dark, using the curfew as a club to beat down a community packed with jittery, unhappy people, some of them prepared to act out their frustrations.

"I'm between a rock and a very hard place," Cheecha sighed. As the senior member of the Hispanic Council for Justice, it fell to Cheecha to handle negotiations and keep the two parties from each other's throats.

"We have a few badasses who've gotten out of hand, but usually our community can handle our own problems. Trouble is, we didn't act fast enough, and by the time we got to the troublemakers it was already out of hand."

It had started with the arrest and detainment of three young men who had turned out to be innocent bystanders wrongly accused of a convenience store robbery. Their arrests were due to the fact that they were a) men, and b) Hispanic, a perfect example of profiling gone wrong. They were roughly shoved to the ground, handcuffed by six police officers and hauled off to jail despite the fact that each of the three was 20 years younger and 30 pounds lighter than the three habitual crooks they had been mistaken for, and who were later arrested on robbery charges.

The community reacted badly to the profiling and rough handling.

There were a couple of serious fights and reciprocal beatings — one angry young man, then a solo cop on foot patrol — followed by a torched police car. Then came curfew and patrolling pairs of burly cops in cruisers, slowly crawling the neighborhoods after dusk to enforce the "all clear" mandate. For residents of The Flats, nights became rituals of huddling against the dark as the community remained indoors, out of sight, transparent to the city, the people in power, and to the majority whites.

"Like they've always wanted," Cheecha said bitterly. "We just disappear."

Jake hung up and went to shower and get ready for work, but his mind was on Rilertown.

He thought about the conversation off and on during the day, but by the time dinner rolled around his thoughts had turned to the tire business and matters closer to home. Dinner with his mom and dad came and went. Jake retreated early to his room to read and grab a good night's sleep in the sanctity of his bedroom.

Night has a habit of visiting our demons upon us. They come in assaultive packs, like wild dogs on the hunt, relentlessly circling, snarling and nipping at our heels, tormenting us with nightmares' diabolical twisting of truth. Our personal horrors become Technicolor panoramas, playing on endless loops that again and again bring the dogs to our throats as the dark grips our souls.

Often, Jake woke in panic, sweating, panting, grasping at his bed clothes and imploring the static image of Sam Huff in full protective football gear gazing down from the wall above his bed to do something to help.

But help never came, and as the dawn forced the dark into retreat, Jake would confront another day.

"Lost in thought, eh?" Sam said breezily, easing back into the booth across from Jake. It took Jake a few moments to bring himself back from the tangled knot of memories and emotions. Sam seemed to understand, and she watched the scowl on her godson's face slowly dissipate as whatever was on his mind floated back into memory.

Lunch arrived. Dan's daily special was one of Jake's favorites, a towering three-decker club sandwich with extra bacon surrounded by a hillock of well done French fries. "Burn 'em," Dan would yell to Jose, the diminutive assistant cook who worked the fryolators at lunchtime — and Jose would reliably turn out a batch of fries cooked precisely to Jake's liking.

Jake's mood lifted. The awkwardness disappeared faster than the mound of fries. Thoughts of newspapering, Rilertown, race riots and a host of other memories evaporated.

The two tucked into the meal, wiping mayo from their mouths and chattering about the upcoming Bruins and Celtics seasons. They talked about their beloved New England Patriots. The Pats had lost three of their last five games the previous year, went 8–8, and missed the playoffs. But it was a new year, and as Halloween approached the Pats were sporting a 6–3 record, oozing promise and bringing fans out in droves.

Sam was a longtime season ticket holder to Sullivan Stadium. She alternated taking Jake or his dad to the games. Jake was due to join Sam for the Bills game in two weeks, so the talk centered around injuries, the teams' strengths and weaknesses, and odds of a Pats' victory.

Jake glanced at his watch.

"Oops. Nearly quarter of two. Gotta go," he said, sliding from the booth and following Sam out the door. The two parted in front of the shop with a hug and a promise to head to Foxboro early in time to tailgate and "load up on pre-game festivities," which meant burgers, beer and bullshit with thousands of rabid football fans just like them.

He was in a great mood as he strode through the door and into the showroom, whistling and wondering how many touchdowns Tony Eason would throw. He didn't notice the man studying the display of snow tires until he was nearly upon him.

Hearing Jake's footsteps, the man pivoted. Jake stopped and stared. Since returning to Silvertown he had unsuspectingly bumped into many people of his past — high school buddies, former teammates, even former girlfriends — but no encounter startled him as much as seeing Dan "Les" Moore standing in the showroom of his family's business.

Chance Encounter, Serious Talks

Moore spoke first.

"Hey, Jake. Good to see you," he said, extending his hand.

Jake took the hand in his, grim-faced, and gave it a perfunctory shake.

"Les."

Les had received warmer greetings from union stewards. Not a great start.

He cleared his throat.

"Look, Jake, I know you're pissed, and I'm sorry for what happened. I'm here to try and patch things up, but I'm also here to buy snow tires. No kidding."

Jake considered telling Moore to shove off and take his business elsewhere — maybe the new chain store down the road would have time for him. Jake surely did not. But he shrugged. Business was business, and he decided to sell Moore a set of tires, hand him over to a mechanic who had an open bay and send him on his way.

"Great. What size?" Jake said, easing into sales mode and leading Moore to the display of tires.

They talked for a few minutes. Moore chose his tire model and handed his car keys to Jake so the mechanic could bring the car into the bay and make the change.

"Look, Jake, you and I need to talk…." Moore said.

"No, Les, we do not *need* to talk," Jake angrily turned on him. "At least I don't, and I think you've already said more than enough.

"You think you can come in here to my family's business, making all nice with your 'I need snow tires' bullshit? You think that negates what you did to me? You hung me out and helped that prick Zamboni flog me in public. You lost your way, forgot what you do for a living — and you humiliated me. You think I'm dumb enough to trust you after that? You've got the wrong guy, Les …."

"Have a beer with me. Hear me out. It's not what you think. Really. You had it all wrong, that meeting in Wick's office. Just let me buy you a beer, and you can make up your mind after that. But please hear me out. As a friend," Moore said.

"Friend? Did you say friend? Helluva word to use to describe someone you completely screwed over," Jake said, stepping closer to Moore and peering into his eyes, unblinking. Moore stared back, also unblinking, and in his eyes Jake saw a man with something worth listening to — or maybe it was something else.

Moore had spent years sequestered in relative monkish celibacy, living a double life as the financial whiz overseeing *The P-R* newsroom in his hometown while quietly maintaining a series of dalliances with male acquaintances. He had been attracted to Jake the first time they'd met — during Jake's initial interview at the paper while he was still a student at Blendhurst — and Moore had spent many an hour thinking of the young man with the deep brown eyes and athletic build.

But Moore saw the futility — and danger — of approaching a man 15 years his junior who was not only an employee but also in a heterosexual relationship; he was clearly straight. So he made the wise choice, keeping a safe distance and cultivating a relationship with Jake built on shared professional values and trust. "Better friends than nothing," Moore had sighed, then eased into the familiar role of finding satisfaction in a friendship with a man with whom he could envision much more.

Jake had viewed Moore as a smart, competent newspaper professional, and a powerful ally. The two had come to respect and like one another based on shared professional values and trust — until the meeting in Wick's office sent him packing for Silvertown.

"Yes, I said 'friend,'" Moore said. "You might not regard me as such, but I sure as hell do you. That's why I'm here." He smiled, "... and to buy snow tires, of course."

Jake paused, thoughtful, studying the floor, and then looked up at Les. In the early years Moore had been good to him, helpful and supportive, an ally before the conflict over the Reigner story. He had become a trusted colleague — and a friend as well.

"What the hell; a beer," Les offered.

"OK. One beer. Six. The Pilot. Main Street," Jake said. He turned and headed to his office.

Shortly before six, Jake locked up and made for the Pilot. The Main Street pub was Jake's favorite after-work haunt, offering cold beer and homemade pub food that perfectly fit a workingman's budget and dietary demands.

He slid into a booth across from Moore, who was halfway through a pint of lager. Jake signaled to the bartender, a high school pal who'd never left Silvertown, and waited for his pilsner to arrive.

"OK, I'm here. Go for it. What do you want?" Jake wasn't feeling charitable.

"No, you tell me," said Moore, who had prepared for this moment and rehearsed it well. He'd best get to it.

"Tell me what you *think* you saw that day in Wick's office. Why was the lawyer there — that's what this is all about, after all, right? You're pissed that the lawyer was there, and that we called her in to cover our asses. You think we set you up. So you tell me."

"Pretty obvious, isn't it? You guys *were* protecting your asses. I put myself on the line for the story, for the paper, but all you could think about was making sure I didn't do something to risk your precious bottom line with a lawsuit. I'm out there, working my ass off, pushing it for me *and* the paper while you and your pin-striped pit bull conspired to set me up and let me take the heat.

"You were all distancing yourselves from me, aligning *The P-R* with those assholes Reigner and McFadden to protect the paper, rather than support me and push the story. The shit hit the fan and you all turned and ran. Nutless, all of you."

Jake paused and took a deep pull on his beer. He looked up and met Moore's eyes.

"You hung me out there for the City Hall vultures to pick at me like the dead rat I was. And after everything else, Les ... I mean, Sabrina's death, and all ... then that ...."

"Wrong, my friend. You were wrong," Moore said, leaning across the table, his voice suddenly taking a commanding edge. "Listen up: we asked the lawyer to join us to *protect* you, not to distance us from you, you idiot."

Jake stared at him, unconvinced.

"We were prepared to talk about our next steps, which, had you bothered to stick around and listen to rather than storm out and quit, would have shielded you from reprisal by those dickheads, and others. That meant we needed you off the story, but only while we sorted out our next move. We were far from done, and we had your back. At least Wick and I did.

"That's right. We were actually standing with you, but in your impetuous, self-absorbed and, importantly, inexperienced opinion, it looked like the opposite.

"Big mistake," Moore sighed. "Big. Damn. Mistake.

"But I understand, truly. You were in bad shape, in many ways, and not capable of reason. We knew that. Why else would we have taken you off the story and given it to that idiot Zabriske, who could fuck up a free lunch? He couldn't find his way through a story without a personal guide and a map.

"Didn't any of this occur to you? Didn't it seem odd that we would suddenly turn on you? If a lawsuit was coming, the damage had already been done. Why would we change course so quickly?

"Then there are the practical issues. You think we'd promote a young guy with a couple years of experience, turn him loose on the best story in the paper's history, then suddenly go soft and run?"

Moore took a breath, shook his head and sipped his beer.

"I tried to reach you, left messages that I know you got, but nada. No, you were safely sequestered in your self-righteous bubble. That's one of the reasons I decided to make the drive up here today. I figured the only way to approach you was face to face."

He paused, smiling softly.

"And I needed snow tires."

Jake studied the bubbles in his beer as they drifted lazily from the bottom of the glass to the foamy head. A single drop of water descended the side of the glass to the table.

He was stunned by the magnitude of his misjudgment.

"You shittin' me?" was the best he could manage.

"Not for a second," Moore said, holding Jake's gaze. "Nope. Not at all."

Jake drained the last of his beer. The silence hung like a fog over the rocky shoals of Jake's world. He felt lost.

"I'm starving," Moore said. "And your glass is empty. What do you say? Looks like these burgers are killer."

Moore scanned the room for a waiter while Jake assessed the situation. He had promised himself to loathe Moore for the rest of his life, forsaking what he'd thought was a friendship at best and a solid professional relationship at least. And now he'd learned that he'd based all this contempt, all this resentment, *on a misunderstanding?*

The waiter approached, at last catching sight of Moore waving his arms.

"Hang on," Jake said aloud, motioning the waiter away. The kid shrugged, scowled and turned on his heels.

"So you're telling me I had it all wrong, that I overreacted and needlessly quit a job I loved … I loved it, goddamn it, and it was the only thing in my life that hadn't gone sour at that point! And I needed it! Work was all that kept me going after Sabrina died, along with my friends at the paper. And now I find out that I threw it under the bus because I misunderstood? All that for nothing?"

A bead of sweat made its way from Jake's forehead along the bridge of his nose. He swatted at it angrily.

"That's why you're here? To tell me what a fuckup I am? How I messed up by quitting a dream job in the middle of an incredible story? To show me what a jerk I am?"

"Only partly, though I must say it's gratifying to watch you struggle with the truth," Moore said. "But that's not the only the reason I'm here.

"Here's the other … " Moore began, shifting in his seat and leaning toward Jake. "Look, I'm sure you've read about the riots in Rilertown. The cops finally went too far, arrested one too many innocent bystanders, roughed up one too many guys who'd had too much to drink.

"Our city's on fire. The Flats are in flames, Jake — flames. There are burned police cars on the side of the road, people in jail who don't belong there. Cops are being told to go hard on an entire Hispanic population under fire. No one's been killed, but it's only a matter of time. Dozens of injuries, a couple of stabbings…. It's a war zone."

Moore took a deep draught and licked a bit of foam from his mustache.

"But we can't get to the story, partly because of the curfew and the police patrols that have The Flats on lockdown, but mostly because we have no one to get inside the Hispanic community and find out what they're thinking. We need to get closer to the story, but we're blocked out."

Jake saw where Moore was leading him.

"Cheecha," he said.

"Right on. Cheecha," Moore confirmed. "Your pal Cheecha is respected, connected, tapped into the community and close to the trouble, if he's not directly involved…"

"No way," Jake interrupted. He knew his friend, and it would be out of the question for him to encourage or participate in violence under any circumstances. "Absolutely not — and even if he wanted to mix it up with Rilertown's finest, Carmella would kill him.

"You want to find out what's up. Why don't you have Zabriske give him a call?" Jake pushed back.

"Tried that. Seems Cheecha has a certain allegiance to a former reporter. He shut down on us; refused to talk."

"So, what ... you want me to give Cheecha a call? Ask him to talk to Zabriske, or someone else from the paper?"

"Nope. I have something else in mind," Moore said, gesturing the waiter back to their table. "But maybe we should order first. *The P-R's* buying, so load up."

THE PITCH

The two ordered burgers and fresh beers, dispatching the waiter so they could continue their talk.

"I want you to come back," Moore said, raising his hands as Jake began to protest.

"Hear me out. Cheecha trusts you, and you know him, his family and his pals. You also know your way around The Flats, so you'd probably be able to get close to the situation without the cops catching up with you.

"Look, Jake. Rilertown's not just a city in a mess; it's my home-town. This matters … a lot — to the paper — to Wick and Mike, in his own, twisted way — to me. We need to expose what's caus-ing all this trouble. A lot of good people are being hurt by all this crap — Hispanic *and* white. A city doesn't just crash and burn without a reason, and we have to get to the cause of this mess to help us all find our way through it.

"We need to explain it fairly and objectively, and find a way to get the key players talking to each other to negotiate a solution.

"So far in your young but illustrious career, you've reported," Moore said. "You've learned how to research, dig and write. This is different. This is community leadership. It's when we do our most important work. You know, pillar of democracy and all that crazy shit you studied in J school? This, my friend, *this* is when we earn our paychecks."

Jake countered.

"I'm sure all this is true, Les, but I've moved on. I'm done with all that. I'm part of my family business now, back in my home-town, and I'm committed to this place, my mom and dad, my sister. So, much as I understand your situation … and I really do … there's not much I can do to help you. I couldn't leave my dad in the lurch; it's inventory time."

Their food and beer arrived, and Moore and Jake half-heart-edly got to work on the burgers and fries, washing them down with swigs of ice-cold beer.

"There's something else," Moore said. "And it has to do with Sabrina."

Jake's skin went cold. Mid-bite, he lowered his burger to his plate.

"What did you say?"

"You heard me. The girl who hit Sabrina, Sally something or other, you know, got off with a light swat. McFadden and Reigner made that happen. Turns out the girl's father is pals with Reigner's aide, Ted Price, so the City Hall machine clicked into gear. Someone made a call to the DA's office, probably to the judge, too, and, well, you know how things work in City Hall......

"The kid was only, what, 19, but the accident with Sabrina was her third accident in a matter of months. The two others involved booze. There's reason to believe the accident with Sabrina did, too. Looks like she got a pass because of who her daddy knows. Given her track record, she should have been doing time for Sabrina's accident, certainly not just community service.

"We got a tip a couple months after you left, and started to dig, but files started disappearing." Jake slumped in the booth as the ghosts of Rilertown's power structure revisited, inflicting him with gnawing torment that cut to his soul. Anger's molten lava coursed through him, leaving him flush-faced and with sweaty palms. His gaze narrowed as he spoke.

"So those fuckers tucked it to me in the worst way they could, huh? They always win, don't they? Elections, contracts, all the graft and corruption, and they even got Sabrina's killer off? They must have loved sticking it to me. Bastards.

"I had them by the short hairs. Their careers were over; they were toast. And then, what, Thompson just dies? I know there's no way to connect McFadden and Reigner to Thompson's death, and maybe it was the New York mob that knocked him off for opening his yap.

"But it's just wrong that those two pricks continue to play the system and keep on their merry ways, untouched. There's no limit to what bastards they are."

"Right you are," Moore said. "How very right you are.

"But here's the sad truth. That's a story you'll never touch. It's personal for you, so no way could you be objective about it. Somebody else is gonna handle that one, though I'm sure it's buried so deep that only a miracle will help us get it on the record and expose them.

"But I thought you'd want to know, and, truth be told, I thought it might just motivate you to come back and help us tackle the Reigner administration once and for all.

"I'm not sure we can get to the story on the girl who hit Sabrina, but I'm damned sure we can find out the real cause of the racial problems in Rilertown. It doesn't take a Rhodes Scholar to trace the issue to Reigner and McFadden, and their racist, corrupt and selfish administration."

Moore leaned back in his booth. Time for the close.

"Come back, Jake. Come back and help us make them accountable. Help us take them down … for the paper … for the city … or you … and for Sabrina."

Moore pushed his plate to the side of the table and paused, staring at Jake.

"I need the little boy's room," he said, rising." Just think about this for a minute. I'll be back."

His appetite gone, Jake pushed his unfinished burger to the side and pulled his beer close. Memories and emotions raced through his brain as he tried to absorb what he'd learned.

He thought of Sabrina, lying in the road, crumpled, damaged beyond repair, dying — and how her memory had now been tainted by the far-reaching evil of Rilertown's elite.

He thought of Cheecha and his family, huddling in the night as Reigner's police patrols slowly cruised the barrio, licensed warriors in Kevlar vests, nightsticks and guns at the ready to repress an undeserving, powerless population.

He thought of the long reach of Reigner and his gang, how they controlled the city, how much they profited from their iron-fisted rule, and how arrogant they'd become.

But *this?* This was personal.

Reigner and McFadden had suppressed the facts surrounding Sabrina's death, twisted them to suit their needs. A call had been made, favors were requested and granted. Agreements had been struck, ensuring permanent allegiance from the girl's father and further solidifying Reigner and McFadden's grip on their city.

Their city.

"Bastards," Jake said aloud as Moore returned, sliding into the bench opposite Jake.

He stared at his beer mug and watched the bubbles rise to the surface. Freed from the depths of the mug, the bits of carbonation rose to the surface and dissipated into the frothy head.

"I'll do it," Jake said. "But I'm going to need a week or so to get organized. This is going to really mess up my family, but I'm in.

"Let me make one thing clear to you, Les. I'm not doing this for you, or for me, or for Rilertown. I'm coming back for two reasons: One, to report on the cause of the riots and, if that's where the story takes me, to lay the blame at the feet of city hall; and two, for Sabrina. I'm doing this for Sabrina, and for her memory.

"It's what she'd want me to do."

Jake left his parents' house before dawn the next morning, drinking cup after cup of coffee at Sam's regular breakfast hangout, waiting for his godmother to make her daily appearance.

Sam didn't disappoint, crossing the threshold at 6:27 and feigning shock when she spied Jake.

"Well, to what do I owe this distinct honor?" she asked, clapping Jake on the shoulder and then turning somber when she saw the look in his eyes.

"Looks serious. Let me grab a coffee. You good?"

Jake nodded. "Actually, no. One more. Large. Black. And thanks."

Moments later Sam returned with two cups of steaming coffee. She took a careful sip and nodded to Jake.

"Let's have it."

"I'm going back to the paper." The words poured out in a torrent of anxiety, pain, regret, confusion and conflict. He spoke without pause for nearly 15 minutes, then sat back in his chair and took a sip of coffee.

He looked exhausted and felt sick.

"So, what do you think?" he asked Sam.

"What do I think? Me? Oh, what I think doesn't matter a lick. But I can tell you what I see, and what I know.

"First, here's what I know: You're not cut out for the tire business, Jake, that I know for sure. You're — pardon me, and you know I love you like the son I'll never have, but this is the truth — a shitty businessman. Your heart's not in it, and if it's not, well, it just isn't. And that's bad for business. You can take it from me. I don't see you selling tires in Silvertown. It's been great for you for a while, as a place to regroup and recover, but not for good. Nope.

"I see you in some dingy office late at night working away on the latest hot story, or, notebook in hand, wandering City Hall in search of some political hack to torment, or knocking on some-one's door who really, really doesn't want to talk to you.

"I see you pounding a keyboard, or on the phone interrogating some poor schmuck who's trying desperately, failingly to outwit you and keeping you from learning what they know. I see you digging, probing, analyzing and explaining complicated stuff to readers who depend on people like you to help them understand.

"I see you making news, Jake, in the purest sense of that term — yup — making the news. That's where your heart is. Mostly. "

She paused.

"It's also lying in the gutter where Sabrina died," Sam said, plac-ing her hand on Jake's. "A loss like that … of a love like that … who among us can really understand? But it's clear to me that you also need to be as close to her as possible. And though she's gone, there's a piece of her still in Rilertown … unfinished business in Rilertown. Yup, that's the place for you, my boy. You need to go back to Rilertown, get back to work, and somehow — no matter how long it takes — retrieve your wonderful, young heart from that gutter and get it back in your chest.

"You're coasting here, biding time as you heal, and you've done a damned good job at it. I see it, and so do your mom, dad and sister. Anyone who knows you has known it all along. You came home to heal. But now you're strong again, and ready to get on with the rest of your life. Tire merchant? Not you, my fabulous godson-scrivener. Not by a long shot."

"But my dad …." Jake protested.

"Will understand," Sam interrupted. "You can trust me on this, my boy. I know your dad like I know my messed up golf swing. He understood all of this long before you did."

Jake arrived at the tire shop before his father, pacing between the office and showroom while glancing down Federal Street, eager to see the familiar panel truck bouncing down the road, yet at the same time dreading his father's arrival. Shortly before 8, the truck — with the "Ketcher's Tire" lettering recognizable from a distance — turned off Federal and parked on the side of the road. Moments later his dad walked in, Styrofoam cup of coffee in hand.

"What, no *Globe* today?" he asked his son. "You were in late last night and out before I got up today. Where'd you get off to at such an early hour?"

He caught Jake's gaze and stopped.

"Jeez. What's up?" He'd rarely seen his son so flustered, so distraught, certainly not since the awful days after Sabrina had been killed.

Jake told him, anxiously pacing as the elder Ketcher sat on the corner of his desk, staring at the floor and nodding. When Jake was finished his father looked up and smiled. "First things first," he said, holding his arms open and welcoming his only son into his accepting embrace.

Jake Samuel Ketcher, veteran newspaper reporter turned tire shop manager, former student, amateur athlete and ex-lover of a complicated woman who stole and trampled on his heart and then shattered it, came completely unglued in the arms of his 59-year-old father. Bereft, devastated by regret, tormented by confusion, conflicting emotions and loyalties, he clutched at his dad and leaked salty tears that soothed his soul while dampening the shoulder of his father's blue work shirt.

His dad held him silently, patting his shoulder and absorbing his son's grief as Jake dispensed it in massive, purifying waves. Jake gasped, taking a deep breath. Minutes passed. The clock on the wall ticked, shattering the stillness yet failing to disturb the moment between father and son.

Slowly, the angst abated, and the tears subsided.

"Better?" his dad asked. "Good. Now, I have something to tell you."

Jake wiped his eyes on his shirtsleeve cuff and sat next to his dad on the edge of the desk. The two faced the wall in parallel stance, gazing to the unknown but embraced by words from head to heart, together. "When you were born, I celebrated with Sam. We went out, bought expensive cigars and went to our favorite bar. I got quite drunk …" the elder Jake laughed, "shitfaced, actually. Good thing Sam was driving, else we'd probably not have made it home. We toasted your arrival, your name, and of course your mother for making the whole thing possible — at least her part of it," he smiled at Jake. "After buying drinks and having drinks bought for us, I offered another toast — to you — to what you'd become — to your future — and, importantly, to becoming more than I'd ever imagined for myself; I toasted your potential. I remember going on for quite a while. 'My son will be football captain.' 'My kid will lead his generation.' 'He'll be president.' And, as Sam reminds me, 'My son will be much, much more than I could ever hope to be.'

"I've always been your number one fan — of your successes, and talents, of course, but mostly of your potential. I suppose I haven't always shown that as much as I should have, but I'm workin' on it.

"But here's the truth: I saw this moment coming long before you did. You? A tire merchant? In Silvertown? It's a nice, quaint idea, Jake, but please. You're a news guy. It's in your blood, and I can see it, and so can your mom and your sister. Sam, too.

"You worked hard to give yourself a shot at a career. You paid your dues, most of 'em, anyway, and you've been lucky to find work that means something to you. You've put a lot of yourself into becoming a reporter, Jake. You can't waste that. No, you can't waste it, and maybe it's time you got on with the business of your business.

"And you know what? You're damned good at it. Even I can see that, a small town tire merchant like me. You've learned well, you are respected and valued, and you've built a following among your readers. And there's the idea of finishing what you started. You have work to do — but not here.

"Hell, I paid for your education, didn't I? You'd think I have the right to expect some return on my investment."

Jake was overwhelmed by his father's wisdom and magnanimity. "But dad ... inventory..."

"I've handled inventory in this pissant little business pretty much all my life, Jake. You think I can't continue to do just that?

"We're good here," his dad said, clapping his hands to knees and rising from the edge of the desk. "Fact is ... we're better than good. We're perfect.

"So. When are you leaving, and when can your mother and I help you get back to Rilertown to start looking for a place to live?"

INTO THE BREACH, AGAIN

It took Jake three days to find a new apartment in Rilertown and, one week later, two hours to move in. His parents, sister and Jake formed a convoy for the 45-minute Sunday afternoon drive down Interstate 85 from Silvertown, three cars transporting a young man's world into a familiar setting with a horrific past and an uncertain future.

The unfurnished apartment had been freshly painted. A trip to the second hand shop yielded a bed and enough cheap furniture to make the place feel like home. It lacked the space, layout and charm of the apartment Jake and Sabrina had shared, but this suited Jake. A new place would give him a clean break, and a fresh start.

Beth laid her motherly hands on the place, adding feminine touches to make a comfortable haven out of what otherwise would have been little more than a place for Jake to sleep. Curtains hung in the windows. A small rug lay beside the bed. A drainage rack rested beside the sink for washed dishes. A matching toilet seat cover, bath mat and extra toilet roll holder gave the bathroom color and a feeling of home.

Pots, pans, and a host of kitchen utensils followed Jake and Sabrina's loveseat and Jake's Panasonic AM/FM radio and cassette player out of the back of his dad's truck. The apartment quickly filled as the four formed a conga line to create Jake's new home.

Jake had phoned Les two days after having dinner with him at the Pilot, and they'd quickly settled on a date for Jake's return. He'd have the same desk, the same beat. Les even offered a small raise, which lifted the young man's spirits and increased his eagerness to get back to work. Jake placed a call to Zamboni, who was typically guarded but seemed enthusiastic to have him back.

"Somebody has to get to this story," Zamboni growled, "and so far we have sucked in epic proportions. Maybe you can come up with something worth printing."

Carrying the last box of Jake's clothes into his bedroom, his mother laid her hand on her son's arm.

"How're you doing, son?" she probed, looking deeply into his eyes.

"It's weird being back, having some of our stuff here, but it'll feel like home thanks to you guys," Jake responded. "I think it's gonna be fine."

"Pizza!" yelled his father from the living room. "I'm starving! Let's eat."

Jake led his family into La Bamba for pizza and beer, entering the dining room adjacent to the bar and stopping to absorb the sight before him. Seated at an enormous table already groaning from the abundance of empty beer bottles scattered across its top were Cheecha, Carmella and their kids, Sarah Turnbull, Phil Buckley, Beebo and Les.

"Welcome home!" they shouted, rising to embrace Jake and his family.

Pizzas appeared from the kitchen and cold beer arrived. Everyone was in high spirits until Jake noticed a solitary figure stroll in from the street and head for the bar.

Ted Price, Reigner's flunky.

Les settled into an open seat next to Jake.

"I was hoping you wouldn't see him," Les said with a sigh. "Don't let him spoil the party. He's not worth your time."

Over the next half hour Jake tried to keep his head in the party, trading half-hearted jokes with Cheecha and his dad, catching up on the latest stories and gossip from his P-R pals, and teasing Beebo about her new hair color — a bright red that made her look older, sadder. "Now you look like your father mated with a rooster," he joked.

But Jake's eye kept returning to Price as the mayor's aide sipped a drink and stared straight at the mirror behind the bar, one eye on Jake.

Jake glared at Price, his mind racing with thoughts of the man making calls to the DA and judge to help Sabrina's killer avoid prosecution. Angered and frustrated, he began to rise from the table, but paused when Les put a hand on Jake's shoulder and eased him back into his seat.

"Not here; not now," he counseled gently.

As if sensing trouble, Price threw some cash on the bar, cast a stony look at Jake and left. Jake tracked him as he walked across the floor, his eyes afire with hostility.

Having watched the drama from the end of the table, Cheecha appeared with fresh beers, an enormous smile and a slap on the back for his returning buddy.

"So, hey, fat boy, you look soft. Gotta get you back to the gym if you're gonna make the team this year, let alone start in right field."

The festive mood gradually returned and continued for another hour before the party began to wind down. Jake's parents and sister departed first, then Cheecha and the kids, heading back to The Flats to beat curfew. *The P-R* staffers left for another bar, and Beebo moved to the pool table, where a bunch of her friends were engaged in a raucous game of team eightball.

Returning from his fourth trip to the men's room, Les sat down across from Jake, surveying the carnage of bottles and plates strewn across the table. Both showed signs of modest inebriation.

"So, how's it feel?"

"Weird, but great," Jake said. "I'm eager to get back at it."

"Same here, but here's a warning. Go easy with the mayor, and with McFadden. They're gunning for you; I'm sure you know that.

"It's also not lost on you how strange it is to see a guy like Price in a place like La Bamba on a Sunday night — and this Sunday night, of all the nights. I'm sure it's the first time he's been here, and I'm sure he was here because he was instructed to be here, to make his presence known, but more importantly, to let you feel McFadden and Reigner's weight."

"Asshole by proxy," Jake said, laughing.

"You got it," Moore replied. "Plenty of that to go around."

"Gotta wonder, though. How did he know we'd be here?" Jake mused. "That I'd be here?"

Les drained his beer, cheeks puffing as he repressed a belch and rose. "I'm outta here," then indicated Beebo who was returning to the table after the pool game concluded. "Looks like your evening's not quite over."

Beebo eased into the seat across from Jake as Les departed. She nodded to the bartender, raising two fingers in a call for more beer.

"Oh, man, Beebo. OK. One more, but that's it. I'm back at work tomorrow, you know."

"Yeah, I know, but I've been trying to get a minute with you all night." The beers arrived, and the two friends clinked their icy bottle necks in a toast.

"To you," Beebo said.

"Look, Jake, I suck at stuff like this, but here goes: I'm really psyched to have you back in town. I consider you a friend, you know, and, well, when I saw you at Sabrina's funeral I didn't know what to say. I mean, I felt your grief, and I know how much you loved her, and, well, I wanted to reach out to you when you went back to Silvertown, but I didn't know how to reach you, and…"

Jake put one hand on Beebo's. He raised the index finger on his other hand to his lips.

"Shhh. Beebo. I get it. I understand, and I appreciate your support. I know you're my friend, and I feel the same. I'm glad to be back. This is where I belong. And, weird as it is to be here without Sabrina, I feel oddly whole coming here. It's as if she's here with me.

"Rilertown is my home, now. It's where my work is, and there's a lot to be done, but it's where my heart is, too — with the paper — and my buddies — and with friends like you."

They endured a moment's uncomfortable silence that Jake took as a signal to call the evening quits.

"Time for this old boy to hit the sack," said. "Tomorrow's a big day."

They drained the rest of their beers, then Beebo returned to her pool-playing friends and Jake headed to his car. Monday morning loomed.

Jake jumped on the racial tension story.

He cultivated sources among Cheecha's network of friends in The Flats, writing story after story that explained the riots' genesis and their impact on Rilertown's businesses and residents — black, white, Hispanic and otherwise. He patrolled streets of The Flats by day, talking to people in a quirky blend of Spanish and English, often with Cheecha or one of his friends along to translate and make sure he was seen as a friend.

After years of tension with numerous city departments, the Hispanic community had simply had enough abusive, heavy-handed treatment. They collectively snapped, taking their anger to the streets, sometimes violently, as pent up outrage turned to rock throwing, Molotov cocktails and fistfights.

One confrontation involved a young patrolman who found himself surrounded by a group of angry young men. They were friends of the guy whose arrest had started the whole mess, so their nerves were already frayed when the patrolman braked to an abrupt halt, intent on dispersing a gathering small crowd. Words turned to insults turned to shoving turned to fists. When one of the young men produced a knife, the patrolman's revolver was suddenly in his hand. That's when things got ugly. No shots were fired, but the stage was set for dangerous confrontations as both sides prepared for battle.

White against color became a citywide issue. The fight spilled from the barrios of The Flats to Rilertown High School. Jake was the first reporter on the scene when police responded to a massive rumble at the school between whites, blacks and Hispanics. "White against the world," was how one of Jake's friends at *The P-R* described the ongoing conflict. "Seems like anyone who's not white is on the same side, and anyone who's white is the aggressor."

That wasn't so, of course, and Jake's reporting provided stories that brought balance and perspective to the issue. He wrote about a quiet Irish man who ran a fishing tackle shop in the center of the city. Richard O'Malley's entire workforce consisted of Hispanics he had known and trusted for years, and he made a living selling tackle to anyone who shared his love of fishing the Tee's abundant waters.

His business was failing, he told Jake, because people didn't dare shop on the edge of The Flats, let alone spend a couple of hours on the vulnerable and unsafe banks of the Tee.

"Too close to the violence," he said. "You'd be nuts to go down there right now. Even I won't, and I'm considered a friend."

The troubles had exacted a cost, personally, and deeply.

"I've had to let Hector go, and Flor will be next," he told Jake with tears in his eyes. "They are like family to me, and I know these jobs put food on their tables, but what am I going to do? Most of my customers are gone, or at least not coming here to buy."

Some residents reacted with kindness, in contrast to the aggressive responses from city authorities and police.

Jake wrote about a humanitarian organization run from the garage of Rilertown's favorite sporting goods store owner by an easy-going middle-aged man whose son had been injured in one of the fights at Rilertown High. Jim Bontempo — third-generation son of Italian immigrants—collected canned goods and non-perishable items and delivered them to needy families in The Flats to help them through the crisis.

"I feel responsible for these people," he told Jake. "They are my customers, my friends, and members of my community. Unlike City Hall, I don't view them as the problem — not at all. Perhaps it's the other way around. Maybe it's our leaders who have caused this problem. Maybe their actions and words have brought violence to Rilertown. When you typecast an entire segment of the population, when you demonize one specific group, you polarize the community, forcing people to take sides — and, sometimes, to fight.

"Yes, I'm angry at the people who injured my son, but I am more concerned about the cause of this mess than a few cuts and scrapes on my son. He'll recover; what about the city?"

Reigner responded curtly when Jake asked for a quote about the issue.

"Ah, this is a red herring fishing expedition," he said dismissively. He called Bontempo "a disbungled member of the business community who can't adapt to changing times. This is difficult for everyone, even City Hall. But if you think I'm going to let a bunch of Coo-coo Ricans hold the city hostage, you'd best think again. And no, you can't use that last remark."

Jake quoted him anyway, holding to the unwritten rule between source and reporter that required both sides to agree to be off the record *before* a comment was made if a remark was to remain out of print. Reigner, of course, took this as a serious breach of protocol and had his aide call to let Jake know "he had crossed a serious line." That meant he'd have less access to City Hall and would become even more persona non grata among Reigner's ranks.

Jake had long given up caring.

Violence — even the threat of it during protracted lulls in the conflict — plunged Rilertown into an increasingly destructive holding pattern, about to explode.

Skirmishes were often minor shoving matches that quickly ended. Sometimes they erupted into full-scale riots, with dozens of combatants punching, throwing whatever they could get their hands on, and setting fire to whatever was closest.

Tires were the favorite items to burn. The furious flames of burning rubber sent plumes of thick smoke into the war zone, providing a filmy, threatening backdrop to the hatred and unrest.

Six police cars had been torched during the course of the lock-down, and while the National Guard hadn't yet been called in, Reigner made almost daily reference to his "trump card to get these animals off the streets, back to work and into their homes where they belong."

Prevailing sentiment at *The P-R* was that Reigner wanted Hispanics out of his city. By his logic, "back into their homes" meant a return to Puerto Rico, the Dominican Republic, or "whatever Central American shithole they came from."

The mayor's invective escalated the conflict. Battles continued through peaks of violence and spells of uneasy silence. Sometimes three or four nights would pass peacefully as the city rested. Then a skirmish would take place and the clashes would begin anew.

Police sirens and police-escorted fire trucks replaced the ice cream trucks that normally patrolled The Flats' streets on early summer nights. Ambulances began making runs into The Flats with armed police escorts. The summer basketball league — with its grueling practices and popular round-robin tournament — a fixture among black, white and Hispanic students — was abruptly canceled, meaning hundreds of testosterone-laden young men suddenly had time on their hands and no outlet for their energy.

School ended for the year, removing at least one potential venue for fights. The city braced for a long, hot summer. *The P-R*'s editorial pages called for calm and urged both sides to exercise restraint.

Using Cheecha's contacts in The Flats, Jake's reporting gave the debate about the tensions a balanced — and therefore neutral — tone, and offset the foolish opinions Wick insisted on spewing on the OpEd page.

Competing coverage on the pages of *The Hazelton Gazette*, meanwhile, was predictably one-dimensional, focusing on the damage. Lacking an insider like Jake to report from within the city, *The Gazette* published wire stories that dutifully recorded the number of arrests, offered details of fires that spread from tires to tenements, and provided quotes from the police department PR flack without bothering to delve into the cause of the problems. They published a graphic on page one that charted the estimate value of damage from the riots, laying all the blame at the feet of people who were burning down their own homes, businesses and churches within The Flats' borders.

Lazy *Gazette* reporters covered the story from the safety of their desks miles away and pumped predictable canned quotes from City Hall into their cursory coverage: "We are saddened by the lack of sense of community that residents of The Flats seem exhibit." "We implore civic leaders of the Latino community to call for peace." and "We are grateful to the men and women on our police and fire departments who are working hard to bring peace to our city."

The P-R covered the damage, too, but Jake wrote story after story about innocent people targeted by overzealous police, and an otherwise quiet, peaceful population frustrated by oppression to the point of breaking. Each story seemed to elicit the same response from City Hall and the police department — "we will lift the curfew, we will stop the patrols and we will end the random arrests, if and only when these criminals stop rioting."

Reigner stopped providing Jake with daily malapropisms for him to quote, opting for "no comment." He directed inquiries to the police chief, who was having the time of his life expressing his racist attitudes by unleashing the most violence-prone dogs in his kennel with unrestrained glee.

"Fuck 'em, and this is off the record" was Chief Burns' reliable pearl of wisdom whenever Jake could corner him long enough to ask a question. "These assholes want a fight, they'll get it. They seem to forget who has more guns, bullets and power, and we're happy to remind 'em."

Jake sensed trouble the minute he entered the newsroom.

Normally reporters were heads-down focused, heads swiveling from notes to their typewriters as they banged away at their IBMs, churning out stories even at the ripe hour of 7:30 a.m.

Not today.

An eerie quiet hung over the newsroom, its filmy pall turning the reporting staff into a nervous pack. They seemed shocked, nervously distracted, like politicians with election night jitters.

"What's up?" Jake asked BD on his way to his desk.

"Oh, man ... what a shitstorm. Zamboni's outta here ... been suspended, but you didn't get that from me. Transferred, actually, to Silvertown, which is more like being fired. Banished to the junior leagues.

"Ooops sorry," he added, remembering that Silvertown was Jake's hometown, and that he had done a stint at *The Eagle*. "You gotta admit, though, Silvertown's the cheap seats compared to Zamboni's front row in Rilertown."

"What happened?" Jake probed.

"Look at Betsey."

The wire editor was hunched behind her computer terminal. She seemed smaller, frail, somehow lesser, and her beet-red face broadcast her humiliation and culpability like a neon admission of guilt. Rounded shoulders sloped to nervous, twitchy hands that now and then grasped at a box of Kleenex well on its way to becoming empty as she pounded away at her terminal's keyboard.

"They got busted?"

"Yup. Big time. Apparently happened late yesterday when Mike copped a quick feel in the lunchroom. Thought no one was watching. He was wrong. I was here picking up a new scorebook, and Gladys was up Les's butt about the paper's fraternization policy.

It was pretty quiet in the newsroom so you could hear her pretty clearly..." (BD paused to grin) … "'specially if you happened to be hanging just outside Les's office.

"Someone apparently walked in on them, passed word along, and Gladys pounced. You know how she loves a staff controversy, and she loves to tuck it to the newsroom. To hook a big fish like Zamboni, though? She's nearly orgasmic. Looks like Betsey and Mike are on the outs, and since Mike's the senior manager, it's mostly his fault, so he's outta here like Vladmir."

Jake spotted Les entering the newsroom. The managing editor stopped, cleared his throat, and addressed the staff.

"Newsroom meeting," he bellowed. "Fifteen minutes. Conference room." He quickly moved to his office.

Minutes later Jake and his colleagues crowded into the conference room. It was standing room only for the nosiest gang in the city, an excited collection of what Spiro Agnew referred to as "nattering nabobs of negativism." No group rises to the challenge and adrenaline rush of disaster like a newsroom. Nowhere does word travel as fast as within the confines of a daily newspaper, where secrets are common knowledge, confidences fair game for water cooler chitchat, and harmful rumors traded like kids share baseball cards.

Today, the reporters already knew the overarching story; they were after the juicy details.

The P-R's senior management team occupied the head of the table.

A surprise visitor, Bill Surety — Jake's mentor from *The Silvertown Eagle,* sat to Les's right. Wick Dunn sat to Les's left. The three of them, seated, appeared tiny before the gleaming specter of Gladys McAvoy, who stood behind them, her radiant countenance and stony glare in happy evidence as she celebrated a major coup.

Gladys appeared an oasis of bliss in a desert of misery, compared to the other three who sat at the head of the table. She had center stage and took command. "OK, silence, please. We have an announcement to make.

"Senior management has decided to make a *temporary* change in newsroom leadership due to circumstances that we will not discuss in this meeting, or subsequently."

She puffed herself up, straightening the lace cravat at her neck.

"We are fortunate to have clear policies that support internal transfers within the company for instances where management changes such as these are made necessary by circumstances that are well beyond the purview of what is deemed acceptable behavior in terms of widely accepted legal and policy structure. Before turning this meeting over to Publisher Wick Dunn and Managing Editor Daniel Moore, I would like to remind each and every one of you that you are all bound by this company's employee manual, specifically the code of conduct therein. I advise you to periodically refresh your memories so you are acquainted with policy and our required behavioral code."

Gladys paused for maximum effect, smoothing a wrinkle that didn't exist on her blouse and boosting her chin toward the ceiling.

"None of you is above the broader interests of this newspaper."

Someone stifled a giggle.

Betsy groaned from her seat in the far corner, dabbing the corners of her eyes, which were hidden by a pair of enormous sunglasses. She slumped in her chair.

Wick took over.

"Thank you, Gladys. I'm sure these good people are all very aware of company policy and your — sorry, our — employee handbook."

He stood, beckoning Gladys to sit. She did, reluctantly.

"Effective immediately, news editor Michael Zamboni has been reassigned to *The Silvertown Eagle*, where he'll direct the news-gathering efforts of our sister newspaper. We have asked *The Eagle*'s news editor Bill Surety (nodding to Surety) to take over day-to-day operations of *The Post-Recorder* while we handle a number of internal administrative issues."

Internal administrative issues? Jake wondered. *As in how to break up the tawdry affair between our married news editor and annoying young wire editor who is bawling her eyes out and going to pieces in the corner of the conference room at this very moment?*

"Les has a few words, now."

Les took his cue, and rose.

"Look, people. It's business as usual around here, and I'll thank you to not speculate about all this stuff. None of that's going to help us get a newspaper out. I want you to meet your new boss, a man most of you know and all of us respect. So let me turn the meeting over to Bill for a few words, then we'll wrap this up."

Bill stood and offered an awkward introduction.

"For those of you who don't know me, I'm a pretty open-door kind of guy. I'm cut of the same cloth as Mike in many ways; not so much in others. I'm here to do the same as the rest of you: put out the best damned paper possible, six days a week.

"Expect me to take up right where Mike left off ..." he began, interrupted by a flurry of faint snickers and furtive glances at Betsey that implied the inadvisability of assuming Mike's entire list of responsibilities. "... as far as stories we're following and daily agenda. I'm here to help you put out the best damned small daily newspaper in the state. We have work to do, and it starts now. We'll have our daily editors' meeting at 10.

"I guess that's about it. I'm looking forward to working with all of you. Let's get at it."

"I'm sure you all have questions," Les resumed, rising to wrap up the meeting. "I'm equally certain I won't answer them, so spare all of us the time and pain of awkward exchanges. We'll keep you all posted as we figure out our long-term plans, but for now I'm not going to belabor the point. We all have roles that need our immediate attention. We have a paper to get out. I suggest we all get to work."

Gladys got in a parting shot.

"I have placed copies of the updated employee manual at the back of the room if anyone would like one. Please pick one up on your way out. Meeting adjourned."

Jake approached Surety as the reporters flowed from the conference room, shaking his hand and taking him aside.

"Fancy meeting you here," Surety smiled glumly. "Not sharing details, so don't ask," he said, pre-empting any attempt by Jake to pry details about the shakeup.

"What's this I hear about you carrying the load as *The P-R*'s star reporter? What has the world come to?"

"I see you haven't lost your edge, Bill," Jake teased. "Just doin' my bit. You know, race riots, dirty cops, crooked city hall … it's not the tough stuff like you're used to up in Silvertown, though. Exposes of bean suppers, investigations into county fair space allocations for the sheep exhibits …."

The kid learned quickly, Surety thought, noting Jake's use of sarcastic banter and acknowledging his adoption of the casual swagger typical of veteran reporters.

"I hope your copy's as sharp as your wit," Surety said, fixing Jake with a stare that was part in good humor and part something else. *A challenge?*

"Guess we'll find out, won't we?" Jake said, clapping his mentor on the back and heading to his desk.

After four months of unrest, the mayor finally accepted Cheecha's suggestion to seek an independent mediator to oversee talks and resolve the stalemate between The Flats Association and City Hall. The two sides began the task of finding common ground, and, ultimately, answers to issues that threatened the long-term prospects for Rilertown.

The Chamber of Commerce director and the head of the local United Way chapter had barked loudly and relentlessly into Reigner's reddening ears about how the troubles were affecting business. Fall arrived in Rilertown, and some businesses were already erecting Christmas decorations. No need to upset the important holiday shopping cycle with the untoward specter of civil unrest.

Once he was convinced that the city's economic prospects were at stake — not to mention contributions to his re-election campaign — Reigner begrudgingly appeared at the negotiating table, hand extended behind a false smile.

An uneasy calm settled over The Flats. The police responded by lifting the curfew on weeknights and reducing night patrols by half. Peace, at least for the moment, returned to Rilertown.

One night Jake was working late, fine-tuning a story about Eduardo Rivera, the eldest son of a single mother of three who had been roughed up by police as he walked to his home from the corner store. His arms loaded with a bag of groceries, Rivera had been hustling along the street to his family's apartment before the Tuesday night curfew descended. Two cops in a patrol car saw a young Hispanic male running along the street. They flipped on the lights and siren, hit the gas pedal, and cut the young man off as he hustled along the lower wards. Seconds later they had him in handcuffs, a spilled gallon of milk washing over a loaf of day-old bread on the sidewalk and into the trash-strewn gutter as they shoved him in the back of the cruiser and off to police headquarters for questioning.

Days later Jake spoke to Eduardo, who was still too rattled to venture from his apartment.

"I went to the store to buy milk and bread for my brother and sisters," Jake quoted him, "and I wound up a criminal. Made up charges because I went out to buy food for my family? It wasn't even curfew yet, and I had done nothing wrong. Nothing. What is wrong with these people?

"I lost my job because of this. My boss decided he didn't want a criminal working for him, and even though I did nothing wrong, I lost my job." Eduardo was near tears; once an impoverished janitor at one of the city's textile mills, now reduced to accepting donations from one of the city's food banks so his family could eat.

"Now look at us. What am I going to do?"

Jake finished typing the quote, pulled the last sheet of paper from his typewriter and sighed.

"Same shit, different day," he said to himself.

He was putting the cover on his typewriter when he noticed Lucinda headed his way. The two had spoken often since his return. In anticipation of their ritual Jake reached into his drawer for the hand cream as she approached.

"Hola, Jake. How're things?" she asked, accepting a dollop of cream and rubbing it into her leathery palms as she rested against his desk.

"Great, Lucinda. How are you? Your family? I'm sure it's great to have the curfew lifted weeknights. Makes it easier for everyone, huh?"

"Oh, yeah, you bet. It's been hard to get home from work at night. I'm one of the lucky ones, though. I still have a job."

Jake nodded. "It's been rough on a lot of people. In fact, I just finished writing a story about a young guy who was busted while heading home from shopping a few days ago, before the curfew was lifted. Cops arrested him and scared the hell out of him. Lost his job over it…"

Lucinda interrupted.

"You spoke to Eduardo? He's my cousin's son. Good kid, but he is very unlucky. He finally found a good job at the mill, after many years of struggles, and now he has lost that, too. He was the source of money for the family. My cousin depends on him. And after everything he has been through."

"Everything he's been through? What's up?" Jake probed.

Lucinda settled onto his desk, preparing for what looked like a long story.

"Eduardo used to work at a hotel up the valley a few years back — a good job, night clerk, maybe assistant manager one day if he had continued.

"But then that girl died…

"Girl? What girl?"

"She was, how you say, *una prostituta?* Eduardo said he had seen her many times at the hotel. She would come to meet men there. One night, she met several men at the hotel, Eduardo said, and she died. Eduardo learned about it when he went to work the next day. The cleaner found her, and someone called *la policia.* They said she just died.

"Police said she died alone and of natural causes. But Eduardo, he said…

"I am saying too much. It is the past." She dropped her feet to the floor, preparing to return to work.

"No, please. Continue," Jake encouraged, reaching for notebook and pen. His mind drifted back a year to the day he had taken over the general assignment beat for Rich Tennenbaum. Tennenbaum had left a stack of files in his care about pending stories and ongoing investigations. One of them involved the death of a young hooker. It had been the source of persistent gossip around the county that she had died not of natural causes, but from foul play.

Tennnenbaum's words came back.

"There were rumors of some major political players involved. Couple of big names, so I was told, but nothing specific."

"Go on," he told Lucinda.

"Eduardo is a good kid with a kind heart," Lucinda said. "He felt responsible, as though he should have said something. But he was silent. Afraid."

Jake leaned forward, pen poised above paper.

"He said she was not alone. She did not die alone. There were men with her, and Eduardo knows this, and he knows who they are. He also knows he should have spoken, should have told police what he had seen, but fear kept him silent, made him weak, afraid.

"I am older, and he trusts me. He told me what had happened, what he saw, and how he had kept quiet because he was afraid of what would happen to him and his family if he spoke. But the pressure was too much for him. He knew he could not keep his job and remain silent.

"So he quit his job, ashamed and afraid that the men would come looking for him. They know that he knows, and they are, as he told me, very powerful."

Jake scribbled in his notebook. She noticed.

"Oh, you cannot say I told you this. There would be trouble ..."

"Lucinda, please. You can trust me. I'm only just making notes so I don't forget all this." Indicating his notebook, "This is just for me. I am not going to use your name, but I would like to talk to Eduardo about this, quietly and confidentially — and soon."

Jake quietly explained the rules of reporting and what "off the record" and "for background" meant: If Eduardo would talk to him, he would use the information as facts for the story; Eduardo would not be named unless he agreed to it. Jake would seek other sources to provide quotes and corroborating interviews to shape the story and provide verification of the information Eduardo shared.

He paused.

"You understand?"

She nodded.

"Look. Just ask him to meet with me — just to talk. I promise I won't put his name in the paper unless he tells me it is OK.

Lucinda, Eduardo sounds like a good kid. He saw something he knows was wrong, and he should have spoken up at the time, but I understand why he didn't. Look what's been happening in The Flats. No one in your family, in your entire community, gets a fair shake from this city. I understand that he felt he couldn't speak up. To face people so much more powerful, so ruthless … I get it. There is no trust between The Flats and City Hall.

"But now it's time to speak. Tell him he can trust me. Tell him I am fair and I will not expose him to danger. Tell him to speak out for the dead girl. She deserves that much. And tell him this is a chance to show this city what you and your family are really all about."

Lucinda looked deeply into Jake's eyes and quietly assessed the young man who had become her friend.

She decided to trust him.

"I cannot say that he will agree to meet with you, but I will ask him," Lucinda said, rising from his desk and returning to the labor of a minimum-wage worker whose back was bent from the endless pressures of an unsympathetic world.

Jake watched her go. He fished through his desk, searching for the stack of files Tennenbaum had left behind. He soon found the one labeled, "Hooker/South Cranfield." Inside, wedged between the pages of a beefy police report, Jake found notes he had taken when he and RT had spoken months earlier:

"... death of a hooker in a hotel in South Cranfield about three years ago. Cause of death was natural ... head in a pillow....

"... nosed around on it ... couldn't get anything concrete... rumors of some political heavyweights involved ... Zamboni ordered me off the story ... maybe you'll get lucky.

Maybe you'll get lucky.

He rose, slid his chair neatly into his desk, slipped the file in his briefcase and headed home.

The next day passed with no word from Lucinda, and so did the next, and the next after that. Jake dutifully filed one-off stories that popped up on Surety's radar screen. He spent free time re-reading the file RT had left behind and researching background on the dead hooker case, calculating where to begin. He started with a visit to the country coroner's office so he could read the report on the young woman's death.

"Death by asphyxiation" read the report's findings, with the "accidental death" box checked.

Ana Chandrakar was 20 years old when she died in the spring of 1975. A native of Jaipur, India, she came to the US as a promising scholarship student to pursue a degree in marketing at the nearby state university. A brief story in a local daily newspaper about her death and an accompanying tiny obituary contained scant details of her life. She had come from a conservative Hindu family, the oldest daughter whose surname carried considerable meaning in her culture: gracious, God's favor, resurrection, playful, wanted, favored, beautiful, graceful, strong, clever, full of pride and bright.

The story quoted her college roommate, Beth Andrews: "She was so full of life — so full of promise. I don't know anyone as sweet and kind as Ana. This is a horrible loss for all of us who knew and loved her."

The story was passive, poorly reported and written, thin on sources and full of holes. Jake clucked his tongue in disapproval. It was typical crappy journalism produced by an overworked, underpaid small town scribe who was too busy and poorly trained to know how to source a story or ask questions. What resulted was bland, spiritless information.

"Local police are investigating the death of a 20-year-old exchange student in a South Cranfield hotel last night whose body was discovered by a hotel maid. Ana Chandrakar, of Jaipur, India, apparently died of incidental asphyxiation, according to initial police and medical examiner reports..."

The Medical Examiner's report was predictably sterile, clinical, and unhelpful.

Other than the fact that she was dead, the woman had otherwise appeared healthy: no signs of physical trauma, all internal organs normal and unremarkable, no positive findings in the toxicological report, so no drugs or alcohol were present. There was no sign of sexual trauma, though the woman had recently been *heavily engaged in sexual activity,* the report benignly stated.

So a healthy young woman just dies in a motel room? Jake asked himself? *That's it?*

Ana would have been 30 now, been back in India, working, or perhaps wiring money to her family from a well-paying job in Boston or New York. A promising young woman in untenable circumstances; a life prematurely snuffed. Jake instantly felt a kindred responsibility for her.

He noted the signature on the report: Richard Jamison, ME.

For 22 years Jamison had been reappointed time and again to the plum job as Bloomfield County Medical Examiner. He had a reputation as an acceptably competent ME with well-developed political acuity. Jamison needed the former skill set to perform the duties of his job; the latter, to keep it. The death doc's legendary butt kissing was the joke of the county employees, who gifted him with the nickname "Pucker." This charming moniker had two possible interpretations: the act of pursing one's lips to kiss the ass of those more senior, or, less complimentary, a description of an anus. Either fit just fine, most agreed.

The ME's domain reached from the Hazelton-Rilertown border of Bloomfield County roughly 30 miles north to the edge of

Silvertown, Jake's hometown. Jake knew the turf — and Jamison — fairly well from his days at papers in both cities.

"Pucker" managed his relationships with the county power brokers like an LA talent agent handles an A-list actress: with cautious deference and soothing, and boundless capitulation. Jake had encountered Jamison over other incidents and the contact had nearly always been unpleasant. The pudgy, irascible ME clearly had no use — and no time — for meddling reporters, or for that matter, anyone who didn't offer Jamison clout he could use or information he needed to get his work over with so he could head home to drink fine wine from his impressive collection. He was the consummate political hack: competent enough to keep his job, yet lazy and dependent on the powers that be to retain it.

Jake closed the file and handed it back to the clerk.

His next stop was the police station in South Cranfield, a tiny town of little significance halfway between Rilertown and Silvertown. South Cranfield was known for two things: The Paradise, a cruddy roadside "restaurant" frequented by long-haul truckers who ducked off Route 85 for a bite, a beer and a bit of exercise with one of the "dancers" who kept the transient clientele occupied; and the Pines Motel, where Ana had met her end.

Entering South Cranfield's tiny cop shop on the town's Main Street, Jake encountered a pleasant young desk officer who was more than happy to break the boredom of another day with a legitimate inquiry from the Fourth Estate.

"How's it going?" Jake opened with a smile, flipping open his wallet and displaying his press credentials to the officer. "I'm looking into the death of Ana Chandrakar and would like to have a look at the file. Can you help?"

Jake was used to Chief Burns' obstructionist blockade at the Rilertown police station, where obtaining anything more than details from the daily police log required submitting a Freedom of Information Act request. In South Cranfield, however, a question from the media meant something to do other than crossword puzzles and doodling on a pad of scratch paper to pass time.

The officer happily complied.

Moments later Jake was seated at a small desk near the duty officer with a half-inch file before him. Ana Chandrakar's name was on the tab, and the file included photos of her body at the scene. Jake tensed when he studied them.

So young ... and so pretty. What a shame.

He scribbled notes from the report, which also included details of the scene, results of interviews with the motel cleaner, who had found the body, and the hotel clerk on duty at the time: Eduardo Rivera.

The cleaner's comments were unremarkable.

Rivera's were anything but.

The woman had booked the room shortly after 7 on a Tuesday evening. She had arrived with no luggage, paid in cash, and had headed straight to the room. As far as Rivera knew she spent the time alone, he told police, though her room was well out of sight of the office since it was situated at the far end of the motel's right wing. *Yes, it was possible that she received visitors,* but the young man had not seen any guests enter the room. No one inquired about her at the front desk. She had not asked for a receipt, so Rivera had not given her one.

All "asked and answered questions" half-heartedly posed by cops ill-equipped to handle such inquiries, Jake noted.

Lousy questions usually elicit useless answers. As with reporting, cops acquire most of their valuable information not from initial queries, but from the follow-up questions. Sometimes, the best tidbits surface by just watching and waiting as subjects squirm and fidget during the interview. *First to talk loses* after asking a tough question, goes the crucial interview technique maxim. Good cops and reporters learn to ask and then sit, watch and wait for their subject to spill the beans.

The investigating cops on this case, however, had apparently missed the training session on effective interviewing. The investigation notes were porous and thin, and begged for more. Jake filled in some of the obvious gaps from his conversation with Lucinda and other information he had learned.

He studied the photocopied page of the reservation book from the date of Ana's fateful stay. Some entries contained names and such details as car registrations, while others were simply "cash" and lacked details. Ana's listing simply contained the room number, "one night" and "cash."

Jake jotted down the room numbers written next to each reservation and the guests' names. He would check the hotel next, and underlined "The Pines" in his notebook.

The report also contained a copy of Jamison's findings but little else. Jake handed the packet back to the desk officer, thanked him and left. Next stop: The Pines.

Jake parked in front of the motel's office, a mottled white box that rested between two 200-foot wings of rooms like a jetliner's cockpit. A weed-infested fieldstone walk led to the office door, marked by a light that glowed dimly even in the daylight hours. Its lens displayed an impressive collection of deceased insects that had also slept their last at The Pines.

Whoever was in charge was putting little effort into making The Pines presentable.

What a shithole.

The Pines was an oddity, as often a haven for travelers in search of a respite from the long, open stretches of Route 85 as for truckers and locals in search of a place to bed employees of The Paradise. It was the region's most notorious "no tell motel", where unpublished hourly room rates were paid in cash.

Bill Brown had built The Pines in the 1950s to benefit from the region's developing tourism. He bumbled along with a 50 percent occupancy rate during high season for years, barely breaking even but providing a place for him to live and a meager income. Route 85 and The Paradise came along a decade or so after he opened, adding two important revenue streams to his business.

Happy to accommodate the sound of opportunity knocking at his scuffed door, Brown bent the rules of conventional hotel/restaurant management he'd learned in his two-year college hospitality program by creating two methods of registering guests. He dutifully recorded income from legitimate sources along with guests' names, home addresses and car registrations on one side of the ledger; on the other he simply listed transient renters as "cash" with no further details.

The inconsistent reporting methodology made it easier for him to provide information to his accountant for tax-reporting purposes while protecting the anonymity of his cherished cash-paying customers, some of whom were regular. The daily receipts tally he submitted to his accountant listed only legitimate reservations. Cash transactions were simply ignored, the proceeds pocketed and unreported. This helped Brown keep his refrigerator stocked with 16-ounce cans of Schlitz while affording him permanent membership in the lowest possible tax bracket.

The left wing of the 24-suite motel was reserved for respectable itinerant travelers and their families; the right wing for hourly customers and their guests. Many a high school student had forked over his or her allowance and kissed their virginity goodbye in The Pines' simple rooms.

It was best to create a moat between such dissimilar constituencies, Brown believed, and he carefully managed any spillover during peak demands to keep complaints to a minimum and the occupancy and turnover rates as high as possible.

Sitting in the motel's parking lot, Jake flipped open his notebook and scanned his list of registrations. Legitimate bookings with names had been assigned to rooms on the left. Reservations listed as "cash" were on the right.

At 3 p.m. on a Wednesday there were only two cars in the parking lot. One, just to the right of the office occupied a spot labeled "manager." Another was parked in front of the last room on the right, Room 24, where Ana had been found dead.

Jake flipped his notebook shut and stuffed it into his jacket's inside pocket. He exited the car and headed for the motel office.

THE END OF A LIFE, REVISITED

The small bell over the motel office door rang noisily when Jake entered. A middle-aged guy with a prodigious beer belly in worn jeans and stained t-shirt appeared from behind a beaded curtain; a rural motel manager wrapped in clichés — two-day stubble, tousled, thinning hair, unfriendly, cold eyes. *Fish eyes,* Jake thought: *Dead eyes.* All that was missing to complete the picture was a cigarette butt dangling from the guy's lower lip. As if on cue, the guy produced a pack of Marlboros and a lighter and fired one up.

"Help you?" the guy asked, clearly disinterested.

"Yeah, I'm on my way through and might be looking for a room tonight. How're you set for vacancies?"

"You're kidding, right?" the guy said, taking a drag on the cigarette and blowing smoke at the ceiling. "Look around."

"Oh, OK, Sorry," Jake said. "So how much for one night?"

The guy's eyes narrowed. He leaned his elbows on the counter, drawing unnervingly closer and sharing a whiff of stale beer breath. "One night, or less than that?"

It took a moment for Jake to follow.

"No, just a night. I'm on my way through, as I said." The guy looked over Jake's shoulders at his car parked 50 yards away. A professional skeptic.

"Mass. plates. Where're you from?"

Tactical error on Jake's part. *Time to lie.*

"Oh, that's my sister's car. I'm from out of state, New York, actually, and I'm driving north to Burlington. I don't feel like doing five more hours behind the wheel tonight. Saw your sign off 85."

The guy eyeballed Jake mistrustfully.

"Thirty — cash; $40 if you use plastic."

"OK. I'm not sure, though … I mean, I don't know if I'm going to stay or try to log another couple hours heading north. It's still early. Is there a place to grab something to eat nearby?"

Brown smirked.

"Only place in town's The Paradise. Not sure I'd call it a restaurant, but you can eat there. Most people drink. Some go for the entertainment. Some people hire the entertainment and come back here for an hour or so." The desk clerk flashed a weak grin. He nodded out the window toward the car parked in front of Room 24. The guy was becoming a wellspring of tourism guidance.

After a few more minutes of spiritless chat Jake returned to his car. Casting a glance to his left, he noticed the car that had been parked in front of Room 24 was gone.

Foregoing the temptations of an early dinner at The Paradise, Jake's next stop was the Rilertown library, where he collected a stack of books and settled into a table near the window in the austere building across the street from City Hall.

He flipped open a textbook on forensic pathology and scanned the index for "smothering" and "asphyxiation."

"Bingo," he said aloud when his index finger hit paydirt. He began to scribble notes.

"Accidental smothering: most fatal smothering is accidental. An epileptic or intoxicated person may smother himself accidently by burying his face in a pillow or covering with bedclothes," he wrote. That would explain the large amount of cotton fibers removed from Ana's mouth and nasal passages discovered during the autopsy. He paused, remembering Sabrina's warnings to keep her clear of hard objects during grand mal seizures and her head turned to the side, away from pillows and bedclothes that could make it impossible for her to breathe.

"I can suffocate if I am face down when I'm having a seizure, baby. Be sure you turn me to the side...."

Jake read on.

"Homicidal smothering. Homicide is possible where the victim is incapacitated by drink or drugs, very weak or old, in ill-health or when the victim is stunned by a blow. Usually the mouth and nose are closed by a hand or cloth, *or the face may be forced into a pillow...*"

"Holy shit," Jake loudly blurted, eliciting an abrupt "Shhh!" and disapproving scowl from the librarian.

"... or the face may be forced into a pillow ..."

There was more.

"Autopsy: Obstruction by bed clothing, pillow, etc., applied with skill, may not leave any external signs of violence, especially in the young and old, except signs of asphyxia.

"When a face is pressed into a pillow, the skin around the nose and mouth may appear pale or white due to pressure, with cyanosis of the face ... the head and face may show intense congestion and cyanosis with numerous petechial hemorrhages ..."

Jake flipped back through the pages of his notebook and compared the notes in the pathology text to Jamison's report.

Cotton fibers in Ana's nose and throat. Evidence of cyanosis in her face, and a reference to petechial hemorrhages, which another text defined as "a tiny pinpoint red mark that is an important sign of asphyxia caused by some means of obstructing the airways."

All the symptoms were present and accounted for in the autopsy report, though the ME had failed to connect the dots.

Why?

Medical reporting wasn't Jake's forte; nor was investigating questionable deaths — but he was quickly learning.

The next day he headed to the state university, a sprawling green campus built around a huge football stadium in a town huddled against the banks of the Tee north of Rilertown. Clusters of high rise dormitories stood like awkward human warehouses where thousands of cows once roamed, providing housing and entertainment to a student body of 25,000. Locating the administration building, he scanned the directory and headed to the alumni office to track down Beth Andrews, Ana's roommate.

A couple of hours later, after working his way up the administrative food chain to convince the assistant director of alumni affairs to give him Beth's address and home phone number in Pennsylvania, Jake made his way back to his car.

A parking ticket graced his windshield.

"Shit," he muttered, grabbing the ticket and grimacing at the $10 fine.

But the ticket — a "non-reimbursable expense," according to Gladys's detailed P-R handbook — turned out to be a worthwhile investment when Jake reached Beth by telephone at home later that night. The young woman — now married with an infant daughter nursing at her breast — was at first reluctant to discuss her friend but soon decided to trust Jake. She was forthcoming and direct.

"Ana was a sweetheart, one of the nicest people you'd ever meet," Beth told him as Jake encouraged her to "help Ana receive justice."

"I know she was hooking on the side to pay for her education. It tore her to pieces, but she saw no option. We would sit up for hours and talk after she'd return from work — sometimes talking through the night — and she'd cry. She felt awful about it all, horrible, really, and hated herself for having to sleep with strangers to give herself a chance at a better life.

"You have to understand — where she came from, her family, her religion, the way Indian society regards women — it was all so very complicated. She was a deeply principled person, so it was so ugly, so awful for her to go to sleep at night knowing what she had become. It was all contrary to what she stood for, what she was all about."

Beth paused. Jake could hear Beth's infant daughter gurgle in the background.

"She saw it her only way out of a very difficult situation. She came to the US on a full academic scholarship. She was very bright … the first in her family to go to university, you know.

"Then came the budget cuts as the recession hit. Foreign financial aid went first, of course, and Ana found herself with a choice: either forget a degree and head back to India, or find a way to pay for it.

"She looked for jobs, tried to sign up as an au pair with one professor, even waitressed for awhile, but everything took too much of her time. It threw her whole life out of balance. She realized she would have to extend her stay in the US to work and get a degree, and that simply wasn't possible, as far as her family was concerned. She was very dedicated, an amazing student, so smart...."

Beth went on about Ana's competence and commitment, painting a vivid picture of a conflicted woman who, facing untenable circumstances that led to tough choices, made the difficult decision to survive by compromising her morality and ethics.

"It devastated her, but she saw it as the only way.

"I did what I could to help her make peace with it. I reminded her that one day she would look back on this time, and it would all fade. I reminded her that hooking was not who she was, but just what she had to do. It was an act of desperation that provided a simple solution. We talked about options to replace the money she got from hooking, but we never found an answer. It became the only thing we talked about, sadly.

"And then ... she was gone."

Jake asked about the night Ana was found by police and the days that followed.

"The police asked me why I thought Ana was in the motel. I didn't see any reason to tell them about her moonlighting. What good would it do? It would have ruined her reputation as well as her family's. It would have destroyed their memory of her, so I didn't tell them.

"I told them she sometimes booked a hotel room to get away, rest, or study without distractions. Funny thing is that would be just like Ana. It made the lie all the more plausible. Was that a mistake? I don't know, and it's a question I will ask myself for the rest of my life."

"Beth, did Ana talk about any regulars?" Jake probed.

Long pause. Big sigh.

"Yeah, there was this guy from down the valley — some big shot. She despised him, but she said he was very connected and paid well. He would call her, set up a meeting in the hotel — the same place she died — and she'd meet the same group of men every time. She made more in one night with that guy and his pals than she'd otherwise make in a week, but I could see how it troubled her, punished her."

"Punished her?" Jake pressed.

"Yeah," Beth answered with a sigh. "It seemed they liked it rough, from what Ana told me.

"It went on as long as I knew her. I think she sort of fell into a routine with them, and it seemed to bother her less as the time went by.

"She said the guy who contacted her was a big golfer, some hotshot involved in business development. She thought he was a jerk, but she wasn't afraid of him. The others, though, well she said she thought they were very powerful men and there would be big trouble for her if word leaked about … about, well, you know … their meetings."

Jake hung up after speaking with Beth for several more minutes and sat staring at the ceiling, deep in thought, considering his options and plotting his next moves.

BREACH OF PROTOCOL

Jake spent the next morning fruitlessly chasing down rumors of a fish virus that was threatening the annual shad migration up the water company's fish ladder and into the Tees' spawning grounds upstream.

A fisherman heading to his favorite spot near the Rilertown Water Power Company fish ladder's exit chute had come upon a collection of dead shad rolling about in an eddy below a rock in the river. The sight of dozens of dead shad with bloated bellies bobbing on the water alarmed the fisherman. He alerted water company authorities through a night watchman who shared the fisherman's love of cold beer and fresh shad. He, in turn, filtered word out through the city's fishing community. A couple days later someone dropped a dime to *The P-R*, and Surety assigned Jake to find out what was going on.

He talked to water power officials, faculty at the university agricultural college, and the regional director of the Massachusetts

Fisheries and Wildlife Authority, reaching dead ends. Toxicology tests on the fish were negative. Unexplained deaths, the Wildlife spokesman said.

"Looks like it was just a bunch of dead fish," he told Surety. "No story there, best I can tell."

Surety wasn't thrilled to have invested precious reportorial resources on a red herring. You fish, you catch, in the world of newspaper management. There is no room for empty nets in the columns of a daily newspaper.

"Great. Just great," Surety said, pen tapping impatiently on his desk. "So what else do you have for me?"

"Can we talk in your office?" he asked Surety, and followed the man into the cramped space next to the wire room.

Jake had pursued Ana's story well outside the boundaries of typical newspaper protocol, keeping his research to himself and quietly reporting on the story while filing reams of copy on randomly assigned stories to meet his unstated quota. Now he faced a decision: continue his solo expedition or bring Surety up to speed.

He trusted Surety, so he owned up.

"Bill, there's something I've been working on … a story that Tennenbaum worked for awhile then abandoned."

The editor scowled, unhappy to learn his protégé had gone rogue.

Settling into the chair across the desk from news editor, Jake briefed him on his progress.

"Here's what I've learned so far…"

An hour later Jake leaned back in his chair, having revealed what he had learned, outlining his progress and explaining his plans for additional research.

Surety didn't look convinced.

"I know this is using a lot of my time, but I think it's worth following. There's something here; I just know it, and I think I know how I can get it nailed down. I've got a source I need to talk to."

Surety studied the young reporter.

"So why am I hearing about this now? You've been spending P-R time and money looking into a story and you don't tell the news editor? What's with that?"

Jake explained Tennenbaum's parting advice.

"He suggested that I keep my eyes and ears open, and he also told me that Zamboni had ordered him off the story.

"I wasn't pursuing it at all. It was buried in a file in my desk, until I got a tip about Eduardo … you know, the kid I interviewed who was roughed up by cops a couple weeks ago … and started to put things together."

Jake talked for a few more minutes, doing his best to convince Surety to let him continue working on the story. He provided details of Eduardo's remarks to police that conflicted with what he had since learned.

"Sounds like you have a shred of something here, but if you can't get the kid to talk, there's really no story. Sorry, Jake, but I can't have you spending your time on a solo expedition that doesn't produce copy. You have to earn your keep, and that means filing stories I can use. You can have a week, but keep me posted."

He leaned forward and fixed Jake with an unblinking stare.

"No more secrets. Got it?"

He wasn't finished.

"And what about that industrial safety piece Zamboni assigned you to? Where are you on that?"

Jake sighed. Weeks earlier, prompted by an injury to a worker on a paper mill production line, Zamboni had assigned Jake and fellow reporter Paul Dzkiekonski to examine the manufacturing industry's safety track record. Jake and "PD" made headway through their initial questions of state and federal safety officials but hit a dead end during a disastrous meeting with the city's industrial safety liaison.

"Not much there, really," Jake told Surety, testing a passive approach.

"I hit a dead end ... need to get some momentum back, find someone to talk about safety trends in the city. It's tough working on it alone, and since I don't know when PD will be back…" Since Surety was new to *The P-R*, Jake summarized PD's mental breakdown that occurred during their meeting with the city's safety overlord.

Jake reconstructed the day, one of the worst of his career.

PD — a quirky general assignment reporter known for his dogged determination as a reporter and as a moonlighting, amphetamine-popping front man for his punk rock band, Choking On Magnets — had begun to fidget nervously during a high level meeting with the safety manager as Jake fired questions. They were making headway in their primary objective of obtaining a look at a stack of statistics the manager was guarding like the king's larder when PD became visibly agitated. Jake cast increasingly worried glances at PD as he struggled to gain the manager's trust.

Then, just when the guy turned the papers so Jake could get a look and scribble some notes, PD came completely unglued.

"I have to get the fuck out of here!" he screamed, scooped up the papers from the shocked manager's desk, tucked them under his arm and rushed across the office. He fled through a door that he thought led to the exit but actually led into a storage closet. He slammed the door shut behind him.

The manager glared at Jake.

"What's this? Stealing documents? Is this the way you operate?"

In an instant, all the trust Jake had carefully worked to construct dissipated into the murky mist of PD's sudden departure from reality.

"Honestly, I have no idea what's going on here," Jake stammered apologetically, crossing the room to coax PD out of the closet and to return the documents. He knocked on the door. "Paul. Come on out. It's OK. Paul…"

Several seconds passed before the door opened and PD sheepishly emerged, his typically disheveled hair and mangy beard in remarkable further disarray, and with a wild look in his eyes that looked to Jake like serious trouble.

"Gimme those," said the manager, ripping the documents out of PD's quivering hands and ushering the two out the door and into the corridor, slamming the office door behind them.

"What was *that?*" Jake asked PD as they exited the building. His questions failed to elicit a response. PD had slipped into some sort of ambulatory coma and was muttering unintelligibly.

The P-R's temporary leave of absence policy kicked in, and PD retreated to his studio apartment under the care of a mental health professional who proclaimed him "upset but stable" and recommended two weeks of rest. Word in the newsroom was that PD soon would be back, but Jake wasn't so sure.

One day he took a call from his unstable friend just before deadline.

"You're not gonna believe this," PD said breathlessly. "I've been listening to Toxic Demise for 26 straight hours, drinking coffee and sitting in front of the mirror. I've made a new friend. Ready for this? It's a fly. Name's Alex. He's cool. Just hangs out with me...."

PD's instability imperiled the story's momentum, Jake explained, privately celebrating the disruption.

It's *probably* a good thing. This story's a dog.

Surety shattered Jake's rambling reverie by slamming his empty coffee cup on his desk. Impatient with what he perceived as wasted time, Surety quickly brought Jake back to the present. Jake forged ahead, working to appease Surety while completing his outline of a story that had ceased to interest him.

He tried to dissuade his editor from pursuing the story.

He failed.

"You and crazy man spent time on this story, so write what you have," Surety growled. "I don't have the luxury of writing off hours of your time."

Jake shifted tactics.

"How about giving me some help wrapping it up? I was able to dig up some statistics on industrial accidents, and I have a good bunch of background outlining the mills' safety records, but it's really just a bunch of history, and numbers. Pretty boring."

That ought to get him to drop the story. Why bother with a boring story full of statistics? A burger without meat is just a bun.

Surety wasn't biting. He smiled sweetly at Jake.

"Nice try. Give me 36 inches. See the art department for some graphics. We'll run it Saturday morning," he said, consigning the story to the worst possible day for publication. At 36 column inches, the piece would be twice the length of Jake's longest article and would be published on the lousiest day possible. Readers tend to forego long stories, and the Saturday morning edition was death valley to reporters; the dumping zone for boring, poorly written stories with zero impact — just like this one.

"You got it," Jake conceded, rising to leave.

"And Jake," Surety added. "One week on the hooker story. That's it."

Two hours later Jake was pounding away at his typewriter, sorting through notepads of notes and copies of documents about the safety records of Rilertown's manufacturing sector — a pointless exercise of recitation that Jake approached with the enthusiasm of a trip to the dentist. Paragraph by tortuous sentence, he constructed the story in a desultory act of duty.

His ringing telephone interrupted his joyless march.

"Ketcher," he said, cradling the phone.

"Mr. Ketcher. It's me. Eduardo Rivera. My cousin said you wanted to talk to me."

Jake's heart raced. He reached for a pen and notebook.

"Hey, Eduardo. Thanks for calling. Yeah, I have a few questions to ask you … did your cousin tell you what I'm working on?"

"Yes, she did," the young man replied. "But I'm afraid to talk to you. I mean, Lucinda told me I can trust you, but I'm scared. First the police pick me up, and now this … You understand that this involves very powerful people. I'm not sure."

"Please, Eduardo. Just meet with me. I can come to you, or we could meet someplace, anywhere you want … how about this afternoon…?"

"No," the young man said emphatically. "I do not want to be seen in my neighborhood with you. It is not good for me. There are many eyes watching in this neighborhood, and people talk. I will come to you — to your office — at 4. I will meet you at the back door, at the employee entrance, where my cousin goes to work. Four o'clock." He abruptly hung up.

At 3:45 Jake began watch on the picnic bench outside *The P-R* employee entrance at the rear of the building, the sun filtering through a bank of fluffy clouds, warming his back. He nervously fingered his press badge, which doubled as a passkey to the back door and hung around his neck on a Doobie Brothers lanyard. He was lost in thought about Ana, the industrial safety story, and Sabrina, so he didn't see the young man quietly approach from the side of the building.

"Mr. Ketcher...?" Eduardo said, startling Jake.

Moments later they were seated in *The P-R*'s conference room, cups of coffee in front of them. The room made Eduardo seem smaller than his 5'5" frame. Jake opened his notebook and jumped in. He explained how the interview would proceed, giving Eduardo broad latitude for "off the record," "not for attribution" and "for background only" protections. He provided an overview of what he had learned about Ana, her history and family, and what he had pieced together about her death so far, quietly sharing details in an easy conversational tone to put the man at ease.

He worked to gain the young man's trust and confidence.

"I want you to tell me what happened, Eduardo, in your own words. Your name will not appear anywhere in this story unless you want it to.

"I am going to take notes, but they stay in this notebook unless you tell me it's OK to use them. OK? So you're safe. No one will know you talked to me unless you say it's OK. I promise.

"Just tell me what you saw."

Eduardo drummed the table with his fingertips and stared at Jake.

He paused, gathering his thoughts.

"Lucinda said I can trust you. OK. So I will. But you understand: these men covered up a murder, so I don't think they will care about me. I am in danger, Mr. Ketcher, and I am afraid. That means my family is already in danger, and it will only be worse if you write this story.

"But these men cannot go unpunished. She died with them, and she seemed so sweet, so kind. Every time she came to the motel…"

For two hours Eduardo revealed to Jake what he had seen the night Ana died — as well as other nights like it when she had met the same men at the motel. He spoke in clear, even tones, occasionally with anger and often with remorse.

"She always spoke nicely to me. She was polite, embarrassed … I could see it in her eyes," the young man said.

"I was not on duty when they found her. I learned about it when I went to work the next night, and I knew the police would be there to speak to me. They came just after my shift started — my hours were five until midnight — and questioned me for a long time."

He grew quiet.

"I told them I knew nothing, other than that she rented the room farthest from the office, which is why I did not see anything. They asked me if I had seen her before. They asked me if I knew anything about her, why she was at the motel, or what she was doing. I told them I knew nothing, that I just booked the rooms and took the money. But that was a lie. I told them many, many lies."

He shook his head, distraught.

Jake saw the opportunity to press for more.

"Did you see the men, Eduardo? Do you know who they were?"

Eduardo paused again, drumming the table.

"Yes. I saw them all, but I only recognized two of them. I saw them, clearly, but I do not think they saw me. They never came to the office. But I could see them from the office window, every time they came to meet her. Yes, I know who they are. Who doesn't?

"One was Rilertown's city council chairman, McFadden. The other was Reigner, the mayor."

THE REST OF THE STORY

"Are you 100% sure, Eduardo?"

The young man nodded. "I see these men's faces on TV and in the paper all the time, usually talking about my people as though we are rats in their city.

"Yes, I am sure it was them. I will remember their faces until my dying day — but not as Rilertown politicians, as men who were with that young woman when she died."

"Did you see them enter the room?" Jake asked, urging Eduardo to recreate the scene.

"Yes. They parked around the back so their cars wouldn't be seen, as usual, but they had to walk along the front by the office to get to the room. Mr. Brown lets the bushes grow by the far end of the building so people cannot sneak out without paying. They have to walk past the office. Most times the clerk is behind the registration desk, out of sight from the sidewalk, and we don't see most people as they make their way to the rooms. But I felt … responsible for the young woman. She was…"

The young man paused in obvious distress. Second thoughts? "What is it, Eduardo?" Jake asked. "Tell me."

"It's just that she was so young, so pretty ... and she seemed so nice ... so kind to me. And now I know she was a student at the university, so she must have been very smart as well. She was not a common prostitute, Mr. Ketcher. I have seen others at the hotel who were, but not that young woman. No. For her to have to make money doing such things must have been very difficult, and to die in such a way..."

"Yes, I know," Jake said, pushing harder. "That's why I want to get this story. These guys are responsible for her death, or at least they're witnesses. They've gotten away with this for years. This is my chance — our chance — to make them responsible for this — and for all the stuff they've done to hurt people.

"Your arrest. The horrible things you and your family and friends have been put through ... all due to City Hall's racist attitudes and policies. McFadden and Reigner have brought so much misery to Rilertown — even my girlfriend's death," Jake allowed. He related how Sabrina had died, and how Ted Price had arranged for Sabrina's killer to receive a light sentence.

"And of course there is Ana and her memory," Jake concluded. "She deserves a defense, someone to speak for her. You're right: she was beautiful, smart and good hearted. She didn't deserve to die at all, let alone as she did. So you see how important this is. But I have to get this absolutely right. There can be no error, no mistake in whether they were there at the moment she died. I will have to talk to the cleaner, of course, and a couple other sources to find out who the others were.

"Did you see the other two as well? Can you identify them?"

"I saw them clearly ... and many times. But I do not know who they are," Eduardo conceded.

"Do you think you would recognized them if you saw them again?"

"I will remember those men's faces forever," Eduardo said, "as well as my shame for not telling the truth to the police."

Eduardo paused, kneaded his temples. "But you cannot use my name. I cannot be identified by these men. I don't care what happens to me; I care about my family. These men would target them. You don't know what it's like to be like us. No one will protect us. Anything could happen; I have seen it. It is a risk I cannot afford. I'm sorry, Jake, but you can't say I told you any of this. You are free to use this information if it will help you, but keep me and my family out of it. Please."

Jake placed a hand on Eduardo's forearm.

"You're doing the right thing now, and that's what matters. You're doing just fine, Eduardo. You're telling the truth, and it's not too late. Can I use this information as coming from an anonymous source, just not use your name?"

"And say the information came from someone at the motel?" Eduardo pursed his lips and shook his head. "Any fool would figure it out, and these men are not stupid. I was the only night manager, Jake. No one else would know who was with the young woman. No, this would bring more trouble to my family, and I cannot let that happen. I'm sorry."

The two spoke for another half hour, and Eduardo rose to leave. Round-shouldered and dour-faced, he was the picture of defeat.

Jake walked him through the vacant newsroom and out the front door, convincing him it was safe to exit the building and walk down the hill to the bus stop. "Don't worry. You won't be seen. It's nearly seven o'clock. It's dark outside and everyone's gone by now."

The two exited the double doors entering the building's portico, chatting about the story and what Jake planned to do. Jake reached to open the exterior door when Eduardo stopped. He stared, ashen-faced, at the display of photos on the wall. "These are the men and women of the Rilertown *Post-Recorder*," read the headline over the display.

Eduardo pointed to one photo displayed prominently in the center.

"That's him," he said, pointing to Zamboni's photo. "That man."

"What do you mean, Eduardo? That's Michael Zamboni, my boss. What about him?"

"He was with Ana, and the other men ... at the motel that night. And many other nights like it."

Jake hustled Eduardo out the door and onto the bus then took a long walk to gather his thoughts.

The day had turned sour, and the temperature plummeted 15 degrees by nightfall. Numbed by Eduardo's revelation to the point of being immune to the chill, Jake walked to the crest of the hill behind *The P-R* and looked down on twinkling lights of the city below.

Reigner.

McFadden.

And Zamboni — Zamboni who had called Tennenbaum off Ana's story, not to preserve precious P-R reporting resources, but to protect his own ass. Jake's mind reeled as he struggled with it all and contemplated his next move.

He had the identities of three of the men. Now he needed the fourth. But Eduardo's refusal to speak on the record threatened the story's foundation. He still had work to do.

He thought back to his interview with Beth Andrews, Ana's college roommate.

"She said the guy who contacted her was a big golfer, some hotshot involved in a major business development. She thought he was a jerk, but she wasn't afraid of him. The others, though, well she said she

thought they were very powerful men and there would be big trouble for her if word leaked about about, well, you know, their meetings."

He recalled his talks with Beebo, her relationship with Thompson and to his dalliance with a prostitute.

"See, Thompson and me, we used to be an item. He's a dick, but he's rich, always buys the drinks, and is great in the sack. At least he was until he moved onto some other chick, some hooker he liked to brag about, as if renting a hooker required talent."

Thompson.

Prostitute.

Bingo.

"Well, hello, Blake," Jake said out loud. But Thompson was dead, and the others at the motel that night would hardly confirm his presence.

I'm going to have to confirm this from another angle.

What to do?

"I'm way over my head," he said aloud as he stared down at Rilertown's rugged skyline and across the dingy brick tenements of The Flats. Night had forced the city's ills into the shadows. Jake knew he needed more if he were to take on this powerful troika and forever alter the city's profile. He needed someone to help complete the picture — someone in the know, someone he could trust.

"Beebo," he said, rising and making his way down the hill to his car.

Beebo was predictably tucked away in a darkened booth at La Bamba. A half empty Corona rested in front of her, a slice of lime suspended halfway between the bottle neck and rock bottom. She nodded to Jake then at the beer. "Grab me another of these, willya?"

"Sure," Jake responded, "but let's talk somewhere a bit less public. There's a booth at the rear, by the pool table. I'll grab the brews and meet you there, okay?"

Jake walked to the bar, paid for two Coronas and then joined her in the bar's darkened recesses.

"So what's up, Jake? Long time. You finally decide to start dating?" Beebo shot him a lascivious grin. She was halfway to drunk. Jake knew he needed to move fast before the booze completely took over.

"Thanks for the compliment, Beebo. When I decide to put myself back on the market you'll be the first to know. For now, though, I'm still active in the monkhood." He smiled at the young woman, marveling at yet another color she had imposed on her hair, this one an incandescent green.

"Nice do, you. You look like your father mated with a parrot."

She smiled dismissively at the familiar dis.

"So you've said in the past — many times, in fact. But the mere thought of my dad copulating with anything makes me ill..." she said with a shudder. "You said this was urgent. So what's up?"

Jake swore Beebo to secrecy then outlined the story about Ana's death and the four men who were with her when she died. He left out the names, telling her only that he knew who three of the men were and was after the identity of the fourth.

He shared Beth's description of the man who contacted Ana to arrange for her services.

"Big shot golfer, business development, and a jerk. Sure sounds like our boy Blake Thompson, doesn't it?" Jake said.

Beebo quietly studied her beer bottle as if it held the answer — or as though seeking refuge within the bottle and its chilled, alcoholic safety, invisible among the bubbles.

She took a deep draught, then rested the bottle on the cardboard coaster.

"Blake was into all kinds of weird shit," she said slowly. "A whole boatload of very, very weird shit.

"I'm pretty sure he was connected to the New York mob — at least that's where he got his investment money. I have no idea how he made his money otherwise. I mean, he never really worked that I saw, only golfed and partied with other big shots, always picking up the tabs.

"It was like he had an endless supply of dough."

The tone of her voice turned apologetic.

"He was great fun for awhile. Like I said, he always bought the rounds and he was great in the sack. But then I found out about the hooker, as I told you. Ana, you say her name was?"

Jake nodded.

"Yeah. That was it for me. I wasn't about to risk coming down with some disease 'cause my squeeze was fishing in dirty ponds. No way. Even I draw the line somewhere, Jake."

She smiled faintly, and straightened her shoulders.

"You are asking me if I know anything that would tie Blake to this woman's death. Well, maybe I do, and maybe I don't. And if I do, I'm sure a bright boy like you can figure out what that means for me, only daughter of Rilertown's chief of police. You're a friend, but you're asking me to put my sorry butt on the line for you. Assuming I do know something that would help you, if I were to take such a drastic step, I want to know what's in it for me."

Jake had anticipated this moment.

"Look, Beebo, I know you and your dad aren't exactly on great terms, but if my guess is right on this story he would be in a position to either cement himself as Rilertown's shining example of police excellence or go down with the ship. He's going to have to decide whether to help take down two of his bosses, or cover their asses.

"He's gonna face a choice, just like you are, and I'm betting he'll follow the law, straight-liner as he is. So it's down to you.

"You can help, or you can sit by and watch as the tide rolls over you and pulls you out to sea."

The young woman stared at her bottle.

"Then there's this, Beebo: A young woman died; little younger than you, actually. She had promise and made some tough decisions to give herself a shot at a better life. Had she been allowed to simply finish her education, there's no telling what she'd be doing right now. She just got a bad bounce and didn't recover.

"Sound like anyone else you know?

"And there's one more thing." Jake paused. "This is me asking, Beebo. Jake. Your friend. Gotta ask yourself, how many real friends do you have in this world? When you get around to counting them, how about starting with me?"

Beebo looked up. A tear had gathered in her right eye and now made its way along the edge of her nose. She wiped it away with the back of her hand.

"OK," she said.

In the course of two more beers Beebo gave Jake a notebook full of details. Blake's mouth was the only thing more open than his wallet when it came to nurturing political and business relationships.

"He told me he had rented this chick for three clients a bunch of times. He bragged about it, like it was some major conquest or something."

She looked from her bottle to Jake's eyes.

"I mean, what kind of a jerk brags about hiring a hooker? As if anyone can't make a phone call, find a girl who's willing to do just about anything for a few bucks…"

"Did he say anything else about her?"

"Just that she was smokin' hot, and Indian, or Pakistani or something…"

"Did he ever say who the other guys were?" Jake pressed.

"Nope, but there was a photo, a Polaroid he snapped one night at the hotel while they were all drinking and carrying on. He took a bunch of them. He loved to take Polaroids. I've been in a few of 'em," Beebo smiled sheepishly, "but I managed to get my hands on the ones he took of me. They weren't what you'd call family photos — nothing I'd like circulated to some nosy reporter or, God forbid, my father.

"Blake said the other guys were pissed that he took their photos, and they demanded that he get rid of them all. He gave all but one back to them; said he kept it as insurance. I got a good look at it when I was scooping all my photos from Blake's collection when I hit the road."

"You're killing me here, Beebo," Jake said, "Who were they?"

"Your buddies Reigner, McFadden and your dear boss Michael Zamboni."

Jake's mouth went dry.

"Jesus, Beebo. You've known me for how long? And you've known I work for Zamboni. You know much I despise that jackass. And yet you just get around to telling me this now? Holy shit."

"Yeah, some friend, huh?" Beebo allowed.

"I held out on you, for sure, but go easy, champ. You think I'm gonna stick my neck out, the alcoholic, disenfranchised and despised daughter of Rilertown's finest, and implicate four powerful men, each of whom would delight in crushing me as sport?

"Why would I? There was no story, Jake, not until you dug into it, not until you figured it all out. I'm thinking you knew that I would have what you need to wrap this up, somehow. That's why you saved me for last. You have the gun. And you have the targets. You needed someone to put a bullet in the chamber so you could pull the trigger. And the photo is the bullet."

Jake leaned closer.

"Do you have it? The photo?"

"I'm a sucker for sentimental mementoes, particularly when they're photos of a dead former boyfriend with his mates at a murder scene. Do I have the photo? You bet your sweet ass I do, sugar. Now, how about another round?"

Jake slid the photo across Surety's desk and sat in silence as the news editor picked it up and studied it.

The color Polaroid depicted three men clearly enjoying themselves. There was Zamboni, loosened tie against his white shirt as he slouched in a chair in the nondescript room, grin on his face and bottle of beer in hand. His feet were planted on the edge of a coffee table strewn with bottles and an overflowing ashtray. To the left, sprawled on a small sofa, were McFadden and Reigner. The three looked as though they were sharing a joke, with big smiles and a general air of joviality.

"Jesus fucking Christ."

"Yeah, you've already said that," Jake countered. "Twice, in fact."

"Let's talk this through, Jake. Mike was there, in the room? We're gonna have to get Les and Wick involved eventually, but, oh, man ... this a murder investigation, fer Chrissake ... and it's been dormant for, what, 10 years? I'm not even sure what the statute of limitations is..."

"Six years for manslaughter, Bill. No limit for murder two or murder one. I checked."

Surety played with his tie and studied the ceiling.

"OK, so here's where we are. You have the motel clerk placing Reigner, McFadden and Zamboni at the motel the night the girl died, right?"

Jake nodded.

"But that's off the record, right?"

"Right."

"You have this photo of the three of them in a room, but no confirmation where or when it was, right?"

"Yup."

"You have the ME report, which only specified that she suffocated, but ruled out foul play, right?"

"Right again."

Surety stroked his chin.

"So you have a bunch of loose ends that you need to tie together if we're going to take down not just the mayor and city council chairman, but also one of the executives of this newspaper. I mean, holy shit, Jake."

"I know, I know," Jake conceded. "So here's what I'm doing next."

Shortly before six Jake parked around the corner from The Pines. Soon, a rotund middle-aged woman made her way out of the motel office and onto the sidewalk that ran along the side of the road. She turned right, as Jake expected, and walked toward the bus stop.

Jake exited his car and followed on foot, catching up with the woman as she strolled in the dim light.

"Mrs. Williams?" he asked, startling her. "I'm Jake Ketcher, from the newspaper in Rilertown. Eduardo Rivera said I should talk to you." He displayed his press credentials and spoke quietly to the woman, who at first appeared guarded but then relaxed as Jake explained his interests. She shrugged and accepted his offer for a cup of coffee at a nearby diner and a ride home, then followed him to his car.

Mary Williams was typical western Massachusetts working class: a hard worker, dedicated homemaker, wife and mother; born of strong, reliable parents who raised her right and did their best to send her into the world with a good heart and strong constitution. She attended South Cranfield High School, where she met her husband, Bobby. After graduating they married straight away and settled into a respectable though challenging working class life. They soon had two kids, a daughter and a son who were now both grown and gone and had spouses of their own. Both children and their partners were regulars for Sunday dinners at the plain but pristine house that Mary and Bobby Williams had called home for nearly 40 years.

She had landed the job as cleaner at The Pines when Bill Brown bought the place years earlier and proved perfect for the job. To Brown's delight, Mary knew how to clean, was solid and reliable, didn't demand regular wage increases and rarely called in sick. Importantly, she also knew how to keep her mouth shut.

Bobby needed the car to commute 20 miles to work each day, so Mary used the Valley Bus Association to get to and from work Mondays through Fridays. Her life was a predictable grid of solid, reliable, unremarkable schedules. Week in and out, not much changed in Mary or Bobby's lives.

Mary, on the honor roll of attendees at the South Cranfield Methodist Church, was morally repulsed by the shenanigans that went on behind The Pines doors, often complaining to Bobby about the wicked ways of the motel's transient business. But jobs were hard to come by in western Mass., and since Bobby's overtime as a university maintenance worker had disappeared as quickly as the hair on the top of his head, principles took a back seat to necessity. Moral convictions don't put food on the table or pay the oil bills.

"Live and let live," read the slogan on Mary's key chain that held two keys: one to her house, the other to The Pines office. She placed the key chain on the table that separated her from the nice young man who had convinced her to have coffee with him.

She smiled at Jake.

"It was awful, that young woman dying like that, in that place," Mary said, wrinkling her nose as though detecting a foul odor beneath the diner's tattered table. She paused as the waitress brought two steaming cups of coffee, thanking her and then turning back to Jake. Waiting for the waitress to move out of earshot, she poured three tiny vessels of cream into the cup, added three packets of sugar and stirred slowly, scowling.

"But that all happened years ago. And I told the police everything I knew. Why are you asking about it now?"

"Please, Mary. Just tell me what you found that day," Jake said, producing a notebook. "Let's just say that I've come upon some new information. Something that raises new questions about what happened in that room — something that might answer the question of how Ana Chandrakar died — something that might give her justice.

"So just tell me what you can remember, please. I'm going to take some notes, OK? Just so I keep everything straight."

Mary nodded.

"I came to work, as always, 10 a.m. I work 10 to 6, with a half an hour for lunch, that's my deal with Mr. Brown, always has been." She took a sip of coffee and seemed to steel herself, shifting in her seat and adjusting the worn collar on her faded print dress.

"I started with Room 28. Always do. I knocked on the door to make sure the room was empty. When I opened the door I knew something was wrong straight away. It was clean. Not a lick of dust, paper or dirt in the sitting room. It was as though no one had been there. It was very unusual. Odd. I knew it had been occupied the previous night. It was marked so on the day sheet — that's my list of rooms to clean.

"So I went into the bedroom, and that's when I found that poor, poor girl…." Mary paused, shaking her head and grasping her coffee cup with both hands, drawing from its warmth.

"She was lying on her side, under the covers, and I spoke to her, thinking she might be asleep. Then I spoke louder … and then I knew … I just knew she was dead. I scampered quick-fast back to the office, told Mr. Brown. He called the police. I knew enough to leave the room be, and I locked it behind me when I left and didn't touch a thing.

"I was shaking I was so upset, so terrible. I've never in my life seen anything so horrible.

"That poor girl. To have died like that."

"Like what," Jake prompted.

"Alone. In a motel room, all alone. And so young…."

Jake paused for a moment to allow Mary to collect herself.

"Could you describe the room?"

"Well, I guess I could," Mary collected herself, took another sip of coffee and continued. "I know that room — every one of 'em, actually — as well as I know my own home. "The door opens to a sitting room, where there's a TV, arm chair, sofa — you can pull that out into a bed if guests have children, though that's pretty rare — a couple of end tables, a coffee table and two lamps. Lovely paintings in that room, two of 'em."

"That's great, Mary," Jake interrupted. "I'm going to show you a photo that has three men in it, but I want you to see if the room looks familiar to you. If you recognize the men that's OK, too, but I'm more interested in identifying the room at this point."

Jake placed the photo Beebo had given to him in front of Mary. He watched her face closely as she scrutinized the picture.

"Yes, sir, that's Room 28, all right. See? Behind that man with the beer in his hand? The painting of the waterfall with the table and lamp to the right. Every room's basically the same, but the paintings, tables and lamps and all are slightly different in each room."

"Mary, if the police or the district attorney asked you to identify that room from this photo, would you be willing to tell them the same thing?"

"I don't see why not if it's the truth, and it is. So why not? But what does this have to do with that young woman."

Mary's face grew pale as Jake related the details of what he had learned and what he suspected, saying that he believed that Ana might not have died a natural death. He omitted details about Reigner, McFadden and Zamboni, saying only that he was trying to figure out the relationship between the men in the photo, the room, and the dead young woman. A middle-aged cleaning woman from the countryside knew nothing of death, corruption and the players in the political shenanigans that routinely transpired in a city less than an hour from her home. As Jake presumed, she wouldn't recognize Reigner and McFadden from the photo, let alone Zamboni.

They finished their coffees and left the restaurant for Jake's car. They two drove in silence for 15 minutes, and Jake turned into the driveway of Mary's home. He stopped the car and killed the engine. They both sighed and exchanged glances.

Mary exited the car, stooping to speak before she closed the door.

"Mr. Ketcher, I am a simple woman. I might not be well educated, or know the ways of the world all that well, but I know right from wrong. I know when something's rotten from the smell. And this smells horribly. It stinks, in fact. Yes, it stinks to high heaven. If those men were involved with that young woman's death, I will do everything I can to help you give them what they deserve."

She closed the car door and leaned into the open window, pudgy elbows splayed across the sill. She fixed Jake with a no-nonsense look.

"As I said, I may be simple, but I am honest. I've looked the other way long enough at The Pines, and I've tolerated all sorts of nonsense that Mr. Brown seems perfectly at peace with: the comings and goings, the unregistered guests who pay but go unrecorded so he doesn't have to pay taxes ... it's all very shady and rotten. It's disgusting what's going on in that motel, but I need this job. I have turned my head for far too long, and that's not like me. I may be just a cleaning woman, but I live my life so I can die with a clear conscience, and I can be very determined, as Bobby would tell you, when I get on my high horse and I know what's right. Right's right and wrong's wrong … and all this is flat out wrong.

"Besides, that poor girl needs someone to speak up for her. I have a daughter, Mr. Ketcher, about the same age as that young girl would be today. Yes, sir. I will speak for her. You can count on it. To do anything less for this poor dead girl just wouldn't be right."

She straightened, adjusted the collar of her frayed coat around her neck in a gesture that could have been as much for protection as for warmth, then leaned again into the open window across from where Jake sat.

"You just call me and tell me what you need."

Jake watched Mary walk to her front door and enter her home. He grinned wryly, knowing that Mary Williams, a woman of modest means, far outside the power construct where McFadden, Reigner, Thompson and Zamboni ruled and resided, held the key that could dismantle their house of cards.

He started his car and headed back to The Pines for another chat with Bill Brown.

Instantly smelling trouble, Brown glared at Jake as he entered the motel office.

"Help you?" he asked, once again displaying anything but an inclination to provide assistance.

"Hope so," Jake said. "I was here a couple of weeks ago..."

"Yeah, I remember," Brown interrupted, quickly dispensing with the façade of customer service. "Kinda figured you weren't interested in a room. What do you want?"

"The truth, for starters, Mr. Brown," Jake countered, showing Brown his press credentials and drawing a dismissive shrug in response. "I'm looking into the death of Ana Chandrakar."

He placed the photo of Rilertown's elite on the counter.

"This is a photo inside Room 28 of your motel. Do you recognize any of these men?"

Brown glanced at the photo and back at Jake.

"What if I do?"

"Well, I'm just wondering why you wouldn't have told the police that these three guys were with Ana, not just on the night she died, but on several previous occasions at your place of business. I think the police would be very interested in knowing that, too, and the police station is my next stop. Thought you might want to have a chance to talk to me first, though."

Brown looked as though he had just been served notice of an IRS audit. His face glowed a deepening pink, and tiny droplets of perspiration quickly gathered on his forehead.

"So what? I have a lot of customers here. Some regulars. What they do in a room they rent is their business, not mine. And this was, what, eight, 10 years ago? You expect me to remember guests from that long ago?"

"Besides, I'm not here all the time, only work days. My night crew would probably know more."

Brown wasn't going to make this easy, so Jake decided to take a longshot. Based on what Beebo had shared with him and what he knew firsthand about Thompson's methods of doing business he figured his guess was a fairly solid risk.

"Look, Mr. Brown, I know about the deal Blake Thompson had with you," Jake began, fudging the details but including enough facts to sound convincing. "You kept Room 28 available for him when he called. The girl showed up, paid for the room, and he paid you to either look the other way or be absent when he and his pals showed up. You pocketed the cash and kept your mouth shut. I know they always took Room 28, 'cause it's farthest from the office and the road — the most discreet.

"I know about your cash reporting system, and, shall we say, your lack of full and fair disclosure of reportable, taxable revenues for your fine establishment.

"I know that violates tax laws and would probably mean at the very least some hefty fines if you were to get audited — if someone was to drop a dime to the IRS, that is."

He paused. Brown was sweating heavily now, and licking his lips. *Lizard man in a filthy Hanes wife beater.* Jake was enjoying himself.

"But that's not why I'm here. I'm here because a young woman died and I think these three guys — plus Blake Thompson — were involved. And if you want to keep this miserable little love shack open for business, your best bet is to tell me what you know. Now."

Brown pondered his fate for a moment. Being of limited intellect yet in possession of impressive self-preservation instincts, even he was able to quickly deduce that his options were limited. He contemplated the young man who stood before him: strong, handsome, confident and obviously a veteran warrior of the newspaper wars, master of a craft that Brown knew little about but feared and respected. Then he caved as stupid people caught in the wrong nearly always do. Under the right pressure, people like Brown would rat out their mothers to save their hides.

Brown was spiraling now. He envisioned an image of the Pines a year from now, shuttered with a "US Internal Revenue Service Seized Property — Do Not Cross" banner of yellow tape blocking access to the empty motel office.

"Look, all I know is that Thompson asked me for a favor. Yeah, he tossed me some Celtics or Bruins tickets a few times, and there might have been a cash bonus or two because I gave him and his buddies special attention, but I just reserved the same room for them whenever he called...."

Brown was rattled; he spoke rapidly.

"Honest. I didn't see them the day she died. I wasn't on that time of night, and I had absolutely no knowledge of who was here or what happened, just as I told the cops."

"So, that's Room 28 in the photo with Reigner, McFadden and Zamboni?"

"Yes, it is."

Following rules of public information disclosure under Massachusetts law, Jake submitted a Freedom of Information request to Mayor Sidney P. Reigner's office two days later, asking for a copy of the mayor's daily calendar for the month of April 1975. He then submitted a similar request for McFadden's calendar and obtained a copy of city car pool records for the month.

The mayor and city council chairman — working through the city attorney — posed strong objections to the requests but were unable to stop the City Clerk from fulfilling his duty to follow state laws and provide the Fourth Estate with the information Jake sought. Two weeks after submitting the requests Jake got a call informing him that he could pick up the results at the clerk's office the next day.

He did so, then retreated to *The P-R*'s conference room, where he spread the documents on the table.

McFadden and Reigner's calendars for Friday, April 25, 1975 both listed "strategy meeting, 4 p.m." and identified the evening hours as "unavailable." The city car pool listed the mayor's limousine as occupied from 4 p.m. on, and also listed a sedan released to McFadden at the same time. Both cars were returned to the car pools shortly after 10:30 that night, according to the records.

Jake checked the signature on the mayor's car release: Ted Price.

Les joined Jake in Surety's office, closing the door after he entered and taking a seat next to Jake.

"I've already briefed Les on what you have so far," Surety opened, "but bring us up to date."

Jake cleared his throat and began.

He could place Reigner, McFadden and Zamboni in room 28 of the Pines Motel from the photo Beebo had given him and verification from Mary Williams and Bill Brown.

He could show that the mayor and council chairman had both taken city cars from the car pool the day Ana died, returning them later that night.

"Great," Les said. "So what do you have to tie them all to the room the night she died. Can you prove they were there?"

"Yeah. I've got the night manager, Eduardo Rivera, placing all of them in the room with her, or at least entering the room at some point that night. But he's not on the record...," Jake began.

"Jake," Surety added. "You have to either get a witness to verify they were there or some physical evidence to prove they were involved. Circumstantial evidence ain't gonna get this done. Otherwise all you have is three powerful city leaders meeting over a few beers in a motel room at some point in time — maybe unrelated to the hooker's death. And you have McFadden and Reigner both using city vehicles after hours coincidentally. Not exactly Pulitzer material."

Les took over.

"You're still not there, Jake.

"It looks bad, sure, but it's not a crime nor highly unusual for two civic leaders to meet with the head of the local newspaper. In a motel room, sure it's weird, but that's simply not enough to go with a story. At least not one that connects the three of them to the hooker's death."

"Ana," Jake said angrily. "Her name was Ana, and she was not just a hooker. She was a talented student with friends, and someone's daughter…"

"I know, Jake," Les said. "I know that's what you believe, and it's probably the truth, but that's no story. As for the rest of it, we can't run a story based on your hunches. So unless you get someone to identify them and to place them in the room the night she died, I'm afraid you have a big, fat zero — at least as far as we're concerned. You've got more work to do before the paper will get behind this story and run it.

"So my advice: Get at it, and get what you need." Les tapped his watch. "Tick, tock … clock's running."

In Pursuit of Justice

Jake drove out of the city in the predawn hours on a sleepy Saturday morning. He rolled along familiar streets into the hills around Rilertown, past the reservoir where he and Sabrina had strolled among fallen fall leaves. He parked in the lot at the top of a hill overlooking the city and shouldered a backpack that contained a thermos of coffee and two enormous sweet rolls.

After an hour's walk, Jake rested on a flat rock perched on an outcrop overhanging the valley below. He scanned the landscape, poured a cup of coffee and cradled it as he rested against the rock and watched the sun rise. Steam rose from the cup into the chill.

Vast stands of pine trees covered the sloping side of the mountain, giving way to rows of birch, maples and oaks that covered the valley floor. All the deciduous trees had shed their leaves as fall gave way to early winter — nature's cycle of life and death. Far below, the terrain leveled off where the river took over and snaked through the valley's center to the north. Rilertown rested south the along the Tee, and the morning sunlight created a peaceful veneer over the city below. No signs could be seen of the potholed streets, crumbling buildings or broken streetlights that defined the city from up close; from a distance, the city looked quiet, calm — pristine, even.

From a distance, dawn's misty still and night's dense shroud tell lies about the city, Jake mused, masking the urban ills and struggles he had come to know so well.

Jake had known his share of challenges in his young life — Sabrina's death being the worst — but he'd been raised believing that fairness, justice and honesty generally prevailed in the ways of the world.

"Give people a chance to do the right thing, and they generally do," was one of his dad's favorite sayings. Jake reflected on that truism as he stared down the valley.

The sound of a rock loosed on the footpath leading to Jake's hidden spot wrested him from his revelry. He smiled as a figure appeared.

"Right on schedule," Jake said. He poured a second cup of coffee and handed it to Cheecha as he sat beside him on the rock.

"I trust you have my breakfast roll," Cheecha chided. "You'd better not tell me I climbed all the way up here for nothing but you."

Jake handed him a paper bag containing a sweet roll that was still warm, bursting with cinnamon and honey, and slathered with sugared icing.

"Perfect," Cheecha declared. He took a huge bite out of the roll and washed it down with a gulp of coffee. "Breakfast of true champions."

The two sat in silence for several minutes before Cheecha spoke again.

"So where you at, Jake?" he asked in the vernacular of close friends who often know answers to such questions but probe nonetheless. Open-ended queries often take us down the most fascinating paths, particularly when close friends are concerned. "You, the story ... all of it."

Jake thought for a moment, organizing his thoughts. "Fuck it," he said, and then talked. And talked.

He shared his frustrations with the story, and his failure to secure the missing detail that would tie Reigner, McFadden, Thompson and Zamboni to Ana's death. He lamented that Sabrina's killer had walked free, and spoke with annoyance that Zamboni had violated not just the vows of his marriage but company policy for his affair with Betsy yet had only been transferred, not fired. He whined about Ted Price, for manipulating the system and shilling for Reigner and McFadden; about Pucker Jamison for failing to conduct an authoritative, responsible autopsy; and about Chief Burns for running a racist, violence-prone police department.

"Doesn't anyone get punished for the awful things they do?" Jake moaned.

Cheecha took another slow sip of his coffee and nodded.

"Look, Jake, I know how you feel. I mean, it's gotta feel crappy, knowing what you know but not being able to tag these guys and make 'em pay. But let's separate the issues. The story you're working on is different than what happened to Sabrina. She just died, man. She just died, and that's it. Yeah, the chick who hit her was in the wrong, but it wasn't an act of evil. She, like Sabrina, was at the wrong place at the wrong time, and that's it.

"This, though. Well, this is different, and you and I, my friend, well we know that. These guys suck — big time. They are pure evil, and they've created a whole boatload of misery for other people. I live in the unrighteous cesspool that proves it very single day." Cheecha turned to look at his friend.

"Yeah, this is different. They used that young woman like they use everyone else. They pay so they play, and what, no one gets to call them out on it? Well, my wonderful reporter friend, that is just wrong, and you are in a position to stop it. No, it's not OK, and you can make it clear that it is very fucking much not OK — not at all.

"So my question to you is this: What are you gonna do about it?"

Jake's answering machine message light was blinking when he returned to his apartment. Calls to his home phone were unusual; messages even rarer.

It was Beebo.

"Hey, sport. Well, this is Santa Claus calling with an early Christmas present for you. It's 11:30 on Saturday morning. Where the hell are you? Call me as soon as you get this."

He did, and Beebo said her news was too big to deliver over the phone.

"La Bamba ... in an hour. Bring plenty of cash, 'cause I'm thirsty and what I have for you is gonna cost you."

"So, you ready to hear a story?" Beebo asked, a long-necked Bud clutched in her right hand, and her left fingers drumming on the tabletop. "I was right here on Friday night," nodding at the pool table, "shooting pool, getting guys to buy me drinks and chatting with friends, when a young woman approached me and asked if I was Police Chief Lester Burns' daughter.

"'That would be me,' I told her, 'but whatever he's done ain't my problem.'

"She told me she needed my advice, which turned out to be one of the worst understatements I've heard in a while." Beebo stabbed at the plate of chicken nachos, popping a cheesy mound into her mouth and chewing as she talked.

"Name Sally Wheeler ring a bell?" Jake shrugged. "Well, it should. She was the chick who killed your girlfriend."

Jake stopped writing and stared.

"Go on."

"Sally was with friends, hanging out and drinking, when one of her friends pointed me out. I guess this chick Sally had told her friends about a pickle she was in, and she told me a story I knew you'd want to hear as soon as she began."

"What pickle?" Jake probed.

"Hold on; hold on," Beebo said, wiping her fingers on a napkin and reaching for more nachos.

"She tells me she's in a bind with City Hall over the accident, and proceeds to tell me about a shit storm involving your pal, Ted Price."

Jake nodded, encouraging Beebo on and struggling to understand her as she gorged on nachos. He pushed the plate out of her reach. She frowned but continued.

"You probably know all this, but Sally's father is some sort of low-level political hack and is friends with the mayor's aide. After she was charged with Sabrina's death, her dad asked his pal Teddy Price for help. Seems daddy didn't envision little Sally making best friends with the best of Massachusetts' medium security prisoners, and he went to Price to help fix the situation."

Sally had met with Price, who agreed to make some calls to see if he could get her charges reduced from involuntary manslaughter to driving to endanger. The subtle change meant a world of different in terms of penalties and the blemish on her record; important distinctions for a woman of 20 just starting her adult life.

"Price got it all fixed, as you know, but it came with a 'price,'" she said, grimacing at the pun. She pulled the nachos close and scooped another overloaded chip into her mouth before Jake could protest.

"Jesus, Beebo, will you just tell me?"

"OK, OK. Basically, Price has been extorting sex from this chick ever since the case was settled. Told her he could always get the DA to bring new charges based on new info, which of course is total bullshit, but poor Sally bought it.

"She's been delivering the goods to Price from time to time, but after things apparently got even weirder she decided she had had enough. She's done with it. Fed up. She's basically a good kid who's in difficult situation, which is why she turned to yours truly, being the expert on crappy, abusive relationships and all, and also being the police chief's eldest and only daughter.

"She perked up when I told her I was friends with the city's star reporter — yes, you. I told her you'd do anything for Sabrina's memory, and that you might be able to kick a shin or two if she agreed to talk to you. No guarantees, but I at least got her to give me her number."

"You think she'll talk to *me?*" Jake asked.

"You? The sweet-talkin', smooth-lookin' stud of *The Rilertown Post-Recorder?* You bet she will," Beebo said, sliding a piece of paper with a phone number across the table.

Jake called Sally from La Bamba's pay phone. He approached her gingerly yet firmly, eager to hear her story but repelled by the thought of meeting with her. Normally he would have spent a soothing moment or two building rapport with an interview subject. This time, however, he shrugged off her stuttered apology and stuck to business.

"Beebo says you have a story to share. Something that'll shed light on a string of City Hall irregularities I am investigating. Soooo…"

Sally agreed to meet him at the bar in an hour. Jake returned to the table to buy Beebo another round and wait.

He instantly spied Sally as she ambled from the bar's entrance, scanned the room and headed to the table where Jake and Beebo sat. A mix of disgust and pity washed over Jake as he studied her face and body language. She was probably a pretty girl in a different light and under different circumstances, but the events of her life had added years to her tired countenance. She exuded a fatigued, embattled vibe that softened Jake — another victim in a city full of them, this one of circumstance and fate — another defeated, lost soul.

Sally nodded to Beebo and skeptically regarded Jake as she joined them.

Jake stared at her, expressionless. "Damned if I'll give this woman a shred of kindness or absolution," he thought.

"I guess you probably hate me, don't you?" she began, taking the seat next to Beebo across from Jake as though forming an alliance — or perhaps for safety. "I probably deserve it.

"I suppose Beebo told you what's been happening to me ever since the accident. Payback, right? That probably makes you happy. 'My girlfriend's killer, a sex slave to a city hall predator.' Just what I deserve."

She shifted nervously on the cracked leather seat.

"I'm sorry, Jake. I really am. I feel awful. I wish it had been me who died, not your girlfriend. Most of me died that night, too. Just so you know, my life has been total hell since that night, and not just because of what that asshole Price has been doing to me.

"I can't forget any of it. I can't sleep. I can't forget the way it sounded, felt, all of it," she was crying softly, now, "and I can't forget the image of you, collapsing on the sidewalk with all those people around you. So lost...

"I'm so sorry — for all of it. I should have just taken my punishment. Maybe I would have had a chance to get on with my life after I did jail time for what happened; maybe not. But my father convinced me he could take care of it, and really, what was I supposed to do?"

She looked like a woman in search of answers, but Jake had none for her, nor would he have been inclined to provide them if he had. He braced himself, then spoke — calmly, evenly, but with edgy, subdued contempt.

"You took something from me that you can never replace, and that I'll never, ever have again in my life. Do you understand? You took my true love from me. You killed her, and you destroyed a big piece of me in the process. So if you come here looking for me to forgive you, forget it. I'm not in the business of forgiveness, 'specially for you.

"But if you have something to give me that will help you move along, get over whatever it is you're dealing with, then speak up. I'll use it if I think it's relevant, but I'm going to name you. No hiding. No bullshit protection of anonymity. Not from me. Not ever.

"Just tell me."

She did.

For a chance at redemption, Sally quickly agreed to being named, and promised to testify; she even agreed to submit a notarized statement as an affidavit to prove she would remain on the record and accountable to what she had to say.

Not long after she initially spoke to the mayor's aide, Price had called her under the guise of needing more information for her court case. They met in a nearby café, and Price had been direct, demanding and explicit.

"He was so full of himself, so confident and, well, arrogant," Sally said, dabbing the corner of her eyes as she sipped a glass of water Beebo had brought for her. "He just told me what he wanted, and said there was no option for me.

"He grinned at me as he spoke, like he was getting off on making me squirm. He treated me like a whore, and somehow he knew I could never tell my father — or anyone, until now — about what he demanded. I'll never forget it. He said if I told anyone he would just deny it. Who would believe me, a stupid nothing, compared to a powerful man like that?

"So I did what he asked, and I have, ever since.

"But I have morals, and standards, and a soul. Even I have a limit.

"Last week pushed me over the edge. Until then it had just been casual, quick sex, but Price started to get weird. He wanted to do things to me that hurt, as if he was punishing me. He's into kinky shit that's just too much.

"I realized this was only going to get worse unless I did something to stop it.

"That's when I decided I needed help. Bumping into Beebo turned out to be the best luck I've had in a long, long time. One of my friends who was with me Friday night told me I could trust her and man, was she right," Sally smiled softly at Beebo, then returned her gaze to Jake.

"So that's about it. I've basically been a sex slave for the mayor's aide for over a year, an on-demand whore.

"Now that I've told you all of this, I have question for you: Can you use this to make him stop?"

"I can do a helluva lot better than that," Jake promised, closing his notebook and standing to leave. He tossed three $10 bills on the table. "I'll be in touch," he said, then nodded to Beebo and left.

Jake was at his desk before 5 a.m. Monday morning, early even for a devout morning person.

He spent hours retracing all of his interviews — Beth, Beebo, Mary, Bill Brown, his original facedown with Blake Thompson — reviewing his notes and looking for holes he could fill by further questioning. He labored through the documents — the ME and police report, motel register, calendars from Reigner and McFadden's offices, and the city car pool records — when his eye fell on the last item: Ted Price's signature on the car pool record.

He folded the piece of paper and placed it in his pocket, grabbed a notebook from his desktop, stuck a pen in his pocket and hurried out the back door to his car. Moments later, he parked in the city hall lot and made his way to the mayor's office, surprising Ted Price when he entered the room.

"Price, you and I need to talk," Jake said, not bothering to hide his contempt for the mayor's front man.

"Mayor's out," Price said.

"It's not the mayor I'm here to see. It's you."

"Really? Well, why don't you make an appointment," Price countered, leaning back in his chair and grinning arrogantly. "I'm sure you can see how busy I am."

"Not for long, Ted," Jake pressed. "I figure your time in City Hall is about up, and your buddy Reigner's, too."

"What the fuck're you talking about?" Price's grin vanished behind a squint.

"I'm talking about extortion and being an accessory after the fact to murder," Jake said, leaning close. Price went pale.

"Sally Wheeler — your squeeze on demand. I have the whole story; how you fixed her charges after she killed my girlfriend and how you've been enjoying her charms ever since, extorting sex."

He slid a photocopy of the picture of Reigner, McFadden and Zamboni across Price's desk. Price picked up the photo and stared at it, rattled.

"Recognize that, Price? It was taken at the Pines Motel a few years ago. It's your buddies and my ex-boss, hamming it up. Remember the Pines? It was a regular stop on your drop 'n' bop circuit. That's where you took Reigner on April 25, 1975, and it's where either he, McFadden or Zamboni killed Ana Chakrandar.

You remember who Ana was, right? The young Indian student that your dear friends used to boink from time to time, before something went wrong in that room and she died."

Price fingered the photocopy and shoved it back across the desk toward Jake.

"Bullshit. You got nothing," Price said. His eyes revealed something other than his usual confidence. That was all Jake needed.

"No, Ted. I have it all, and I'm going with it. You're fucked, one way or another, and I'm going to make sure of it. Question is, how bad's it going to be? Losing your job, or going to jail? It's kinda up to you."

He reached across the desk, looming over the aide, and tapped his index finger on Price's right temple. "Think, Teddy ... this is your last chance to save your dumb ass. Time to spill it."

Panic set in.

"What about me?" Price begged, instincts for self-preservation trumping arrogance and entitlement.

Amazing, Jake thought, *how quickly the agents of the rich and powerful turn on their masters when threatened.*

Jake stood silently before Price, deploying one of a seasoned reporter's most effective tools: *Remain quiet, and stare. The first to talk always loses.*

Price lost.

"I wasn't even involved. I'm nothing but the mayor's aide. I was only driving that night, fer Chrissake!"

Jake zeroed in.

"Here's the deal, Price. You talk to me, on the record, and you tell no one about this conversation — not the mayor, not your wife, not your priest, if you have such an influence in your miserable life. You tell me the entire story in detail. Then I leave, and you shut the hell up.

"I go away and do my thing, but your mouth stays shut — absolutely closed.

"Be very clear about this, Price: I already have this story; two stories, actually, if you count Sally Wheeler's little tale about the two of you as a separate piece. Come to think of it, that'll make a nice sidebar.

"I'm going with the story about Reigner, McFadden and Zamboni whether you talk to me or not, but you're going to look a lot worse if you don't. You'll do jail time.

"So you tell me what you know, I leave and after I nail down a couple other details this story takes the mayor down for good, and McFadden and Zamboni, too. You talk, and maybe I forget about the extortion deal you had with Sally Wheeler. Maybe you don't go to jail for extortion, but you're done with her. You get it? Done. You leave that girl alone, Price, permanently. Don't even call her. You do, and I promise you I'll do everything I can to plant your sorry ass in jail.

"I'm not after you, Ted. You know what I want. Reigner and McFadden. And I think you're smart enough and selfish enough to give 'em to me."

Price did as Jake expected.

On the night of April 25, 1975, he had driven the mayor to meet McFadden and Zamboni for drinks at a bar near South Cransfield around 5. He drove Reigner to the Pines around 7 and waited in the car as usual, parking at the back of the hotel next to Zamboni and McFadden's cars.

"I don't know when they arrived, but the mayor told me that Thompson was already there, and that he had 'already set the table' for the night's entertainment."

Shortly after 9 p.m. the mayor scrambled from the hotel room and appeared at the side of the car, disheveled and flustered.

"He told me to get his stuff out of the room, that there'd been an accident, and that he was going to wait in the car to make sure his fingerprints weren't in the room. He jumped into the back of the car, kind of huddled there in the dark.

"When I got to the room, McFadden and Zamboni were leaving. They were a mess, frantic. Thompson was there with the girl, and he'd put a ton of stuff into a plastic trash can liner: bottles, glasses, the ashtray, clothes, towels ... and told me to get it all out of there.

"He told me to not touch anything, and to stay calm and just help clean the place up and get out.

"He said something had happened to the girl while the mayor was screwing her. Said she had just died. An accident, he said.

"I stuffed the bag into the back of the car and drove the mayor back to Rilertown. On the way he was a complete basket case. I've never seen him like that — bawling and jabbering. Told me it was just sex, harmless, that he hadn't meant to kill her. Said he was sorry, thanked me for being the only person he could really trust, all sorts of crap like that.

"I dropped him off at his home just before 10, got rid of the bags of stuff in a dumpster near the fire station and returned the car to the car pool," nodding to the car pool receipt in front of him. "Just like the log says.

"I went home and made like nothing had happened.

"It was an accident," Price pleaded. "I'm sure it was."

"*You* called the ME, right?"

"No, I didn't. I asked the mayor if he wanted me to call Jamison, but he said it was already taken care of. He didn't want any possible trace to him. He canceled all his meetings for the next couple of days. Stayed home. Called in sick, which he's never done before, so he could hide and do damage control."

Jake glared at Price and imagined the pleasure of punching him in the face. Instead, he asked a couple of follow-up questions and jotted notes, enjoying making the mayor's aide squirm and sweat.

Then he made Price repeat the entire story, pausing to ask clarifying questions and backtracking when Price was inconsistent. He scribbled more notes and added underlines to important quotes he had already circled, his gaze alternating between Price's sweaty face and a notebook that contained Jake's ultimate prize: retribution and justice, all recorded in sweet, excruciating detail in a cheap reporter's notebook emblazoned with *The P-R*'s logo.

Reminding Price to keep their conversation confidential, Jake closed his notebook and left the aide staring at the blank space before his desk, envisioning the City Hall sand castle slowly being consumed by crashing, ambivalent waves.

The drive from Rilertown to Silvertown shadows the Tee River, snaking on a north-south axis along the riverbank through fertile fields and across the flatlands of Bloomfield County.

Late-morning traffic was light, and Jake completed the drive in 45 minutes, pulling into an empty parking space in front of *The Silvertown Eagle*. He deposited a couple of coins in the meter — enough to allow him to park for an hour. He wouldn't need that much time.

Zamboni was in the middle of the busy newsroom, hunched over the wire editor's shoulder, eyeballing a story on the computer terminal when he spotted Jake approaching from across the room. He straightened, a smirk crawling across his face.

"You lost, little boy? Or just seeking a break from the big city for the day?"

"Your office," Jake said. "Now."

"Who the fuck are you, telling me…?"

Jake tossed the copy of the photo of Zamboni, Reigner and McFadden on the desk. The wire editor looked at it then ping-ponged back and forth between Jake and Zamboni as Zamboni snatched the image from the desk. He stared at it, then raised his glare to meet Jake's unblinking scowl.

Zamboni glanced again at the photo. Smirking, he slipped it into his shirt pocket, turned, and strode toward his office.

"Follow me," he grunted over his shoulder.

"You can keep the photo, Mike," Jake parried. "It's a copy. I have the original safely stored."

Zamboni was a typical Machiavellian bully. He had an uncanny ability to justify his conduct, bizarre philosophy and the abuse he heaped upon nearly everyone he encountered.

"I hate everyone in the world on deadline," he loved to brag, *"even my mother — especially her, if she calls on deadline. She ought to know better."*

Like all bullies, Zamboni was long on bluster and short on substance, but he wasn't stupid.

Cornered, he first tried bravado.

"So what do you think you have here? An old photo of me, Reigner and McFadden? Big fucking deal. Since when is a photo of a local paper's editor with city officials a newsworthy event? I know you're relatively new to this game, but I sincerely hope you don't think this is something newsworthy or substantial. Is this why you made the long drive from Rilertown, to show me a picture of me, the mayor and the council chairman having a laugh over a drink?

"This means nothing."

Jake proved otherwise, outlining what he'd learned and placing Zamboni at the scene of Ana's death. Zamboni stared beyond Jake's head as he spoke, lips stretched thin, his eyes barely perceptible through tiny slits.

Zamboni shifted tactics, trying threats.

"You're over your head. We'll eat you alive, any one of us."

Jake smiled and shared details of the web of information people had willingly given up to bring matters to light.

"You're a bit of a legend, Mike. There's a long list of people eager to see you crash and burn. A bunch of them are more significant and powerful than you are, and they're more than happy to see you take the fall. This story was fairly easy to construct, once I had the details wrapped up — and thanks to RT's notes on how you tried to squelch the story."

Zamboni rose to his feet and in an instant was around the desk with scarlet face and clenched fists. Jake prepared for the assault. Zamboni stopped inches short of Jake and assessed the younger man — taller, stronger, fitter. *This would not end well for me,* he thought.

The punch never came.

His options depleted, Zamboni shrunk smaller than his 5′5″ frame.

What now? Fight? Obstruct? Run?

As the years had passed Zamboni had contemplated his choices countless times, alone in the dark, curled on the bed next to his sleeping wife, alone, tormented. He had considered leaving, simply packing and running north, perhaps to Canada, for safe haven and a chance at escape. But the prospect of competing in a new world, of leaving his dysfunctional family and demanding job, and finding a way to make a living in a foreign land, was too much for a man accustomed to complete control over his life. He thrived on ruling the newsroom like a medieval landlord; abusive, unforgiving, unwavering. So he continued to work long hours, hiding from the truth and the elements of his life he found intimidating and frightening, finding safety and security in repetition and familiarity.

Now, he retreated to his desk, a defeated man.

Jake looked at his watch, realizing he still had more than half an hour left on the parking meter. He could take his time, enjoy the moment. He spelled the story out for Zamboni, who sat, fingers kneading his temples, causing the pockmarks on his jowls to rise and fall, gather and race apart. All the swagger was gone, and Zamboni looked more a lost, tormented soul with a face ravaged by adolescent acne than the powerful voice of a daily newspaper who also moonlighted as part of a political machine.

"You're probably enjoying this, aren't you?" A smug smile crossed Zamboni's face but was soon erased by his usual scowl. "It figures it'd be you who'd unravel this story. I should never have put you in the GA slot ... friggin' RT leaving turned out to be the beginning of the end, huh? Ironic, isn't it, that I'm the one who gave you your big chance? A shot at a story way too big for your talents, then, but I allowed you to develop, taught you what you needed to learn to fuck me over in the end."

Zamboni sighed and leaned back in his chair.

"When a man knows he is to be hanged, it concentrates his mind wonderfully," Zamboni quoted. "Samuel Johnson. Eighteenth Century British. I think he got it right.

"So what's your move, Jake? How's this going to play out?"

"Like this, Mike. You're going to tell me everything — everything. I'm going to take notes, and I'm going with the story after I talk to the medical examiner and find out why he fudged the

ME report. That's the last piece, but I'm sure you know I don't need it to make the story.

"For your information, I already have it all — nailed down tight, just as you would demand. You're right: I learned well — how to report, write, all the things you taught me.

"Les, Bill and Wick also know, and they're on board with the story. They're just waiting for me get back from this meeting so I can to wrap it up in nice, tight prose: You, McFadden, Thompson and Reigner, with Ana the night she died. Thompson overseeing the cleansing of the room after she died, and the three of you sterling community leaders heading off into the night to save your illustrious asses.

"I have confirmed through a third party that the mayor was with the girl when she died, and that's enough for me to run with it. Or, I could let it hang … just leave it that the three of you were all with her, and let you all take the fall from the DA's investigation. I'm sure that would make your family happy. I can tell you that Betsey is already less than thrilled."

Zamboni again began to rise from the desk.

"Bad idea, Mike. Smarten up, sit down and consider your situation. First of all, if you think getting tough with me's a good idea, bring it on. I'd welcome the chance to plunk you on your ass, and I think you're smart enough to know you'd wind up on the losing end.

"As for the bigger picture, you think Reigner and McFadden are going to save you? You think it's worth protecting them any longer? I have the story, Mike — all of it — and I'm going with it, with or without you. So yeah, you could continue to protect them."

Zamboni leaned back in his chair, thoughtful.

"Or you could just tell me what happened."

"What do you want, Jake? Money? I have access to plenty of money. A phone call; that's all it would take, and you'd have enough dough to make a bit of silence well worth your while."

"Oh, man. You're a piece of work, Mike. Unbelievable. Money? You fucking kidding me? It's not about the money, or the power. It's not about you, or me, or even Reigner or McFadden, not as individuals.

"It's the story, Mike. Like you always said, it's all about the story...."

Zamboni fingered his tie. His eyes darted around the room as if looking for a place to hide. The tiny office shrank as he contemplated the end of his newspapering career. But that wasn't the worst of it; jail time was a distinct possibility. Zamboni had been a visitor inside the state's prison system on story assignments and wanted nothing to do with life as a resident there, regardless of how temporary.

Like water finding its way through the rocks along a stream, Zamboni took the only possible path to selfish freedom.

"It wasn't me; it was Reigner. He killed her. I was in the living room. Me, McFadden and Thompson … and Reigner was with the girl…"

Jake enjoyed his meeting with Medical Examiner Richard Jamison almost as much as he had the confrontation with Zamboni.

Jamison was unrepentant.

"Yes, that is my signature, but I did not perform the autopsy, which is fairly common and you would know from the autopsy notes. That was conducted by one of my associates. You would need to speak to her. Unfortunately, she is no longer associated with my office, and I have no idea where she is now. I heard she left the state for a job out west."

Jake realized that Jamison would remain outside of the circle of culpability, as crooked as the rest of the figures involved but with a shield of protection that was neither necessary nor worth the time to crack. He had the story without scorching Jamison's hide. Taking down Reigner would likely end Jamison's reign as ME anyway.

He left the ME's office and headed back to the paper. His phone rang as he settled into his desk. It was Dolores. He had a visitor.

Eduardo Rivera stood by the reception desk accompanied by a slight man in a priest's cassock, who introduced himself as Father Figueroa, spiritual leader of the Holy Name parish in The Flats who had served as parish priest since Eduardo was a child.

"I must speak with you in private, Jake," Eduardo said. Jake led the two men through the newsroom and into the conference room.

Seated next to the priest, Eduardo spoke in even, assured tones. Father Figueroa sat supportively next to him.

"I have changed my mind, Jake." He straightened his shoulders. "I have spoken with Father Figueroa, and also with a lawyer from the legal aid society. I know that I have committed perjury by lying about the men who visited that young woman at the motel. I know I have committed a crime, but I cannot live with the lie any longer.

"I am here to give you permission to use my name." Eduardo glanced at the priest, who smiled softly and laid his hand on the young man's arm in a gentle show of encouragement.

"I stand by what I told you last time we met. I will identify the men in the room. You can use my name."

Eduardo's eyes shone.

"It is the right thing to do."

FINAL REVISION

Jake dressed in his best clothes, for once choosing a tie that didn't clash with his shirt or his corduroy sport coat. He got to work early to prepare for the biggest day of his career.

Les arrived shortly after 7, and the two retreated to his office. Surety joined them a few minutes later, bringing three large black coffees to fuel the conversation — as if anyone needed the jolt of caffeine. Energy was high and an air of anticipation and excitement permeated the small office.

This was serious talk, tense and lean of excess verbiage. Facts, logistics, verifications and cross-checks: all revealed in the glorious, inverted pyramid style that needed little polish to draw *The P-R*'s readers deeply into the story. Some tales tell themselves. This was one of them.

Jake outlined the details of the story from the beginning, presenting his case evenly and quietly, with an emotionless detachment that remained intact until he reached the part about Price's extortion of Sally Wheeler.

"I say we go with Price's story as a sidebar," Surety argued. "Why let this asshole walk, when he manipulated that kid and squelched the charges against her for Sabrina's death at the same time?"

Jake shook his head.

"Like it or not, I gave my word. We made a deal: he talked; I'd forget about that part of the story. He's toast, anyway, Bill; we've heard the last of Ted Price once Reigner goes down. And I am sure he'll leave Sally alone from now on.

"There's something else. I've met the girl. She's suffered enough. Why drag her through the mud of this mess and further fuck up her life. What's the point?"

"Point, is, you had no right to bargain with him," Les said gently. "That really wasn't your call, but it is what it is." He turned back to Surety. "I say we accept what Jake says and move along."

They concluded the review of the initial story and then discussed possible follow-ups. Surety would see to artwork — photos, copies of documents — to accompany the piece on the front page and into the copy and sidebars that would trail onto the page 12 jump. Les would fully brief Wick so the publisher was prepared for "the excrement that was about to hit the rotary oscillator," as Surety predicted.

It's rare for a reporter to find himself involved in a story of such magnitude; even more so for a scribe with relatively little experience. Pursuing a story like this, with the twists, tangles and drama of a John LeCarre novel is exhausting, exhilarating, frustrating and tense — a cat and mouse chase, a chess game and an all-consuming challenge as reporter and editor struggle to carefully construct the story, anticipate questions, fill holes of logic, fact and substance, and prepare for the backlash that is sure to follow.

Les, Surety and Jake covered all this and more in two hours, leaving Jake to the task of his final interview: Mayor Sid Reigner.

Jake had booked a 10 a.m. private meeting with the mayor, reminding Price to keep his mouth shut before Jake had a chance to confront Reigner. Jake was nervous, excited and anxious — but well prepared — as he drove to city hall and entered through the back door. He scurried up the flight of stairs and into the mayor's office reception a minute or two before 10. Eager anticipation turned to concern when he saw the horrified look on Price's face.

"I had to tell him," Price said. "It wasn't fair for you to blindside him, and, well, he had a right to know what was coming…."

His words were cut short by a loud report from inside Reigner's office. Rushing into the room with Jake close on his heels, Price stopped, shocked at the image of Mayor Sidney Reigner slumped low in his high-backed leather chair, his cherished .38 snub nose revolver in his right hand and a gaping, oozing wound of blood and gore in his right temple.

Reporters write in a bubble. Most have a method for creating a private, unassailable space where they retreat to write even the most pedestrian story. You can bang on a reporter's desk while he's writing, threaten him or scream that his eyebrows are on fire, but still he'll pound away, undeterred. Seasoned reporters bang out decent copy — sometimes good, other times superlative — while surrounded by ringing telephones, arguing reporters and editors and the low-level buzz of an active newsroom. Any reporter worth his salt is skilled at creating copy that makes sense while surrounded by madness.

For this story, though, Jake needed quiet. Les gave over his office, and Jake disappeared for an entire day and half the next, surrounded by files, empty coffee cups and a small mountain of reporter's notebooks.

Page after page flew from the typewriter and into a waiting stack. Jake's pace quickened as he followed the outline he, Surety and Les had constructed.

Finally, he typed the last paragraph.

> State and regional legal authorities declined to comment on whether posthumous charges could be brought against deceased Mayor Sidney Reigner,

saying only that all legal options would be exhausted
to 'fully bring this matter to closure, for the city, the
state and for the family of the young woman who
died such a horrible, untimely death.'

Jake drew a deep breath and pressed the carriage return button
one last time.

Reigner's suicide dominated *The P-R*'s front page for two days,
along with stories about McFadden being named acting mayor
until a special election could be conducted, and the effect of
the mayor's death on city affairs. It's not every day that a political legend blows his head off in his office. *The P-R* rose to
the challenge of dutifully reporting on the fallout from such
an abrupt change in the city's leadership, not to mention the
shock that spread through City Hall long after the cleaning
crew purged Reigner's office of the blood, gore and the mayor's
personal effects.

Jake wrote the story about the suicide, but another P-R reporter
handled the McFadden angle. Jake didn't think he could stomach talking to the council chairman; besides, the man carried
his grudge against Jake like a war club and would likely refuse
to talk to him.

Reigner's death delayed the story of Ana's murder and changed
it substantially, so Jake got to work reconstructing the piece.

Working with Surety and Les — with Wick's approval — they planned to break the story the day after Reigner's funeral. They weighed their options: to proceed with the story as part of covering Reigner's suicide, or to separate them into individual newsworthy items. In the scope of cause and effect the two events were inseparable, but the larger story of conspiracy between Reigner, McFadden, Zamboni and Thompson (not to mention other minor players) would have been buried beneath the stunning news of the mayor's death.

Even in death, Reigner found a way to control the message, Jake mused.

They decided to wait it out, let the suicide story run its course, then break the investigation after the funeral was over and the state, regional and federal officials had all retreated from the funeral services. They would return in force once they learned what Reigner and his pals had been up to, quickly forgetting their condolences as they sharpened their swords and set out to dismember Reigner's legacy.

Les, Wick and Surety decided to meet with the District Attorney before the story was published, an unusual concession of disclosure that Wick advised would help the cause for indictments after the story hit the streets. Leave it to the publisher to understand and represent the politics of newspapering.

They booked a meeting with DA William Sullivan the following afternoon. Jake was hurrying along High Street on his way to the meeting when a young woman nearly collided with him as she exited a shop.

Sally Wheeler.

The two stared at one another uncomfortably until Sally spoke.

"I've been meaning to call you." She stepped closer to Jake, looking deeply into his eyes with a grateful, imploring gaze. "It's stopped. It's over. I haven't heard from Price since you and I spoke. I know it was you. I know you made it stop.

"I want you to know how grateful I am. You gave me my life back."

Sally seemed younger, lighter, more alive, than when Jake met with her at La Bamba. The furrowed lines in her eyes were shallower, the shadows gone from beneath. Jake felt a gentle release move through his chest, a deep sigh of forgiveness that surprised him and brought a lump to his throat.

To his surprise, and to hers as well, he reached for the young woman and pulled her close in an embrace that in one small gesture set both of them free.

He smiled at her.

"Live your life," he said. "I'm going to. It's what we do, people like us. So let's both get at it, huh?"

He hugged her again, touched by the tear of gratitude that left Sally's eye and remained on her cheek. He turned and walked on to his meeting with the DA, a bounce in his step and with a lightness of soul that he hadn't felt in many, many months.

The meeting with Sullivan was predictably lengthy and mildly contentious.

"We're meeting with you as a courtesy," Wick opened, making it clear to the DA that in bringing the gift of pre-publication information he expected something in return. The man was difficult, not dumb. He got it, and nodded in agreement. *The P-R* would have a clear runway for the story's takeoff the next day.

The irascible gnome, renowned for his ill temper and domineering manner, controlled the meeting from then on. He refused to tip his legal hand, ruthlessly carving out his turf and simply allowing that he and his staff would take the matter under advisement.

Yes, the mayor's suicide complicated matters considerably.

Yes, indictments would be considered against McFadden and Zamboni. Price's role would also be examined, naturally.

Yes, the meeting would remain in strict confidence out of respect to the newspaper's publishing rights until the story broke.

Jake scooped a few quotes to add to the story and tucked his notebook into his back pocket as the meeting drew to a close.

The P-R group left the DA's office and went straight to a bar to celebrate and plan the final steps before publication. Cold beers and shots of tequila eased the afternoon's angst. Jake drank soda water. He still had work to do.

Exhausted yet unable to sleep, Jake rose before dawn the next day and made his way to his frigid mountainside retreat. Coffee thermos and fresh coffee roll in hand, he watched the sun rise over Rilertown and thought back on the years that had passed.

The photo loop in his mind played images of Sabrina, over and over again. Unpacking, laughing, rolling a joint, berating him, agreeing to marry him, making love, dying. He thought of his mom, dad and sister, the sources of love and support that had carried him through some of his darkest moments, sustaining him with encouragement and a sense of solid foundation that was unshakable despite the emotional earthquakes he had endured.

He thought of Sam, his principal advocate who pulled strings, gently encouraged and, when necessary, kicked his butt to help guide him in the right direction.

He thought of his internship at *The Eagle* under Surety's stewardship, and tools he learned from him that he continued to use every day. He thought of the tire business, of Silvertown, his friends in his hometown and the allure of a simpler, less complicated, slower life.

He sighed, chewed on a bite of coffee roll, took a swig of coffee and allowed his thoughts to dwell on Rilertown: *The P-R* and his friends at the paper, Les, Surety; of his confidants and sources in the community. He thought about Cheecha, his pal, #1 source and valuable second baseman on their softball team. Then he considered Beebo, who was turning out to be more than a casual friend and source.

His thoughts drifted back to Sabrina.

"What would she say?" Jake asked aloud. "What would she want me to do now?"

Jake thought of himself as the young man on *The P-R's* doorsteps only a few years earlier, dressed in awkward clothes and with equally uncertain idealism, pulling on the door labeled "push" as he eagerly entered the world of newspapering. He pondered what it meant to be a reporter — allowing himself to indulge in the pride, satisfaction and understanding of an industry he had trained hard to join and had come to understand, value and love.

He thought of the service he had done to *The P-R* readership, by "inflicting the comfortable and comforting the inflicted." There would be a new mayor, and a new city council chairman. Calm had been restored to The Flats, and Cheecha's stock had never been higher. Rumors circulated that he would soon become the city's first at-large Hispanic councilman.

A tangible measure of civic progress had occurred, due in part to good, honest journalism — a city made a little better by *The P-R*'s efforts to expose injustice, corruption and evil. He felt a familiar feeling, deep within his chest, a sense of pride in his work, but much, much more. It was love — and he compared that love with the heartfelt feeling he carried for his family, their business and all the values they had instilled in him.

Alone in the splendid solitude of the morning sunrise over western Massachusetts, as he drank the last drops of steaming hot coffee and savored the final crumbs of the coffee roll, as another day dawned on a sleepy city struggling to find its way in an ever-changing, demanding world, Jake Ketcher's choice of a course for the rest of his life came into perfect, clear focus.

He tossed back the rest of the coffee, packed his backpack and made his way back along the winding path to his car, and on to *The P-R*. The story needed a few finishing touches, and he had plenty of time. Deadline was still five hours away.

The story broke with predictable impact.

"Reigner, McFadden Implicated in 1975 Death," screamed the banner headline, along with an equally inflammatory subhead:

"P-R Editor, Former Business Exec Also Involved," and went on to quote the DA in great detail from the day's previous meeting.

The story was the talk of the city; *The P-R* phones rang non-stop. County officers started calling, then state officials joined the fray. Readers overwhelmed the switchboard and bombarded the reception desk with letters to the editor.

Sullivan promptly called a press conference to outline his office's investigation. Jake knew what Sullivan would say well before the diminutive DA climbed the three steps to his press-room podium. Jake was center stage at the press conference to bask in the glory and gloat as competing reporters struggled to catch up. Jake noticed Ben Davidoff when he uncharacteristically arrived late, relegating *The Gazette* to the back of the room.

"I have prepared required documents to seek indictments in this case, specifically for Rilertown Acting Mayor Butch McFadden and former Rilertown *Post-Recorder* editor Michael Zamboni, as being accessories after the fact in the death of Ana Chakrandar in 1975," Sullivan puffed.

"I must congratulate Mr. Ketcher and *The Post-Recorder* of Rilertown for his valuable investigative work into this matter," he added, shocking Jake with the unexpected acknowledgement. "Thanks to his efforts, I have also ordered that a new investigation into Ms. Chandarkar's death be opened immediately so any new facts related to this case may be brought to light."

Jake scrambled for his notebook. Such a public acknowledgment was unexpected, as was the announcement that the DA would reopen the investigation into Ana's death. It made for days of follow-up stories, digging and work. The story promised to drive *The P-R*'s front page and would make *The P-R* the state's media darling — not to mention cause a surge in circulation, to Wick's delight — for weeks on end.

The P-R's parent company suspended Zamboni without pay pending the investigation, and the suddenly silent editor retreated to his home in Binnfield, only to find his personal belongings in a heap at the end of his driveway. His wife had had enough of his act. He moved into a cheap studio apartment overlooking the Tee River, alone and unemployed, spending his days drinking cheap whiskey and reading classic literature.

Indictments soon followed, announced by front-page headlines as Rilertown made plans to seek not only a new mayor but a change in city council leadership for the first time in decades. Change came to *The P-R*, too, when Wick announced that Surety would be returning to Silvertown once *The P-R* completed its search for a permanent news editor, which he announced to the staff, "will be completed as promptly as possible."

Wick and Les made the decision public a few days later, following a red-faced Jake from a brief meeting in Wick's office into an all-newsroom gathering in the conference room where he unveiled who would lead *The P-R*'s newsgathering efforts from then on: "I'm pleased to announce that we have reached a decision about who will serve as news editor for *The P-R*," Wick said, tugging at his vest and allowing his booming voice to carry across the room. "Let me introduce you to him: Mr. Jake Ketcher."

The room exploded in appreciation. It was a populist decision that also made good sense, a bi-directional vote of confidence in Jake.

Jake would be the youngest daily newspaper editor in the history of the company. "Maybe even the state," Wick proclaimed with a laugh as the champagne bottles were opened and he offered a toast.

"To the future," Wick said.

"Hear, hear. And to Jake, to his hard work and strong ethics, and to the memory of Ana Chandrakar," Les added somberly.

"To Jake!" said the group.

"To champagne!" shouted Jake.

Jake downed the last of his champagne and returned to his desk to make an attempt to work. A bouquet of fresh flowers rested next to his phone.

Puzzled, Jake opened the card and read.

"Thank you. At last, my family can be at peace, and Ana can rest." Tears sprang to his eyes when he read the signature. Pramod and Vinita Chandrakar.

Jake made his way through his morning office ritual, half a cup of black coffee gone as he scoured the morning's competing editions for news tips and leads. He moved aside the brass nameplate on his desk to make room to spread the broadsheets before him.

"Jake Ketcher, News Editor," read the nameplate, a gift from his mom, dad, sister and Sam.

They had presented the gift in a quiet celebratory family dinner in Silvertown that quickly turned less sedate when Les showed up with a chauffeured van full of reporters from Rilertown. Jake senior, Beth and Jake's sister remained at the party for a while but soon retreated when someone produced a bottle of tequila, limes and a saltshaker.

Jake finished reading the morning papers, then opened his desk drawer to retrieve a pair of scissors so he could clip a story that had attracted his attention in the Times. He stopped and smiled when he spotted a fresh jar of Rose Hip hand cream front and center in the drawer with a note attached.

"Congratulations, Mr. Editor. To a bright future – for all of us. Lucinda and Eduardo."

The surprises continued when Beebo showed up later that morning, unannounced. Her eyes were clear, her shoulders straighter. She had dyed her hair light brown, something close to her natural color.

"So much for the rainbow look, Beebo. Run out of colors from the parrot kingdom?"

She smiled as she sat across from Jake: two friends catching up.

"Just kidding. You seem good," Jake noted. "You look fantastic."

He was right. She did.

"I am. Really good, actually. I'm done with the boozing, the craziness, Jake. Time for little Beebo to grow up.

"I'm heading to rehab. Checking in day after tomorrow. My dad's taking me."

Jake knew resurrection when he saw it. Beebo's dad, the grouchy police chief, taking his little girl to get help she needed to straighten out her life — that the support of a father could matter so much to a tortured yet kind soul in need of a bit of help left him happy. He grinned at his friend.

"Hey, Beebo, that's great. I'm really happy for you … and your dad … and, well, I'm proud of you."

"Thanks, Jake."

Big sigh.

"It's gonna be a long walk, this one, but I'm serious about it. There's a lot I want in my life that's gone missing: my dad, believe it or not; a career, and who knows, maybe even a family one day? Time to get at it.

"Speaking of which, here's why I'm really here. How about having lunch with me? Today, maybe as friends. Maybe something a little bit more some day?" She spoke faster. "I know this might be a bit of a shock, and I know I have a history of moving way too fast, covering too many bases too soon, but I'm talking about a slow takeoff here.

"Lunch, then I go away and get my house in order, and you and I see how that feels. How about we share a sandwich and see what happens?"

Jake paused, then nodded his assent with a grin. "Sounds great, Beebo. Let's start with lunch. La Bamba, 1 p.m?"

"Time's great, but location's not, Jake. I'm done with La Bamba. That's all ancient history now. Let's go someplace that doesn't serve booze — maybe with healthy, organic food...."

She left after they arranged to meet at a local vegetarian restaurant opened recently by a young couple — he, Irish Catholic, she, Dominican Protestant — that had earned rave reviews.

Jake's phone buzzed.

"Morning, Jake," said Dolores. "Your new hire is here. Want me to bring him in?"

"Thanks, Dolores. I'll come get him. Be there in a minute."

Jake pulled the kid's resume from the top of a stack on his desk.

Bill Smart. Bachelor's in journalism, Boston University. Native of Binnfield, which would be both the kid's beat and *The P-R's* next hope for circulation growth. Jake recognized a gaping hole in Binnfield coverage after Zamboni's untimely exit. He thought Smart might be able to help repair the breach. The kid had wowed just about everyone during the interview process — except Gladys McAvoy, of course — and he seemed the perfect fit.

Jake left his office, made his way through the editor's pit and across the blue carpet to reception.

Smart stood by the desk, nervously shifting his weight from one foot to another as he watched Jake approach.

As Jake drew near he noticed an angry pimple erupting from the kid's right cheek. Jake considered teasing him about it, but held his tongue, instead sticking out his right hand in a greeting.

"Hey, Bill. Welcome to *The Post-Recorder*, the best little newspaper in the country. Come on. Let's get you started."

AFTERWORD

This book is fictionalized autobiography; a personal look back at a career and moment in time that meant something to me, and, I think, to others I was close with, people I met, worked with, interviewed and wrote about.

It is also a lament for an industry that centuries ago bound together a fledgling country, then gave rise to some of the United States' most powerful and ruthless publishing czars, then reached its feverish zenith with the publishing of the Pentagon Papers and the Washington Post's intelligent yet controversial chronicling of the Nixon-era shenanigans that began in a nondescript hotel and brought an administration to its knees.

Now, arguably tracking toward its nadir, the newspaper industry is struggling to find ballast for a foundering ship. Late to recognize the looming threat of the Internet, many newspaper companies have found lifelines to revenues and readership by embracing digital media. In addition to newspapers, media companies now publish websites, blogs and other forms of communication as part of the business of transferring information of all kinds from source to consumer.

The '70s and '80s, however, remain the glory days of my newspaper career, and perhaps in the industry's contemporary history as well.

Jobs were plentiful and newspaper revenues were steadily climbing. Inflation-adjusted newspaper advertising revenues hovered north of $40 billion in the 1980s, along the way to a peak of $65 billion around 2000, according to data published by the Newspaper Association of America. These days, including revenue from digital media, newspaper advertising revenues total just $23.6 billion — less than total industry revenues were when the NAA starting tracking data in 1950. That crushing economic shift has caused unprecedented contraction in the sector.

The earlier, brighter days, however, promised jobs, fun and a brand of cocky irreverence to a generation of contrarians bent on raising hell.

And that we did.

My colleagues at the now-defunct *Transcript-Telegram* in Holyoke were young and appallingly inexperienced; a bit odd, smart, curious, unfazed, caring and fun-loving. It was a collegial mess of misfits, each with our own peccadilloes and quirky habits, breathing the same air, enduring the same abuse from crotchety editors, and sucking down beers together after work.

The era spawned an entire generation of young men and women eager to cover the news, cause trouble and commit themselves to lives of poverty while bitching about the work every day. Journalism schools churned out reporters, editors and photographers to feed the 1,730 daily newspapers in the US and the thousands of magazines, weekly newspapers and so-called "specialty publications" that produced decent copy, and generally prospered.

Today, there are roughly 1,300 daily newspapers in the US, and even the mightiest are barely recognizable; shells of their former multi-sectioned advertising-laden, "touch all the bases" selves. In the year (2016) when I am at long last bringing this story to conclusion, the respected *Boston Globe* once again celebrated its 2003 Pulitzer Prize for reporting on the Catholic Priests Sex Scandal with the release of the Oscar-winning movie, *Spotlight*. Around the same time, it was forced to recruit reporters and editors to help deliver the Sunday morning edition when its distribution agent fell down on the job.

How the mighty have fallen, indeed.

The industry has shed jobs at an alarming rate. The number of total newsroom jobs peaked at around 56,000 in 2001 and has been in steady decline ever since, now hovering somewhere around 32,900.[5] Former *St. Louis Dispatch* reporter Erica Smith

5. American Society of News Editors

launched Paper Cuts, a blog dedicated solely to reporting on newsroom layoffs throughout the United States.

Declining revenues reflect advertisers' rapidly developing alternatives for where to spend their money. There is good reason for the mass migration of advertising dollars. Newspaper market penetration has plunged from nearly 125% of US households in 1950 to 37% in 2010[6] while the number and efficiency of online sources surged, posing a tough challenge for folks on the business end of the news industry.

Meanwhile, there's the not-so-small matter of public perception.

Clowns like Donald Trump have made headlines castigating the press corps while thriving on their coverage. "Corporate media" has become a favorite target of a hateful public, to some extent with good reason.

Expecting Roger Ailes to objectively operate Fox News is like expecting Keith Richards to successfully run a sobriety clinic; nothing good is going to come from the allegiance.[7] And then there's Rupert Murdoch, who, having bought and sold US papers, and walked the razor's edge of FCC scrutiny and anti-trust laws, decided that owning *The Wall Street Journal, Barron's,* and

6. *Sixty Years of Daily Newspaper Circulation Trends,* Communic@tions Management, Inc., 2011

7. Ailes was booted out by Fox in July 2016 after allegations that he systematically sexually harassed female employees.

The New York Post among others didn't bring enough influence over his conservative agenda. He bought *National Geographic* as well, sending the global warming crowd — me included — into fits of anguish.

All this feeds mistrust and skepticism among the public, a confused and unhappy bunch of news consumers. It's a bit of a mess in the media business, and print is leading the way into the darkness.

It's become fashionable to rail about how useless and irrelevant the local daily is to our lives. Journalists, once feared but revered, are now often viewed as social pariahs, and critics cast a wide net castigating reporters as shills for sinister corporate interests.

Jobs are scarce, and still low paying, and thus undervalued even from a pessimist's perspective. A 2015 Jobs Rated report ranked newspaper reporter and lumberjack as numbers 200 and 199, respectively, in terms of low pay, availability of jobs, and a trend of massive layoffs across the land. (Consider Eric Johnson, who as a journalism school graduate and former lumberjack, once landed a job as executive editor of Northern Logger magazine, combining the two professions with the nation's worst prospects.)

That's the *bad* news about the state of the industry.

The good news?

Newspapers not only endure but thrive in some parts of the USA, in developing countries, even among the shrinking club of US big city publishers. Here's what legendary investor and business-savvy billionaire Warren Buffett said in 2014, explaining why his BH Media group scooped up 70 papers in the US:

> "Newspapers continue to reign supreme, however, in the delivery of local news. If you want to know what's going on in your town — whether the news is about the mayor or taxes or high school football — there is no substitute for a local newspaper that is doing its job. A reader's eyes may glaze over after they take in a couple of paragraphs about Canadian tariffs or political developments in Pakistan; a story about the reader himself or his neighbors will be read to the end. Wherever there is a pervasive sense of community, a paper that serves the special informational needs of that community will remain indispensible to a significant portion of its residents."

Rilertown is about a paper similar to what Buffett describes: set in the unsexy world of small-city journalism, with its grit, specific focus and single-minded purpose to be a mirror of the communities it serves. And it's about the people who labor on to bring us the news day in, day out.

It's a somewhat wistful look back on a career that tormented me at the time but now tickles me to no end.

The news business gave me an education; some of my best, most enduring friends, countless amusing and horrifying memories, and even my wife (we are former colleagues).

It also gave me this book.

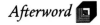

POSTSCRIPT

I landed my first bylined writing job as a pudgy sixth grader at Four Corners School in Greenfield, Massachusetts, penning an advice column for the school newspaper. It was an anonymous column, yet everyone in the school knew I was the tubby wit behind "Dear Flabby."

Insulting moniker notwithstanding, that job launched a 45-year love affair with the news business that continues today. I look back on that time from the perch of a retiree/writer, traveler and evolving curmudgeon with a bit of a chip on my shoulder and a few things to say. Some of those pearls — as well as the curmudgeonly influence — are the underlying reasons for this book. It's also meant to capture a bit of an industry that is vastly different now than it was when I first cut my teeth. The business has a habit of working its way into your psyche and staying there, like French fries on your waistline.

It's worth describing how I got into the profession. Why I would I commit to a career of comparatively low pay and absurdly long hours in a business populated by miscreants, dysfunctional wackos, brilliant thinkers and people who, like me, fell into journalism mostly by accident?

Like Jake, the protagonist in this book (who bears a striking resemblance to me in many respects, and who carries my father's nickname), I smoked and drank my way through junior college before I awoke from my intellectual hibernation and decided I wanted to be a journalist.

While in journalism school at Syracuse University, I got a paid job as features editor of *The Student Association Report* (a leftist, self-edited rag that gave fledgling scribes tons of free rein as well as access to the Student Activities budget, which I used, in one brazen example of raiding the proverbial cookie jar, to assign myself the story of learning how to sky dive. I wrote about the experience, focusing not only on my jump but also on the experienced jumper I rode into the skies with who died after his chute failed to open.)

At *The SA Report,* I learned to write features on deadline, how not to edit someone else's work (owing to my awkward relationship with the young woman who routinely butchered my submissions into an unrecognizable form of drivel), and how to smoke cigarettes, drink coffee, cradle a phone and bang away at a manual typewriter, all at the same time. Writing is an art, not a science. The job requires a certain flair for dexterity.

I bridged my junior and senior years at SU with an internship at my hometown newspaper, *The Greenfield Recorder,* and that cemented my love of the business. I was in love, hooked on glue pots; the clatter of typewriters; crusty, dysfunctional editors; newsroom slang; and the magical allure of gathering and writing news. Here was a way to communicate broadly, to gather, filter and repackage information, and then present it for mass consumption. It was captivating, inspiring, stimulating work, and it was gloriously fun.

Best news of all: I would get paid for it!

Glue pots and manual typewriters were gone by the time I landed my first full-time job in 1977 at the now-defunct *Holyoke Transcript-Telegram,* replaced by sleek IBM Selectric Typewriters and an enormous machine that magically scanned words from our typed pages and converted them into digital files for editors to scrutinize. Few outside of newsrooms of the era will recall Optical Copy Readers (OCRs), but these monsters existed widely in the early days of computerized newsrooms.

The early years of my career were fun, wild and unpredictable. They were also the least financially rewarding. (One of my colleagues at the T-T, as we called it, shamed our publisher after he traipsed to nearby Westover Air Force Base to claim his share of federally subsidized cheese being made available to the region's poor, and then threatened to write about it. He had to show his pay stub to get into the PX, but after quickly satisfying the sergeant on duty that his appallingly low salary made him a viable candidate for charity, he was on his way home with a block of Velveeta on the seat next to him in his rusted car.)

That job, that newspaper, and that city provided the foundation for this book. Readers from western Massachusetts as well as colleagues who made their way through Holyoke on the way to more fertile professional fields will recognize some of the similarities between Holyoke and Rilertown.

In later years I served as editor of a weekly newspaper, *The Marblehead Reporter,* where I abandoned my bias against non-daily newspapers and developed an appreciation for the people who put out not six or seven editions a week, but one. This was a different ballgame played by similar wingnuts following basically the same rules.

A weekly newspaper requires discipline if its staff is to create enough decent copy to fill the news hole — and therein rests the problem. It's like leaving your children alone in a messy house with the threat of retribution if the place isn't spotless when you return by dinnertime. Chances are they'll tackle the job seconds before you walk in the door, but you're still going to have to do the dishes and vacuum if you want to make a favorable impression on guests due to arrive in an hour. Often it takes an adult to finish things correctly. Such is the role of an editor.

But the work was fun and meant something to the community we served. If a newspaper may be judged by the quantity and quality of letters to the editor, *The Reporter* was a vital, healthy beast. Friends and colleagues from that era will also recognize some of the people, anecdotes and memories in *Rilertown* as originating from our Anderson Street hovel of an office.

As the years passed, I made my way into management, winding up as publisher for a group of 11 weekly newspapers in suburban Boston. Owned by a corporate giant with dubious financial and political motives, the business quickly lost its appeal as I moved farther and farther away from newsrooms and their real issues, endless challenges, and generally honest, hard-working, caring people. I'll take a newsroom, darkroom or composition table any day over the offensive, sterile pointlessness of a boardroom.

I left the newspaper business for good in 1996 for the more financially rewarding but professionally frustrating trenches of the commercial newswire business. In 2010, after nearly 14 years with *Business Wire,* I quit my job as Senior Vice President of Global Sales and, with my similarly eager but far more inspirational wife, left the country to see the world, volunteer, and write.

I like where I am now as much as I did when I started working for a living. But when I look back on the early days I recall worthwhile, relevant vignettes, not just of a vastly changed industry, but also of a time when small efforts by small people doing hard work often led to improvement; on some occasions, significant, wholesale change.

Most of the characters, anecdotes and events in *Rilertown* are rooted in reality and mirror things that happened. This is a work of fiction, though. Any resemblance to actual and real characters, events or circumstances is purely coincidental; memories of countless crazy people and moments, embellished by a vivid imagination and decent grasp of the English language. I hope that people who read this and see bits of themselves are, for the most part, amused and not offended. For the ones who deserved more accurate, unflattering portrayals ... well ... screw you. And I say that with all the love, admiration and respect you deserve.

Ask any newspaper veteran to share a story or two, and the conversation will soon turn to the characters within the newsroom:

The lifestyle editor who endured snickers and catcalls when she brought a plastic chair donut to work after successful hemorrhoid surgery.

The nice but malodorous young man whose chronic nasal blockage made it impossible for him to know just how badly he smelled, forcing colleagues to draw straws to pick who would confront the unsuspecting guy and get him to take a shower at least every other day and double up on the deodorant.

The acerbic scribe whose caustic remarks during news budget meetings could be counted on to leave the entire staff holding their sides in laughter with tears streaming down their faces.

They're all in here, recreated, embellished and glorified, captured in print by one man's memory of the magic in a business that, in spite of its many flaws, created something close to perfection by simply being able to get out the day's edition. We did good work, sometimes great, in spite of ourselves.

I wrote this book to recall and reflect, to express how much I miss those days, and also to vent. I wrote it to remind readers that newspapers are worth fighting for. Even in their diminished, horribly altered states, our local rags remain one of the pillars of what's left of democracy in the US.

An interesting factoid: as newspaper readership continues to sink, surveys show that readers place disproportionate credibility and, therefore, faith, in what's in the paper every day, compared to what they see via other media.

There's hope, and there's good reason for it. If you read this book and gain a bit more understanding about what goes into gathering, synthesizing, writing and packaging news, perhaps you'll place a bit more value on your local paper.

Newspapers are like anything else worth valuing. And anything worthwhile is worth fighting for. You read it here first, and from a reliable source: Dear Flabby never lies.

Rilertown

DEDICATION & ACKNOWLEDGEMENTS

My wife Gabi and I are extensions of one another. We fill in the gaps for each other, adding sweetness (hers) and cynicism (guess whose?) when it's needed, and we generally have each others' backs.

Gabi is the voice I listen to most openly and closely. She rounds off my rough edges, as a partner, a father, a friend, and as a writer. A gifted writer and editor in her own right with a wonderful, soft touch, Gabi is my toughest and most trusted critic. Her voice and touch is apparent throughout *Rilertown;* the astute reader will see it and feel it from start to end.

That's why I dedicate this book to her.

I wrote most of the first draft while we were housesitting in San Casciano, Italy, about 30 minutes outside of Florence. The home was a writer's heaven, a stone cottage surrounded by olive groves with a fabulous kitchen and easy, walking-distance access to fresh, local ingredients I could use to whip up the evening meals. Soft breezes wafted through the open windows, and on clear days we could see the Duomo as we walked to town.

Nikki, the property's owner, an artist and spiritualist, had a shaman cleanse the house's energy when she moved into the place, and it had been smudged by burning sage to create a space full of creative, positive energy. I do not, by nature, embrace ideas rooted in the spiritually sublime, but after a month in San Casciano in awe of the words that flowed from my brain to fingertips to Word file, I am a happy convert and a believer.

I began most days between 4:30 and 5:30 a.m., hot cups of coffee by my right hand as I pounded away and turned out chapter after chapter. I often wrote 3,000–5,000 words at a sitting. I would run out of energy, creativity or interest after two or three hours, unplug my laptop, and crawl back into bed with Gabi, who was normally awake by then.

There, I'd read her the day's entry and she'd make notes. Her suggestions always improved the story line, added depth to the characters, and spotted the lazy writing and flaws that go with a first draft. She kept me honest to the book's premise and reminded me tirelessly to stick to its pure intent. I know she braces at some of the crude behavior and language I have painstakingly presented within. It's a British thing, but *Rilertown* is a better book because of Gabi. If it's not to your liking; that's my fault. But if you love it as I do, Gabi deserves a large part of your appreciation.

There are others who contributed to this effort and deserve acknowledgement.

Pete Lawson is a dear friend, fellow writer, and lover of food, culture, people, travel and countless other facets of life that I hold dear. He was the first to read my initial draft of Rilertown and offer notes to help pull the story into focus. Sitting in a coffee shop around the corner from his flat in Brighton, the hour I spent with Pete gave important shape to this narrative that has carried through each subsequent draft, and his subsequent comments have been on target, relevant and useful.

As children, my daughters Kirsty and Emily probably never fully understood what daddy did for a living but accepted my absences and weird schedule as normal: I am happy to know that they are both gifted writers who can confidently turn out thoughtful prose, content, and poetry. I take some measure of responsibility for their good writing habits.

My mom and dad scratched their heads and said, "OK" when I announced I was going to quit being a business major and head to journalism school. I was blessed to have parents who unconditionally supported my psychotic changes of heart, both professionally and personally, and stuck with me nonetheless. From them, I learned what true parents' love looks and feels like. They are no longer with us, but I think they would like this book, or at least the idea that I wrote it.

To my friends and colleagues over four decades in the news business who arrived, disappeared and, in some cases (thanks to Facebook) reappeared, albeit from a distance: Many of you inspired and taught me in ways you could not see and perhaps cannot fathom. I am grateful.

Thanks to the key players at *The Greenfield Recorder,* many of them now gone, who helped shape my early career and set me off on the right foot in a positive direction: Alvin Oickle, Glenn Surrette, Neil Perry, Walentyna Pomasko, Chuck Blake, Irmarie Jones and Charlie Keller. I learned, and I remember who taught me.

A nod to my SU professors who taught me how to write, edit and do it reasonably well while nursing my fifth Utica Club well after midnight: Prof. JT "Jake" Hubbard and Bill Glavin, and to Professor Maxwell McCombs, who had drawn the short card when he found me in his Communications Law class but taught me rules, standards and principles I used throughout my career.

To Tim Lundergan, who came and went several times as a colleague, was my roommate when I was briefly single and who remains a treasured friend, valued reader and respected contributor to everything I write. He remains the only person I have encountered who read the entire *Tower Commission Report* and found a local angle to pursue. #awestruckafteralltheseyears

To my dear friend Vicki Ogden Wallack, and her late husband Bob — colleagues, friends, co-conspirators and like-minded lovers of everything newspapers stand for — who continue to inspire and teach me, no matter how far we are from one another. There's a scholarship in Bob's name offered through the New England Newspaper Association that underwrites internships for aspiring reporters. I like knowing we're all part of an effort to ensure another generation of scribes is trained to pick up where we left off.

To my colleagues and friends Chuck Goodrich, Jim Hopson and Mark O'Neill, who, along with Vicki, Lynn Carberry and me, formed the operating committee at Community Newspaper Company: It was fun while it lasted — sorta.

To Bill Wasserman, Selma Williams, Donna Rice, Paula Bramberg Gaull, Kenny Wooton, David Spink, Lynn Sears and Kenny Hughes: many of the wacky moments we shared together at *The Reporter* found their way into this book. Maybe I'll find space for fictionalized characters of Jackie Oldham, Genie Dinkler and Francis Twohey in the sequel.

Many of these people — as well as countless others — contributed ideas, sources, stories and characters for *Rilertown*.

For all your support, help and encouragement, and for the laughs, memories and incredible, poignant moments, I thank you.

Fittingly last but certainly not least (give me this one cliché, will ya, Dave?) is my trusted, funny and talented editor, Dave Bricker. Your kind counsel, excellent ideas and suggestions, and well-timed and –placed kicks to the tail helped make this book better.